THE QUEST FOR
TERA'LOTH

THE QUEST FOR TERA'LOTH

TARA MIER

ISBN: 978-1-958414-86-6

Hydra Publications

Goshen, Kentucky 40026

www.hydrapublictions.com

I dedicate this book to my husband, Matt, and to everyone who encouraged me on the journey to publication.
You are the true heroes for enduring my near daily doubt that anyone would be reading this dedication, much less my book.

"Show me a hero, and I'll write you a tragedy."

- F. Scott Fitzgerald

PROLOGUE

In the frenzy of darkness and smoke, two Kami men named Zlogarth and Jyneth ran swiftly downward through the rugged cliffs of Mt. Curac. Behind them, flames blasted out of a magnificent mansion.

"Come, we must hurry before anybody catches us. We have to protect the Stones. It must stay sealed," Zlogarth choked through labored breathing as the men continued to descend the mountain, leaving the sound of glass shattering and the sight of flames flickering behind them. Approaching the bottom of the mountain, they were relieved to find that the Giberals had left their carriage free from their shredding pecks.

"Where can we possibly hide these to make sure they stay hidden?" Jyneth looked downward at the calf-skinned sacks resting in his lap, sighing as he knocked on the carriage's roof.

With a swoosh, the carriage flew into the sky.

"I do not know where we will hide them, but we must make sure they remain hidden. Tera'Loth, our world, must stay protected from this evil, no matter what."

EVYNLOTH ALMACKIA

E vynloth Almackia was born in the Marshlands of the Djinn realm, nestled in the middle of a land named Tera'Loth. He came from a poor family and his parents were neglectful, but it was only because they worked hard to survive. Evynloth's parents worked as herb collectors for the greatest Spell-Caster in all the land, Lord Jinn Avestyn. Evynloth's father, Ereous, came from a family among the oldest and wealthiest magickal families in all of Tera'Loth.

The Almackias included many of the most prestigious Spell-Casters and Seers in all the realms. Ereous was a wondrous Spell-Caster, but a stroke of bad luck saw his family without a fortune and him without an education. If a person did not have a magickal degree, they couldn't make a living from their abilities. Evynloth's mother Juliana resented her husband's lack of education and the burden it placed on her. Because of the family's extreme poverty, herb collecting wasn't her only job. Juliana worked as an archivist for the Great Seer Syron Almackia, whom she always assumed hired her out of family duty or pity. Although Juliana had achieved a magickal degree, her gender limited her prospects in a male-dominated realm.

On a fine-weathered day, Ereous was out in the marsh collecting herbs for the apothecary. After he completed his work, Ereous collected mushrooms to go with his dinner. On the way home, an old beggar man approached Ereous looking for scraps. A kind-hearted Ereous gave the man the mushrooms he intended for his own dinner. The old beggar man gave Ereous a piece of hack-root in thanks.

Hack-root was hard to find and good for making tea. Ereous couldn't believe his luck.

In his youth, he loved to chew on the raw roots, which produced a giddy euphoria. Ereous hurried home to prepare a pot of hack-root tea. Ereous chewed the root as he waited for the tea to brew. An instant euphoria hit, but it left him feeling strange. Before night, Ereous was bedridden by illness. Juliana suspected Ereous to have consumed poison mushrooms from the marsh, judging by the purple around his lips. Evynloth and his mother tried every spell they knew to heal Ereous, but they could not heal him as his memory, hazed by the pain, left him unable to remember what he had eaten on the day he fell ill. Ereous, being poor, left his son nothing but a piece of amethyst on a simple black rope.

"This is the symbol of our family," said Ereous through labored breathing. "Wear this necklace with pride."

Ereous died in his wife's arms three days later.

After the death of Ereous, Juliana fell into a deep depression from which she never recovered. Evynloth tried every herb and spell he could think of to bring his mother back from the brink of despair, but he was unsuccessful. With the burden of an ill parent and no income, Evynloth needed to find work. After weeks of searching, Evynloth happened upon a sign posted outside the magickal college known as The Erudition. The sign was an advertisement for an apprentice and servant to Lord Jinn Avestyn of the High Council of Djinn. Seeing an opportunity, Evynloth snatched the sign up for himself and ran off toward the High Council.

After navigating the labyrinth of High Council halls and staircases, Evynloth reached Lord Jinn Avestyn's office. Behind a desk in the entranceway to Lord Avestyn's office sat Lord Avestyn's assistant. He was a tall Druid, not much older than Evynloth.

"I'm here about the job," Evynloth choked as he struggled to catch his breath.

The Druid said nothing. With a grunt, he motioned to the door next to him.

Evynloth walked up to the door with a hand outstretched but stopped himself from grabbing the doorknob, opting to knock instead.

"Enter," bellowed a deep voice behind the door.

Evynloth opened the door a crack and slid inside the foreign domain.

Lord Avestyn—being prone to the classics—decorated the office with the usual things found in the study of a sorcerer: books in strange languages, unlabeled jars filled with unidentifiable objects, and a well-stocked apothecary. In the room's center sat Lord Jinn Avestyn at his desk, scratching away with his quill and mumbling as he always did.

"Excuse me, sir. I am here for the job."

Lord Avestyn did not look up as he motioned Evynloth to sit.

Easing gently into a large plush chair, Evynloth kept his gaze on Lord Avestyn, starstruck by his tall and regal future master. After a strange interview in which his blood was drawn and his mouth was inspected, Evynloth found himself an apprentice of Lord Jinn Avestyn.

In his excitement, he ran straight home to tell his mother, stealing her a loaf of bread along the way for good measure. When he arrived home, he found her passed out from another of her "special tonics". It would be days before she awoke, so Evynloth wrote her a letter while feasting on bread and cheese before retiring to his room to pack.

The next morning, Evynloth awoke early and readied to leave the house. With sadness, Evynloth looked around the only home in which he ever lived. A sigh on his lips, he closed the door, not knowing that this action marked the end of his happiness and his childhood.

Evynloth arrived at Avestyn's castle on a frosty winter's day. The castle was near to his home, so he saw no need to pay for a carriage ride. Besides, he didn't have the money anyhow. Evynloth approached the castle wearing nothing but a simple thin cotton shirt and brown slacks held up by suspenders repaired one too many times.

Evynloth never dressed for the weather and needed proper attire. Lord Avestyn opened the door before allowing his new apprentice to knock. He stood in the shadow of his master, trying not to make eye contact as he felt Lord Avestyn looking him up and down. Next to Lord Avestyn stood a short, fat black dog with crooked teeth that stuck out even with its mouth closed.

Avestyn shook his head, muttering under his breath as he motioned for the boy to enter his domain. "I am not agreeable to noise, boy. You better be near the door if we are expecting company," Avestyn bellowed as he paced the great hallway, allowing his new apprentice a few moments to take in his new home.

Evynloth was in awe of the castle. The tallest man in the land could not touch the castle's ceilings. The staircase stretched for miles, and the grandest purple carpet ran across its steps. Gray marble from the dwarven quarries covered the walls of the foyer. Across the castle's foyer floor lay a mosaic pattern of large, multi-colored, diamond-shaped cobblestones. This was truly the home of a king.

At the slam of the door, Evynloth jumped as he turned to find his master locking the large foreboding doors on his youth, and perhaps his life.

"Boy, you will sleep in my study with my dog, Forge. If you get under my feet, I will turn you into something unnatural."

Evynloth nodded in agreement, trembling as he watched

his master walk down the hall toward his study with Forge at his side.

"Well, come along, boy. Don't dawdle because I hate that as well."

The first few months living with Lord Avestyn were dull. Evynloth learned no magick and spent his days cleaning the castle. If anyone had ever cleaned the castle before, it was a long time in the past. With dirt and cobwebs that touched the ceiling, Evynloth would not die from lack of work.

After months of making his way through the castle, Evynloth found the Library. It was one of the largest rooms in the castle, so big that his own house could fit inside it with room to spare. The bookshelves extended to the ceiling, filled with volumes on any topic one could think of. Evynloth looked at the shelves covered with inches of thick dust. With a sigh, he set to work.

After a few hours of cleaning, Evynloth took a break. In a corner of the room, a dusty old green armchair beckoned him to sit, and he fell asleep before his backside hit the chair.

"*Boy! Wake up, boy!* Where is my supper?" bellowed Lord Avestyn.

Evynloth woke up in a panic; he couldn't see a thing. In the horror of realizing he had slept longer than he should, Evynloth jumped up, still half asleep. "I am sorry, my lord, I only meant to rest for a—"

Evynloth hit the floor.

This was Evynloth's first beating.

Until this point, all Evynloth knew was neglect, but now he could add violence to the list of tragedies that made up his life. Looking up at his master in fear, Evynloth entertained the thought of running away, but having bound himself to serve until he was twenty, running was not possible. Evynloth had signed on with Lord Avestyn to learn the art of magick, but his primary concern was providing for his mother rather than his own safety. Evynloth took the abuse for his mother's sake, but his defeatist acquiescence did not stop him from hoping that this form of discipline might be a rarity.

"Get off that floor, boy. Make my supper now," Lord Avestyn snapped as he turned to leave the room.

On his way out the door, Lord Avestyn threw a book from the shelf, hitting Evynloth in the head. Evynloth picked up the book and read its title, *Tera'Loth: A History*. "History before magick. Boy, get off that floor now. I want to eat."

After a dinner of cold cuts for Lord Avestyn and stale bread for his new apprentice, Lord Avestyn excused his new apprentice to bed, thrusting his tiny body into the study as he locked the door behind him. Evynloth looked around the dim room, lit only by fire. Before the fireplace lay a bed fashioned from straw and burlap sacks, and the sheets he was to sleep in were the same ones he used to clean the fireplace. With a deep sigh, Evynloth laid on his makeshift bed and read his new book by firelight.

As the months went on, Lord Avestyn schooled Evynloth in the ways of magick, and Evynloth became Avestyn's most promising pupil. Each day after his lessons, Evynloth returned to his work as a servant, tending to the castle.

Once, Evynloth was polishing the silverware when he

heard strange noises coming from the ground below the castle. They resembled ghost-like moans. When he questioned the noise, Lord Avestyn told his young apprentice that he was hearing the unwanted souls of the House of Avestyn and if he wasn't careful, he might end up with them. Evynloth dropped the topic at once. Evynloth learned early on how to read his master and did not want a beating. Evynloth now realized the troubles he faced working with Lord Avestyn, but that did not matter so long as his mother could eat.

After a few months, Lord Avestyn gradually warmed up to his new apprentice, but his demeanor changed as soon as he realized Evynloth's magickal abilities could easily surpass his own. When Lord Avestyn moved on to medicinal recipe instruction, which was his specialty, it enraged him when Evynloth mastered a spell in less than an hour. In his jealousy, Lord Avestyn spent the rest of the afternoon beating and torturing his young apprentice. After that, the beatings became a daily ritual, given for the smallest infringements. After a few more months, Lord Avestyn grew bored with beating the boy, choosing instead to shift his abuse to the realm of exploitation. Evynloth began doing the bulk of Lord Avestyn's work, including the Spell-Casting. Lord Avestyn was so greedy and cruel that he kept the money to himself and fed Evynloth the scraps—if Forge didn't get them first.

After three months with little to no food, Evynloth finally reached his breaking point. He endured employment with Lord Avestyn for the sake of his mother, but he could take no more. He was bone thin and now suffered fleas from Forge.

Evynloth longed for the outdoors and the Marshlands. Looking over himself in the mirror, Evynloth realized that there was a real prospect of death. To keep from dying, he decided it was time to escape. It was a Friday, which meant that his master would spend the day dashing across town, collecting orders and money owed before his customers gave it to the tavern or spent it at the market.

On the morning of his escape, Evynloth cooked breakfast as normal, standing by to fight Forge over the scraps. Evynloth's strength had waned so much that he rarely bothered to fight the dog, but today he knew he needed an extra boost.

Lord Avestyn left the house at nine o'clock that morning. Evynloth watched from the study window as the carriage headed toward town. When the carriage was out of sight, Evynloth sprang into action. Evynloth thought of stealing everything of value, but given the state he was in, that was not an option. Traveling light was the only way, but there was something he wasn't leaving without, and that was his amethyst necklace.

A cruel and greedy Avestyn stole the necklace from his apprentice. It sat in his desk under a protection spell, as collateral until Evynloth finished his contract. Evynloth used the last of his strength to cast an undoing-spell on the desk. Uttering the words of the spell, he heard a click followed by a bang. Evynloth did not bother to turn. He knew what happened and who was standing behind him.

When Evynloth had cast the spell, Lord Avestyn appeared in the room, a snarl on his lips. A flash of anger swept Lord Avestyn's face as his voice roared through Evyn-loth's back.

"How dare you steal from me." Lord Avestyn screeched as he put Evynloth under a spell called forestall, rendering him paralyzed. "Well boy, since I can no longer trust you here alone, it's downstairs and below the castle for you. I told you that you could not leave me until you are twenty, and I meant it."

The floor beneath Evynloth rumbled. A circle appeared on the floor around Evynloth's feet. Lord Avestyn chanted until the floor below Evynloth opened, plunging him into the depths of the castle.

In the dungeon, Evynloth found that his new home was a tiny cell, the contents of which were a bed and a stone slab for a seat. Before the slab lay a bench board with levers on it. From above, Evynloth could hear the voice of his master.

"This is your punishment for trying to escape. You will live in this cell for as long as you draw breath," said Lord Avestyn as he coughed and sputtered his words. "In front of the stone seat is a board with levers. These levers control travel between the realms of Tera'Loth and can only work when fueled by the life force of a child."

Lord Avestyn uttered the words of the spell known as wills-overtake, throwing Evynloth, under the spell, onto the stool and forcing him to pull the levers.

"You are to live here in this dungeon suspended in child-hood, pulling the levers forever."

Lord Avestyn laughed as the light from above dissipated, plunging Evynloth into darkness.

IMOGEN THE ADVENTURER

Imogen Welkin was a mischievous girl of thirteen who lived on a farm with her parents Simone and Jonas, her Granny Astrid, and her siblings John and Vivian. Imogen was a natural explorer, due in part to the boredom she faced living in isolation.

Their farmhouse was twenty miles from town, and there wasn't a neighbor in sight. Her grandparents moved onto the land after they married, and her grandfather built the house with his own two hands. Her grandfather's name was Richard, and he died before she was born, but Granny spoke of him so much that Imogen felt she knew him.

Today, Imogen's boredom was far worse than usual. She was on a break from school, but her father didn't get the leave he requested, so that meant no family vacation. With her mother's ban on television during the day and no escape from the farm in sight, Imogen decided that she would hunt for treasure. Having explored every nook and cranny of the barn, guesthouse, and the woods that surrounded the farmland, Imogen went on a mission to the last place devoid of exploration. Her destination was what Jonas referred to as "the abyss"—otherwise known as the attic.

Upon entering the attic, she was met with the welcoming yet repelling smell of mothballs and dust. Imogen's talent was a wild and active imagination. To her, she was not staring at decaying boxes of long-forgotten junk. No, in Imogen's eyes, she was seeing a jungle to wade through in hunt of wondrous treasures.

Before Imogen stood a coat and hat rack. To get to it, she jumped over paint-stained sheets and old newspapers. Jumping upwards, she grabbed the safari hat from the hat rack and got lost in her own little world.

"Onward men. The entrance to the cave is near." Imogen ran full steam toward the grandfather clock that sat against the back wall.

With a thud, Imogen tripped on a purple velvet throw blanket, hitting the ground in pain.

"Ouch, what was that?" Imogen yelped.

She yanked the throw blanket away and unearthed a new treasure. Before Imogen sat a beautiful deep red, cherrywood chest. It looked like what Granny called a hope chest, but it was deep like a sea chest. The craftsman of this fine piece adorned its lid with thousands of tiny purple amethysts. Curiosity piqued, Imogen longed to see what was inside.

With all her might, Imogen lifted the lid to reveal a treasure trove of items. A gleeful giggle shot out of her mouth before Imogen dove headfirst into the chest. Inside the chest, Imogen found many books, clothes wrapped in paper and a barrage of other little trinkets. At the bottom of the chest, she spotted a piece of purple velvet that appeared to be concealing something.

When she unwrapped the purple velvet, Imogen found a book called *The Chronicles of Tera'Loth*. Imogen was an avid reader, so all books excited her.

"I wonder who this chest belonged to?" she said to herself as she opened the book. Written on the front page, under the title, was the name Richard Welkin. "This must have been my grandfather's."

She knew her grandfather spent most of his life as a hopeful yet unpublished author but, despite Imogen's pleas, Imogen's mother read none of his stories to her. Simone said hearing the stories might make Granny sad.

IMOGEN OPENED the book to find the most beautiful handwritten script she had ever seen. Imogen shuffled into a corner, readying herself to read. Sadly, her adventure into a new world was dashed by the call for lunch. With a sigh, Imogen put the book back in the chest and ran downstairs.

After lunch, Imogen took the book from the attic to read in the playroom. She threw herself down onto her beanbag and opened the book. Being so tired from her adventures and a heavy lunch, sleep overtook her before she could read.

As Imogen lay sleeping, she had a very curious dream. In it, she was clutching something in her hand while she was yelling at a blurred figure that stood before her. As Imogen screamed louder, the blurred figure flew up to her face, placing its hands on her throat. Imogen's whole body shook in the hands of this evil being, choking her as she tried to beg for her life. In an instant, she felt herself stop struggling and everything went dark.

Imogen yelped as she awoke with a start.

Someone was jabbing her. "Wake up, sleepy head. Let's go play hide and seek in the woods before dinner." It was her sister Vivian. "Come on, sleepy head. We've only got thirty minutes until dinner."

Imogen hauled herself off of the beanbag with a cheeky grin, pushing past Vivian as she ran for the door. "Okay, the last annoying sister to the oak tree's a rotten egg."

After dinner, John and Vivian escaped to the playroom. It was after dark, and that meant it was time for electronics. Imogen went to visit Granny on her way to the playroom. Granny Astrid was not bedridden, but it wasn't easy for her to get up some days.

Imogen knocked gently on the door. "Granny, it's me. May I come in?"

Imogen waited until she heard a muffled, "Yes," before entering the room.

Astrid lived in a modest-sized room surrounded by her memories. She was a beautiful woman. Even in her fifties, she could pass for thirty. She and Imogen were the only two members of the family with chestnut hair and dark blue eyes. Their eyes were so dark that they almost looked black. Their features were the only similarities they shared.

Imogen rushed to show Granny her treasure from the attic. "Look, Granny, I found a book written by Grandfather Richard," she remarked as she held the book up for Granny to see.

Granny's demeanor changed as soon as she saw the book.

Imogen wasn't sure why Granny looked upset, but she assumed that Granny struggled to think of her lost love.

"That, my dear, is the jewel in the crown of your grandfather's writings. I hope you enjoy reading it." Granny stood up from her chair by the fire and walked toward her bed. "Now, child, I am tired. Please go enjoy your book."

Imogen kissed Granny goodnight and made her way to the playroom. As soon as the door was closed, Astrid reached into her bedside dresser drawer. She unearthed a small pouch that held a single diamond-shaped purple amethyst strung on a piece of black rope. Astrid put on the necklace, clutching the amethyst as she whispered something inaudible. As the last words left her mouth, a man appeared before her.

"Lady Astrid, it has been too long. Why have you summoned me here?"

Astrid stood up from her bed. "She has discovered his chest. I thought you destroyed it instead of hiding it here in my home."

The man bowed his head as he apologized, "I am sorry, child, but there was no time to move it."

Astrid raised her voice, cutting the man off mid-sentence. "You need to fix this before she discovers the truth. We agreed to protect him from Imogen."

The man nodded. "I will fix this for their sake."

The man disappeared from the room as quickly as he arrived. Astrid climbed into bed in silence, still looking toward the space from which the mysterious man disappeared.

"Please fix this, Matthew, before we all suffer by her hand," she said to herself while stowing the necklace back inside the safety of the drawer.

With a kiss on Richard's picture, Astrid drifted off to sleep.

A BEDTIME STORY FROM SIMONE

Imogen entered the playroom to witness her mother wrestling John and Vivian into their sleeping bags. Despite having a large house, Simone could not convince the children to sleep in their own bedrooms. The children preferred to sleep together in the playroom. After years of failing to keep them in their own beds, Simone now allowed the children to sleep in the playroom so long as they were asleep by 9 o'clock, but they never were.

With her babies bundled up, Simone asked the worst question one could ask of three different children. "What story should we read tonight?"

With that, little voices began speaking in unison.

"Mother, we want a scary story tonight. Please, please, please," remarked Vivian.

For a girl of eight, Vivi's appetite leaned toward less

conventional fare. John wanted the usual action-packed story any ten-year-old boy would want.

"Okay, Miss Imogen, you're the tiebreaker."

Imogen thought for a second. "Can we have a new story tonight? I found this in the attic." Imogen pulled the realm chronicles from under her blanket.

When Simone saw the title, it surprised her. "I've not seen this book in years. I think someone's been sleuthing in the attic again," Simone said as she pinched Imogen's nose.

"Mother, why didn't you tell us some of our grandfather's books were in the attic?"

Simone mustered a little grin. "I suppose it was because I loved my Daddy's stories so much that I wanted to keep them to myself," said Simone as she tickled her daughter. "Well if you wanted a scary story, Miss Vivian, then you will find it here in these pages." Simone cleared her throat, opened the book and read. "This, children is the story of the Wizard's Slave-Boy.

"Once there lived a little boy named Evynloth. He lived in the Djinn realm, in the land of Tera'Loth. His parents were not always there for him because they worked tirelessly to support the family.

"After a run-in with some bad mushrooms, Evynloth's father got sick and died. After the death of his father, his mother fell into a deep depression from which she never recovered. It forced Evynloth to leave home to work as an apprentice for the family patron, Lord Jinn Avestyn. Evynloth was only fifteen years old when he entered service.

"Lord Avestyn was, at first, welcoming of his new apprentice, but his demeanor changed as he soon realized Evynloth's magickal abilities surpassed his own. In his jealousy, he became cruel. He beat his apprentice for the smallest infringement. Lord Avestyn soon realized that rather than beating Evynloth, he could just as well exploit the boy's talent for his own gain.

"Evynloth was now doing all of Lord Avestyn's work, including the Spell-Casting. Lord Avestyn was so greedy and cruel that he kept all the money for himself and fed Evynloth the scraps—if the dog didn't get them first. After enduring for three months without food, Evynloth was at his breaking point.

"He stayed in this employment for the sake of his mother and to honor their patron, but he could take no more. Evynloth had experienced extreme weight loss, and his only reward was fleas from the dog. In his desperation, he hatched an escape plan. It was Friday and that meant his master would be out collecting orders before his customers gave their money to the tavern or the market.

"Lord Avestyn left the castle at 9 am. It was time to run.

"Evynloth traveled light. He had arrived at the castle with nothing more than the clothes on his back, and his clothes were now nothing more than tattered rags. However, there was a treasure that he was not leaving without and that was his father's amethyst necklace. His father had given it to him on his deathbed. It was magickal, and the symbol of his family, but getting the necklace would not be easy.

"Lord Avestyn, in his greed and cruelty, had stolen the necklace from Evynloth and placed it inside his desk, under a protection spell. Evynloth found an undoing spell to use on the desk. The spell worked, but Evynloth was thwarted, for when he cast the spell, Lord Avestyn detected it.

"Lord Avestyn appeared in the room before his young apprentice. 'You were trying to steal from me?' he demanded. 'What made you think you could steal from me?'

"Evynloth summoned what little strength he had left to fight for his life. 'I was taking back what was mine. I am not leaving here without it.'

"Lord Avestyn's ire rose. 'My apprentices leave when I am done with them,' he bellowed as he put Evynloth under a fear spell to paralyze him. 'Well boy, since you have shown me that I can no longer trust you, it's down below for you.'

"Lord Avestyn placed Evynloth in the dungeon to do his work. Evynloth's new home was a tiny cell. In it sat a makeshift bed and a stone slab for a seat. In front of the seat sat a bench board with levers on it.

"'This is your punishment for trying to escape. You will live in this cell forever. In front of the seat is a board with levers. These levers control travel between the realms of Tera'Loth, which work only when fueled by the life force of a child.'

"Against his will, under Lord Avestyn's spell, Evynloth pulled the levers in front of him.

"'You are to live down here, suspended in childhood, to pull the levers forever.' Lord Avestyn walked away laughing as he closed the door on his apprentice turned slave for the last time."

With that, Simone snapped the book shut. "That's all for tonight. We will read more tomorrow." With a smile, Simone retreated downstairs to her favorite chair by the fire, ignoring the groans of her children, who were begging to hear another chapter.

Jonas came up behind Simone's chair. "Are they asleep?" he asked as he kissed her neck.

Simone smiled as she watched the flames dance. "You know they won't be asleep for hours. I read them a story that my father wrote. It was about a boy who tried to escape his evil master and got locked in a dungeon forever."

Jonas grinned. "Imogen will be awake until dawn planning his rescue."

Upstairs, the children lay in their sleeping bags.

Imogen gazed at the ceiling, imagining what it would be like to visit a magickal realm. "I would love it if Tera'Loth existed. We could travel there and save Evynloth."

Vivian rolled her eyes as she turned to face the wall. "You're so silly, Imogen. You know Grandfather Richard wrote that story a long time ago. It's made up, silly."

Imogen grinned, still looking up at the ceiling. "I know, but it's still fun to dream."

Despite being the youngest, Vivian was the practical child. Unlike her siblings, she anchored herself in the comfort of reality.

Later that night, with the children defeated by sleep, Imogen found herself within another unusual dream. She was sitting in front of thousands of people, but she could not see their faces. She was holding a blurred object above her head. The crowd was cheering, then the cheers turned to screams. From the distance came a howl that pierced her eardrums. The dream ended, and Imogen woke up with her fingers lodged in her ears.

EVYNLOTH'S RESCUE

Evynloth lived down in Lord Avestyn's dungeon for the next five years. While he was locked in the darkness, Tera'Loth underwent massive changes. The focus shifted toward treating women and children as equals rather than slaves, and trade reopened between the realms.

Four years into Evynloth's imprisonment, there was a historic meeting between the Elves and the Djinn of Magicka. For eons, the Elves had lived in seclusion from the rest of Tera'Loth. After many years of peace and solitude, the Elvish council opened its borders in the interest of trade.

The Elves claimed that their resources were diminishing at an alarming rate, but they refused to elaborate as to how the resources of such a powerful race were dwindling. Their claim was a farce, for the Elves had received a prophecy that Lord Avestyn would take over Tera'Loth and turn the realms over to the Necromancers, with himself as the king of Tera'Loth.

The Elves came to the land of Magicka armed with nothing more than magick. The Elves were cautious to open themselves up to the Djinn, but they did so to find out anything they could about their new friends. The current generation of Elves knew nothing about their new friends, for there were none left alive with any knowledge of the Djinn people of Magicka. Moreover, there was no record in the Elvish archives about the Djinn.

Upon arrival at the High Council building in the Magicka realm's capital, High-Orconia, Lord Einar Teymark, the Elvish representative and ruler of the Elvish realm, met with the High Council members, including Lord Avestyn. The Elves were always curious of Djinn creations, such as the realm travel boxes, and how the realm travel machine got its power, which was a secret well guarded, for the truth was sinister.

Lord Avestyn was the only person who knew how realm travel worked. He was from a long line of great Spell-Casters. His third great grandfather, Lord Horridge Avestyn, was the creator of the realm travel box. Before the use of realm travel boxes, a traveler would take a long—and sometimes perilous —journey to reach another realm. The Elves of Tera'Loth honored the freedom of future generations as much as they honored the freedom of the individual. The Elves suspected how the machine got its power, and it did not take long to discover the truth.

Lord Avestyn, although great in power, was weak for

brandy wine. On the last night of the trade delegation, Lord Teymark approached Lord Avestyn in his chambers in the High Council building.

"I hope you do not mind my intrusion, but I have bought a drink to share with a new friend," he said as he opened his cloak to reveal a bottle of brandy wine mixed with a little Elvish Magick.

As Lord Avestyn gulped the brandy wine, Lord Teymark cast his gaze over the room. Lord Avestyn naturally furnished his chambers with all the darkness that only the cruel would own. The walls of the office were adorned with the heads of dead game and the shelves were stuffed with a plethora of books that paid homage to everything dark in Tera'Loth.

Lord Teymark refreshed their drinks and grinned as he handed off a chalice to his new friend. "I am glad that our two realms have joined forces again."

Lord Avestyn took another greedy gulp of his brandy wine, grunting his approval of Lord Teymark's observation.

Lord Teymark refilled the chalice as he continued to speak. "I know I might be too forward in my asking, but I am a tinker of sorts, and I was wondering what it would take to power a system of travel as big as what you Djinn have created?"

Lord Avestyn's head was gravitating toward the table as he felt the effects of the Elvish brandy wine. He shook his head and burped.

"All right, sir, your secrets are your own," said Lord Teymark as he stood from the desk.

"I would show you out, but I seem to have lost my feet. I would appreciate a case of that brandy wine."

Lord Teymark nodded and bowed in silence. As he moved toward the door, from behind he heard the familiar sound of a head thumping down. He smiled to himself. "Thank you for your hospitality, good sir."

Lord Teymark, not knowing the full extent of the Djinn anatomy, wasted no time in ransacking the chambers before Lord Avestyn woke up. Searching behind the heads on the wall, Lord Teymark came across a secret compartment.

Inside was all the evidence he needed to bring to the High Council. The machine was powered by the most vulnerable of Tera'Loth, the children. Lord Teymark took this information to the rest of the trade delegation. The Elves were furious by the realization that the life force—known as Aura in Tera'Loth—of children was being used to fuel the machine.

The children who were being used were also special, as they were thrice blood—Children of Djinn, Kami, and the blood of their birth race. With all the knowledge in hand, the Elves brought their findings to the High Council the very next day.

At first, the High Council was reluctant to believe this, but they still brought Lord Avestyn before the High Council to stand trial. According to the laws of the Magicka realm known then as Djinn, they needed but a single witness to secure a conviction. The trouble was finding a witness who would submit to questioning by the High Council.

The High Council used a potion on the witness to extract

the truth. They made this potion from a deadly plant, which would age the person who testified if they lied. This was a practice invented by earlier High Council members to secure true testimonies.

After a few months of searching for a relative of Lord Avestyn, the High Council found a witness willing to speak. The witness was Lord Avestyn's cousin, Lady Hedra Avestyn-Sageland. She was one of only a few family members who had discovered how the machine sourced its power, and had split from the family because of it. She had tried to tell the people of the realms what was happening, but her family had silenced her with slander. After her public shaming, she had retreated to live in the Druid lands and had married a Druid named Ells Sageland.

As was the custom, the High Council forbade Lord Avestyn from knowing who would testify against him until the person was sworn in. On the day of the trial, Lord Avestyn came face to face with his long-lost cousin. At first, he believed it was a trick, for Hedra remained as youthful as the day he had last seen her.

"Don't look so shocked, Jinn, the truth is I *am* special, I am thrice blood and I am here to save those I could not all those years ago," Hedra said as she spat at her cousin before drinking the truth potion. The potion made Hedra very weak, so she climbed to the podium with the help of two members of the High Council.

"My dear lady, as per custom, you have taken the potion in order to give justice to another. Please proceed with your truth, but know that if you lie, you will age."

Hedra looked through her cousin as she spoke. "Our family line was and still is the most powerful line in all the lands. When I was eighteen years old, I was cleaning my grandfather's study. On that day, I was cleaning the shelves. They were so dusty, just covered in filth."

Lord Avestyn squirmed in his chair, clearly uncomfortable in Hedra's presence.

"As I dusted the books, I was reading the titles on the spines. I have always loved to read, but my mother only let me read what she chose. That day, I found a book named *The Laws of Realm Travel*. Upon opening it, I found that it was penned by my great grandfather, Lord Horridge. A diagram was drawn on the first page. It was a lever board, with instructions on its purpose."

Lord Avestyn jumped up in protest, cutting off his cousin's testimony. "My dear men, this shrew is not offering us anything. Get her out of here before she embarrasses my family name further."

The High Council member in charge of the proceedings, Lord Alphias, raised his hand in disapproval of Lord Avestyn's interruption. "Please, madam, proceed with your testimony."

Hedra nodded as she continued, "A thrice blooded child can power the machine. This is because their life force is strengthened by being a child of three races. Thrice bloods, or Kami children, are seen as something worth shunning, but they are the only beings who can open portals between worlds. They can do this because they are of mixed race and descendants of the Kami."

The room erupted with gasps. Most did not believe the tales of the Kami, especially in the Magicka realm.

Lord Alphias took off his glasses as he looked down at Hedra. "My dear lady, I am sorry to question your testimony, but with such an accusation I have to ask if you have any proof?"

Hedra gave a slight smile as she reached into her cloak to reveal a book. Every witness in the room leaned as far forward as they could to get a glimpse of the evidence. Hedra handed the book to the man who helped her. Lord Alphias gasped as the book was placed in his hands.

"I took it with me when I fled the house. I was of noble blood, but my family did not give me my rightful place because *I* am Kami, thrice blood. I should not have washed the floors or endured my cousin trying to persuade me to silence." Hedra looked at her cousin cuttingly. "The saving grace for me is that only a virgin Kami can power the machines." Lord Avestyn's face dropped as Hedra said, "Was it Grandfather who suggested you hurt me? Or did you come up with that plan all on your own?"

Another gasp, then a painful silence swept over the room.

The Elves stood and placed hands over their hearts as they bowed to Hedra. Lord Alphias, realizing what had transpired, did not have to proceed any further with the trial. In all of Tera'Loth, there was a single complaint that would allow an automatic conviction, and that was the defilement of another. Lord Avestyn was grateful for not being in the Viking realm, for in that realm, a charge of this nature brought instant death.

After excusing Hedra to the care of the Elves, Lord Alphias passed his sentence. The High Council found Lord Avestyn guilty and sentenced him to life in the Elvish Prison of Loneliness. There, they left him to live in seclusion for the rest of his life.

After Hedra's testimony, the High Council tasked themselves with finding the exploited Kami children and assembled a party. Lord Avestyn refused to cooperate or disclose their location. With little to go on, the party decided that they would search the Avestyn home for clues. The obvious choice was to start in the lower levels of the home.

Upon their arrival at Lord Avestyn's home, the party found the doors to the castle wide open. Lord Avestyn felt no danger because of his great magickal power and the secrecy of the realm travel machine's existence.

As the party, led by Lord Teymark, walked with caution into the abyss, it met them with the smell of hate and violence. The smell of must, like scrunched up wet towels. Lord Avestyn had divided the basement into numerous small rooms with heavy doors and a tiny barred opening to let in air and some light. Every room they approached was empty.

"I knew he would not be this stupid," said Lord Teymark as he reached into his pocket to unearth a satchel and grabbed a small portion of purple dust. Cupping his hands, he whispered some words in Elvish over the dust and blew it out into the room.

"This is a method of tracking from our realm. I hope it will lead us to the children."

The party began to follow the dust, leading them to the

back wall at the end of the hallway. This was Lord Avestyn's last piece of malice. The children were hidden just out of reach. It took the entire High Council, Elves and Witches and Wizards, three days to break through all Lord Avestyn's protection, cloaking, and locking spells.

When they finally entered the hidden chamber, it met them with the sights and sounds of utter depravity. Not all the children down there served the purpose of realm travel. Off in a corner room, the party found a girl named Drayah chained to a dilapidated bed, wearing nothing but a rag that looked like it may have once been an exquisite dress. On the wall next to her were implements of torture, and the room was strewn with blood in various stages of dryness. Drayah was unconscious and near dead. The rest of the dungeon was far worse than the room in which Lord Avestyn had left Drayah.

Along their way through the labyrinth of rooms, the party found many children dead, their organs in jars next to them. Lord Avestyn had deliberately blinded some children, and the party found others covered in deep scars from prolonged and frequent whippings. From the children who were able to speak, the party learned that Lord Avestyn spent most nights assaulting the children indiscriminately for sport.

The girls suffered rape and torture. Many times their defilement lasted all day. Before the party coaxed the children out of the hidden room, a few children took their own lives. Lord Teymark presumed that the children were spelled to hurt themselves if discovered. It scared the children to leave the dungeon. They thought it was a trick. Most of the children couldn't speak, and they were suffering from a myriad of illnesses and starvation. It took a month of slowly taking them outside for the children to realize that Lord Avestyn was no longer in the castle.

A Druid-Elf named Beelay found Evynloth Almackia. Evynloth was suffering from undernourishment, unable to speak from the years of seclusion. The sunlight hurt him. In all the time he was down in that cell, he never knew there were other children working the levers with him. Evynloth had always wondered how the machine worked while Lord Avestyn allowed him to sleep.

After the discovery of the children, the High Council halted realm travel until they could find a humane way to fuel it. With time, the Magicka and the Elves developed a way to make realm travel work without the use of Kami children. Eventually, the children came to the capital, where the High Council reunited many of them with their families. Most of the children were lucky enough to go home, and many of the capital's citizens adopted those without homes. Evynloth was the eldest of the children and a true orphan. He could not return home because his mother was dead, for in a bout of depression, Juliana had forgotten she was cooking and had burned the house to the ground. The High Council arrived at the realization that Evynloth would not find a home, so they decided he would go to The Erudition to live and study for free.

Beelay became a father figure to him, taking the boy under his wing. He would visit Evynloth at the college whenever he could, and sometimes Evynloth would go to Beelay's home in the Mountains of Memory. Evynloth found it difficult to adjust to life outside of the dungeon. He would often lose his temper when he could not find his words or have panic attacks in the night when the other students in his dorm room would blow out his candle light during the night. His teachers recognized his brilliant mind and a flair for Magicka, but others saw him as damaged goods, an oddball not worth associating with. His life seemed to be on a downward spiral with nothing to hope for, but little did he know there was something good on the horizon.

THE TRUTH UNEARTHED

The next morning, Imogen trekked back to the attic to investigate the chest further. As she opened the chest, it met her with confusion. The chest was empty, without a trace of its former contents.

"How can this be? What's going on? This chest was full to the top last night."

In frustration, she hit the edge of the chest, which caused a secret compartment to open. Inside the compartment, Imogen found a book, a small wooden carved box adorned with gems and strange writings, and a key. Imogen pondered the items before her. What were they and why were they hidden in the chest?

The title of the book was, *The Realm Travel Instructicka*.

As she gazed down at what she was holding, questions filled her head. *How did Grandfather get these? Does this mean that the Story of Evynloth is true?* Quickly, Imogen opened *The*

Realm Travel Instructicka and an envelope fell out of it. Inside was a letter addressed to Imogen.

DEAR IMOGEN,

I kept this box a secret from your grandmother, and I hoped you of all people would never find it. If you are reading this, then it means that I have failed you. Though you never met me, I knew you before you were born. My name is Richard Welkin. I am a Seer and I am your grandfather.

I was born in the Magicka realm of Tera'Loth, once known as Djinn. Tera'Loth is the name of our world, your world. The world you know is a lie. Your grandmother and I moved to the human realm to protect ourselves from danger. You descend from what was once a great magickal family.

At the time of writing this letter, I am in my 40th year. Before I was born, the Seers foretold that I would also be a Seer. A Seer is a person in our world who has all knowledge of the future and past, but the visions we have do not always come true. I died when your mother was five years old. I wanted to have a child when I was much younger, but I knew Astrid was the woman with whom I would have a child.

When we married, I was thirty, and she was just twenty. Even though I was a Seer, I still wanted to change the course of the world, even if it meant my undoing. When I met Astrid, I knew unconditional love, and all I wanted was to grow old with her. I had my first vision at age fifteen

. . .

IMOGEN TURNED the page over to find it blank. Where was the rest of the letter? Imogen was slowly piecing together the puzzle upon which she had stumbled. After reading the partial letter from her grandfather, Imogen went in search of Granny.

After locking everything but the letter away in a secret place, she made her way to Granny's room. When Imogen knocked on the door, she startled Astrid, who was sitting by the fireplace, nose deep in a book. Living with the humans had caused her to develop a weakness for the trashiest romance novels ever written.

"Come in," Astrid called from across the room as she hid her book under a pillow like a naughty child. Astrid tried to maintain her poker face. "Hello, darling, come in and give your granny a kiss."

Imogen embraced Granny before sitting next to the fire in her favorite chair. Imogen could do nothing but stare at Granny.

Astrid broke the silence. "I wonder, darling, did you read your grandfather's storybook yet?"

Imogen sensed a strange tone in Granny's voice. "No, Granny, I did not. The strangest thing happened. I returned to the chest this morning only to find it empty." Imogen tried not to cross her arms or look confrontational.

"Well," Astrid said with a slightly snide voice, "that is peculiar. Perhaps your mother moved the things or gave them away?"

Astrid's face changed as she spoke, her eyes glassy and uninviting. It was as if Astrid was oddly happy that Imogen had not had time to read the book. For the first time in her life, Imogen sensed danger from her grandmother.

"What is wrong, dear? You look like you have something on your mind."

Imogen stood up and walked away from Astrid. "I came to tell you dinner is almost ready."

As Imogen turned to leave the room, Astrid took her arm firmly, locking eyes with her granddaughter. "Are you sure that that was all, my dear?" Astrid's eyes were cold and dark.

Imogen stepped backward, releasing herself from the grip of her grandmother's gaze. "Yes, Granny, that's all."

As soon as Imogen left the room, Astrid snapped out of her trance and went right back to her trashy romance novel, giggling like a schoolgirl.

EVYNLOTH'S HEALING BEGINS

Over the next few years, Evynloth focused on rebuilding his life. Happily, Evynloth discovered his family's joy of Herbalism. After spending all that time in the dungeon, he enjoyed long walks in the vast fields outside the capital. When he was out gathering herbs, Evynloth met the most beautiful girl in all the realms.

Her name was Ericka. Her eyes were like the ocean and her hair was a beautiful chestnut. He tried not to startle her so that he could take in her beauty. He would have gotten away with this if not for the dandelion that hit his nose, making him sneeze.

Ericka turned around, looking for the source of the noise. "Oh, hello there. I am glad it is not just me who sees the quality in these herbs. Most people never venture far from the capital, but I find the quality of the soil surpasses anything you find in the outer areas of the capital."

Evynloth stared at her, dumbstruck.

"Oh, I am sorry. Where are my manners?" She extended a dirt-covered hand. "My name is Ericka Alphias," she said, forcing Evynloth into a handshake.

His love for her was instantaneous. He was so overcome with her beauty and inner peace that, for the first time in many years, he could converse with a person other than Beelay. "I find the orange weed is b-better out here. I l-like to use it in p-pies."

Ericka smiled at him. "Maybe you can make a pie for me next time we meet. I love steak and mushrooms."

It was not a smile of pity for his stammer, but a confirmation of absolute love and friendship. Evynloth was always grateful that she did not point out his stutter or berate him for it. That day, they struck up a friendship and love that Evynloth thought would last forever.

In the weeks after meeting in the woods, they were inseparable. Ericka's father was the high wizard Andreas Alphias, and she worked as her father's apprentice in his spell-casting shop. Evynloth spent every spare moment with her. He would even walk her home every afternoon.

The couple loved to stroll through the market in the evenings as a way of winding down. As they walked through the market, as they did every evening, a young man named Xenus Alphias approached them.

Xenus was the son of Lord Genoa Alphias, the head of the High Council of Magicka. Xenus was always vulgar to everyone except Ericka, because she was his cousin. Xenus walked in circles around the couple as they walked the market, taunting Evynloth along the way.

"How's the weather today? Is the air fresh enough for you, Evynloth? Is it sunny and bright up here?" Xenus remarked in the snidest of tones.

"Xenus, do you have nothing better to do with your time these days?" remarked Ericka.

"Come now, Ericka, it's all just fun between old pals. Isn't that right old chap?" he said as he put an arm around Evynloth's shoulder.

"If you want to be around us, you need to be kinder to Loth," Ericka said as she lifted her nose into the air.

Xenus stood back and bowed at Evynloth humbly. "I apologize, my good sir."

There was no sentiment in his apology, but Xenus played along for Ericka's sake. Xenus had loved Ericka his entire life, but he had never gotten the chance to tell her because Evynloth got to Ericka's heart first. The year that Ericka met Evynloth, Xenus went away to train as a doctor with the Elves. Xenus was now busy establishing a practice alongside his father.

After years of hard work and dedication, Evynloth graduated from The Erudition, after which the High Council assigned Evynloth to work for the Magicka Inventions Unit. There, his duty was designing inventions to improve the lives and comfort of the Magicka people.

Evynloth worked in the Unit and saved his money for a year before he plucked up the courage to ask Lord Andreas for permission to marry Ericka. With courage plucked, he went to the market to find a ring. As he scoped out the tables, he could do nothing but shake his head at the options and mutter to himself about backing out.

It was at the table of the jeweler named Madame Juliana Rosewood that he found the most beautiful pearl-shaped emerald set in a white gold ring.

"Who is the lucky lady then, love?" Juliana said with a wink.

Blushing, he remarked, "Ericka Alphias."

Madame Rosewood gave him a little smile as she wrapped the ring. As Evynloth approached the shop, sudden thoughts of fear washed over him. *What if Lord Andreas says no? Moreover, what if Ericka doesn't want me?*

Taking a moment to breathe, he put the thoughts aside as he entered Lord Andreas's spell-casting shop. Evynloth made his way to the office. There, he found Lord Andreas sitting at his desk, huddled over his spell-casting book as he mumbled to himself.

"Excuse me, Lord Andreas?" He was so nervous, one couldn't hear the words pass his lips. Living in the dungeon all those years had made him soft spoken, and he was still taking speech therapy. After emitting a small cough, Lord Andreas turned to see the disruption of his work.

Upon seeing Evynloth standing in the doorway, his face lit up. "Oh, my dear boy, welcome. Please sit down," Lord Andreas remarked as he ran to clear a chair piled high with books and scrawled pieces of paper. "If you are looking for Ericka, she is fighting her way through a week's worth of laundry. Her mother insists she learns to do things on her own, although I am paying maids to do such. Oh look at me, I am rambling away now." Lord Andreas stopped talking to give Evynloth a once-over. "What is it son? You look pale. Are you eating?" he remarked as he resumed his seat.

Evynloth moved to sit down, but given the reason for his visit, he thought it might seem rude. "S-sir, I do not know any other way to say this, so I'll come out with it."

Upon noticing the look of anticipation on Lord Andreas's face, Evynloth suddenly could not speak.

"Well, spit it out, boy. I'm not young," Andreas said with a chuckle.

A flush came over Evynloth's face as he shouted the words at Lord Andreas. "I want to marry her." A look of horror crossed Evynloth's face. That was not how he had practiced his speech, but there was no opportunity to start over.

Lord Andreas smirked a little as he answered Evynloth. "Well, is that all boy? I have known that for years, but even a man as educated as myself finds himself at a loss as to why you waited this long."

With a deep sigh of relief, Evynloth slumped down into the chair. "That did not go at all how I planned."

Lord Andreas smirked as he wiped his glasses. "Life never does, child, but we muddle through as best we can." Lord Andreas put on his glasses as he turned back toward his desk to continue his work.

Evynloth sat frozen in a giddy daze, shocked at Lord Andreas's quick agreement. He was not from money, or a wealthy family. The only thing he offered was true love for Ericka.

Lord Andreas, sensing a presence, turned back to see Evynloth still planted in the chair. "Boy. Isn't there something you should do?"

Evynloth shot up, as if he had forgotten the reason he was sitting in a daze, and ran out of the shop in search of his bride-to-be.

Ericka sat outside in the courtyard, slumped over a washboard with her laundry piled high beside her, grumbling to herself as she scrubbed away. She was not very house proud and would have preferred to be out gathering herbs.

As he watched her working away, Evynloth heard another call her name. It was Xenus.

Evynloth darted out of view to spy on them. Upon hearing her name, Ericka looked up to find her cousin standing before her.

"Hello, my darling," she said as she stood to hug Xenus. "I hope you are behaving." She looked him over.

"Now, cousin, just you remember who the doctor is here then," he said as he touched her nose.

With a smile, Ericka took his arm and strolled through the gardens with Xenus. From the balcony above, her mother and aunt watched on as the children strolled.

"To what do I owe this pleasure, my darling? I feel you have been avoiding me for weeks."

Xenus smiled and chuckled a little as he responded. "You know I am a big important doctor now, my days enriched with lancing boils and inoculations for the poor."

Ericka smiled as she spoke. "Well, you can see all that has been occupying my time as of late."

The pair approached the gazebo, sitting on a bench in front of an emerald-colored bird bath as Evynloth watched from afar. "My darling, I came to ask you a very important question. I know that you have feelings for Evynloth, but..." Xenus got down on both knees as Ericka gasped. "I would love for you to be my bride," he said as he opened a ring box to reveal a large ruby set in a light shade of purple platinum.

Ericka looked up at her cousin and down at the ring in quick succession. A mix of fear and shock drew the blood from her face. "I love you, but I cannot do that to Evynloth, and there are all the marriage laws to consider. We are first cousins."

Xenus shook his head as he produced a writ from his pocket, handing it to Ericka. It was a legal document signed by the courts, granting special permission on the grounds of family purity. Xenus had convinced an overseer that the family was dwindling in numbers and that this was necessary to keep the family going. "You see my love, I have taken care of everything. Now there is nothing and no one standing in our way."

Ericka looked at him and thought about Evynloth. It tore her to think of hurting either of the two men. As she looked back toward the house, she saw her mother and aunt looking on, and then thought she saw Evynloth hiding in the bushes.

After a brief contemplation, she looked at her cousin and shook her head. Standing to return to her laundry, Xenus grabbed her arm. With tears in his eyes, he remarked, "You will regret this, I promise you, cousin."

Freeing herself of this grip, Ericka walked away with tears in her eyes to return to her laundry. When she returned to the courtyard, she found Evynloth sitting next to the fountain with tears in his eyes.

Ericka ran to his side. "My darling, what is wrong?" she said as she grabbed his hand, which he pulled away from her.

"I-I s-saw you with him. When were you going to tell me about that?"

Ericka hit him as she cried, "There was nothing to tell. I am as surprised as you with what just happened."

Evynloth stood up, raising his hands in the air. "Well then, why were you crying? Was it the joy of your upcoming wedding?"

Ericka threw the washboard as she screamed, "No, you fool. I was crying because I am quite sure I just lost my cousin who, for your information, was my best friend." Ericka ran past him and out of the courtyard in tears.

Evynloth was dumbstruck, but he snapped out of his trance when Lady Alphias approached him.

"I won't lie to you, my dear, when I tell you I wanted another for my daughter, but she has made her choice," Lady Alphias said as she snapped her fingers for a servant.

A servant—one of them was never far away—jumped to attention.

"Please drive our guest out to the orange weed fields to find Lady Ericka?"

The servant nodded as he motioned Evynloth toward the gate. Evynloth wasn't sure he would find Ericka. Despite only being gone a few minutes, Ericka could teleport to any place she wanted. There were no limits to how far away she might be.

When the carriage approached the fields, Evynloth breathed a sigh of relief. There Ericka was, sat in her usual spot atop a stump she had found as a child. Evynloth approached her with caution. She was a great spell-mistress, and he was not stupid enough to startle her if he wished to stay alive.

"Ericka, I came to take you home. Please forgive me for acting like a child."

Ericka remained on the stump with her back still turned.

"I went to see your father today. I asked him a very important question, and he agreed."

Ericka looked down at the ground and grinned, but still refused to turn. She calmed down quickly, another of her endearing qualities. Evynloth walked around the stump to face her. Dropping onto one knee, he held out the ring in Ericka's direction.

"Please look up, because I cannot ask a head of hair to marry me."

Ericka burst into laughter as she ran toward him. "Of course I will marry you, you foolish man." she said as she pulled him from the ground. The couple married in the same spot six weeks later.

BEELAY THE HALF DRUID

On a cool and rainy night, Beelay sat cozily in his chair, nose deep in a book, enthralled by the story. The sound of pounding on his door startled him. There were few people left who knew where he lived, thus allowing him to live a relatively peaceful life. As the pounding continued, he put down his book and grabbed a poker from the hearth on his way to the door. Upon opening the door, he met with the face of a woman who had not graced his home in years.

She was a witch, and her name was Afloriana.

"Afloriana? What are you doing here? It is far too dangerous for us to be meeting."

Afloriana bowed in silence with a little smirk on her face. "I am old enough to protect myself. Besides, I used the dwarven tunnels to avoid detection."

Beelay, still dumbstruck, stared at her.

"Am I going to stand in the doorway looking at your open gob all night, or are you going to let me in before someone sees me?"

Beelay blinked and shook his head as he motioned for her to come inside. "I don't think anyone would see you, or be out in this weather," scoffed Beelay as he followed her down the hall.

Afloriana went straight to the living room and sat down by the fire to warm her hands.

Beelay sensed the tension, so he poured her a much-needed goblet of wine. "You would not be here in person if it was not important. To what do I owe this visit?"

Afloriana gulped down her drink. "The Seers have received a vision. They have learned of the Stone's location."

The color left Beelay's face at once. "We did everything we could to stop them. How did they find out?"

Afloriana looked out the window toward the mountains. "We have a weak link, but who it is, I cannot say and neither can the Seers."

Beelay cried out in frustration. "How could they not know?"

Afloriana nodded in agreement. "They know, but they won't tell me. They have seen another vision that concerns the two of us. The Seers say that if we were to find out who spoke out against us, then we would wage war and forget our true mission to stop him from taking over all of Tera'Loth."

Beelay did not even think for a second before running to the hall closet. "Time has run out, so it seems the time has come. I must bring her to Magicka. Only she can stop him. It is her destiny."

-

After dinner and another boring evening, it was time for bed. That night, Imogen slept in her own room. After Imogen was sure everyone was asleep, she went to her secret hiding place and took out what remained from the attic chest. As she stared down at the realm travel box, she decided on opening it.

A single lock on the top sealed the box. She stopped short of putting the key in the lock. She did not know what she was doing and feared what would happen if she turned the key. *What if I turn the key and nothing happens?*

Suddenly, she thought she heard a man's voice say, "You don't know until you try."

Imogen almost jumped out of her skin as she turned around to find a tall man hiding in the shadows. As he moved into the moonlight, a tall man dressed in a fashion foreign to her met her gaze. She thought his clothes were stranger than the fact that an unknown man was in her bedroom.

"May I introduce myself? My name is Beelay, and I am a half Druid. I am an old friend of Richard's."

Imogen looked at Beelay with fear as she shouted, "What are you doing in my room? How did you get in here?"

The door handle rattled.

Jonas, having walked by, had heard the commotion. "Imogen, it's Dad. What's wrong? I hear shouting."

In the hallway, Simone came up behind him. "She's been acting strange. It might just be hormones. Let me talk to her."

Jonas stepped back and nodded. He was not comfortable with the unpleasant facts of life, so he happily handed that job off to anyone else.

Beelay, having sensed a presence, cast a silence spell over the room.

As Simone put her ear to the door, the room suddenly sounded quiet.

"Come on, darling, let's go to bed," said Jonas as the two walked away.

Imogen continued to interrogate this mystery man. "You mean it's all true, everything? I mean I haven't just dreamed all this up, have I?"

Beelay walked a little closer to her. "No, my dear girl. You have not. If it is your wish, then I will take you on the greatest adventure of your life. The truth is, Imogen, there is more to this story than you know, but I don't know if I should be the person to tell you about it. Astrid has to share responsibility in all of this. She is not who you think she is. But that is not my business to say either."

Imogen's mind was bombarded with more questions than ever before.

Down the hall, Astrid awoke with a start, having felt a slight rumbling in the room. Astrid threw her bedside drawer open to find that her amethyst was lighting up on its own. It only did this when it sensed magick was nearby. Astrid got up to investigate.

The last time this had happened, pixies had accidentally crossed into the human realm and scarcely survived her wrath. As Astrid exited her room, the sense of a strong Aura struck her.

"Beelay," she said in anger as she went in search of the half Druid.

Meanwhile, back in Imogen's room, the tension was rising. "I think I need to see Granny," Imogen said as she looked at Beelay, as if he knew the right answer.

"I don't think that would be a wise move, my girl. Astrid and I, we go back a long way. She was once a kind and sweet girl, but now it is hard for her to tell the truth unless it is to her benefit." Beelay looked toward the door.

The handle rattled again.

"Imogen, darling, it's Granny. Please let me in. I need to speak to you."

Beelay placed a finger to his lips.

"Imogen, I know you are not alone, and I think by now you know that I have not been honest, but I beg you, please do not trust him."

Beelay pulled out his wand and pointed it at the door, bringing an end to the distraction.

"What have you done? Is she alright?"

Beelay scoffed at the thought of Astrid being in trouble and the fact that someone might care. "She will be just fine. It is a temporary coma spell. It froze her in place outside the door, and I am glad for the silence."

Beelay walked to the window to observe the outdoors, having not traveled to the human realm in many years. He took in the view with a sigh. "It's still as beautiful as I remember it."

Imogen ignored him as she thought about her choices. Should she go to bed and pretend this was all an odd dream, or should she go on an adventure in search of answers?

As she opened her mouth to give her answer, Beelay smiled.

"Magicka it is, my dear girl." With that, Beelay took the box and key from Imogen and put the key in the lock. As he placed the box on the ground, he whispered some magickal words. The lid to the box shot open, giving way to a beam of light, which then turned into the shape of an arched tunnel.

"Last chance to back out."

Imogen shook her head as she picked up her army surplus satchel. It was her to-go bag, and she never left home without it. "Very well, child. Hold onto my hand as tightly as you can."

With that, the pair stepped into the archway-shaped tunnel made of light, bound for Magicka.

EVYNLOTH'S WORLD UNRAVELS

In the months preceding his marriage, Evynloth continued to work for the Magicka Inventions Unit and quickly rose to the rank of Overlord. For the first time in his life, he felt he was in charge. In time, Ericka gave birth to a child, a girl they named Astrid.

While the family lived in blissful happiness, Xenus did not. He clearly always loved his cousin, but they were not to be. Xenus tried hard to convince his uncle and his cousin that Evynloth was not a suitable husband. He argued that Evynloth was not right in the mind after what happened to him in the dungeon and that his quick temper was of concern. A great part of this was true, but Evynloth could control himself so long as Ericka was by his side—and without the provocations of Xenus.

Ericka was Evynloth's anchor. She was his good in the world, and he would never have hurt her, ever.

Xenus's hatred for Evynloth only grew as time passed, so much so that he thought about killing Evynloth frequently. A week before the High Council was to reopen for the year, Xenus learned that his father would fill Lord Avestyn's seat and experienced joy for the first time in as long as he could remember.

Having applied to join the High Council, Xenus saw no question of his father's old seat going to anyone else. Unfortunately, the High Council was not of the same opinion. They decided, in a closed session, that they should offer Evynloth the seat as a way of apologizing for what he and all the other Kami children had endured.

Evynloth accepted the position with reluctance. He was not sure if he was right for the position, but he did not want to insult the people who had helped him rebuild his life. The appointment of Evynloth to the High Council was the final straw for Xenus. In his rage, Xenus decided that Evynloth had to die.

On the eve of Evynloth's entrance ceremony to the High Council, Xenus went to Evynloth's home under the guise of congratulating him on his appointment. When Xenus arrived at the house, he found Evynloth nose deep in a journal he kept for all his ideas for inventions.

Evynloth, feeling a presence, turned to see who was there.

"Hello, Evynloth. I hope you don't mind. The door was open," Xenus remarked as he walked toward Evynloth.

"No, Xenus, you know Ericka always welcomes you to our home."

Xenus smiled snidely. "Yes, she is always the dutiful hostess, even for family," he remarked as he ran a finger over the mantle.

Evynloth felt an oddness in the air, akin to when he was a captive of Lord Avestyn. It was a feeling of malice. Evynloth tried to shake the feeling off, mustering a smile. "Xenus, what brings you here, my dear cousin?" he said as he rose from his chair.

Xenus looked at Evynloth with a sense of finality. "Ever since I knew what love was, I knew that I only ever felt it for her. My parents were cold in my upbringing, and they taught me nothing but hatred for those outside of our family. For years it was just the two of us together, blissfully unaware of the world. Lost in the joy of companionship.

"Ericka is the only person who ever understood me. She still understands me and has time for me, even with her time consumed tending to a child and a man who acts like his baby daughter. Have the night terrors subsided, by the way? I spent years planning our marriage, but then you crawled out of that dark hole and ruined my future and my happiness."

Evynloth stepped back toward the kitchen. "Xenus, the past is the past. P-please just w-walk away."

Xenus smirked at the return of Evynloth's stammer. *Weakness*, he thought as he continued to walk toward Evynloth. "I went away the year you met Ericka to train as a doctor with the Elves. A single year away from her, and all my plans were ruined."

"Xenus, my friend, I—"

Xenus raised his voice. "You are not my friend. You are an

impediment. I tried to let this go, but my father giving you that seat over his only child did nothing but add fuel to the fire."

Evynloth reached for a cane that was nearby. "You deserve none of this. You are not a member of the high families. You are nothing better than a sewer rat."

Upon hearing the commotion, Ericka entered the room. "What is going on? I heard shouting and now the baby is awake."

The trio exchanged silent and hurried glances.

"Xenus, my love, are you alright? Are you hurt? Is it our uncle or my parents? Please don't say it's them."

Xenus calmed down at the sound of her voice and the words *my love*, but it was only for an instant. "I've hurt no one, Ericka, darling. Not yet at least."

Ericka looked at him with confusion. "What do you mean 'not yet'?"

Xenus bought out his wand and pointed it at Evynloth, chanting strange words foreign to Evynloth.

"No! Xenus! Stop!" Ericka pulled out her wand in defense of her husband, who had been paralyzed from the spell cast by Xenus.

In his bloodlust, Xenus did not see Ericka step in front of her husband. Evynloth broke free of the spell at the very moment Ericka jumped in front of him. Xenus cast the death spell.

With the crack of his wand, the room went dark.

Within the darkness, all that could be heard was Xenus

screaming in agony. When the light returned to the room, Evynloth went rigid.

On the floor in front of him, Xenus sat clutching Ericka's lifeless body. Evynloth, now paralyzed with shock, dropped to the ground beside Ericka. Her lifeless body was already cold, her eyes wide from the shock.

Xenus, in grief and anger, stood up and screamed over the couple. "You will pay for this. I will tell people I came here at the bequest of my dear cousin. Upon the arrival of a telegram at my office, I learned that she was frightened of what you might do to her because you were suffering from your dark moods again. When I entered the house, I found that you were holding her under a spell and killed her before I could stop you," he said as he calmed down enough to fix his hair and clothing.

Trying not to look at Ericka's lifeless body, Xenus continued his speech. "You then motioned for the stairs. You said that you would kill Astrid. Thus leaving me no other choice but to kill you."

Xenus pointed his wand at Evynloth and began to chant, but mid-sentence, Xenus went quiet as coldness washed over his face. His body fell to the ground to reveal Beelay standing there with a rock in his hand. Evynloth looked at Xenus and then at his wife.

In that moment, darkness overtook his heart forever. He no longer felt anything but anger and hate.

Beelay picked Evynloth up off the floor, "You need to run. I am sure someone besides myself sensed what just happened, which means that the authorities will be here at any moment."

Suddenly, the sound of Astrid's wailing came from above.

Evynloth looked at Beelay in coldness as he said, "Please take care of Astrid. I can't take her with me."

Beelay nodded. "You know I will, friend."

Evynloth and Beelay quickly collected what they needed before leaving the house, each running in opposite directions into the dead of night. Beelay wasted no time in heading to his other home in the Mountains of Memory. It wasn't safe to stay in the capital, and he did not trust his housemaid to keep silent about the baby. Beelay arrived at his home safely, but Evynloth did not get as far as he planned. As he entered the Forest of Fortune, something struck him from behind, and he plunged back into darkness.

ASTRID TRAVELS TO MAGICKA

In the human realm, Astrid was in a panic. After the spell Beelay cast wore off, she rushed to her room to summon the mysterious stranger once more. The man appeared before Astrid, furious. Gone was his respectful attitude.

"Astrid, how could you let this happen? After everything we did to make sure she did not learn of Magicka?"

Astrid squared her shoulders as she tried to look intimidating. "Matthew, I was not responsible for this. It was that meddling half Druid," she said as she collected things from hidden places in her room. "You and I both know that if she is successful in her quest, ours will fail. I already sacrificed my husband for this, and if I have to do the same with my granddaughter, then so be it. He meant more than she ever could."

Astrid walked toward her writing desk as she continued

to speak. "The question is, can we stop her without killing her?" Astrid paced the room, playing with the amethyst in her hand. "I think I'll return to Magicka. This realm is of no further use. From there I can make my decision, where I have more resources."

As Astrid collected her things, an idea struck her. It was something that would surely slow Imogen's impending quest. While everyone else in the house slept, she and Matthew cast a binding transportation spell on Simone. With assurances that Simone's comatose body would be transported to a secret location, she and Matthew left the farmhouse.

As they walked to the edge of the field, Astrid looked back at the farmhouse for the last time. After breathing a short sigh, she cast an inferno spell toward it and entered the portal to the Magicka realm. The inferno burned the farmhouse to the ground, killing Jonas and the other children as she swept away the memory of her life in the human realm.

Astrid hoped the news of her family's death and the kidnap of her mother would distract Imogen from the quest on which she now found herself. Astrid thought her plan was foolproof until a realization struck her. How would she make Imogen aware of the fire and her mother's kidnapping without incriminating herself?

When Astrid and Matthew arrived in Magicka, they landed in the courtyard of Astrid's childhood home. The home had been closed up for thirty years, and the pair found it covered in dust, but after a little spell-casting the house was clean and restored to its former glory. Standing in the grand ballroom, it struck Astrid with nostalgia.

The room was untouched. The tables were still arranged as they were the night of her wedding party. Astrid, being deranged, smiled at the sight of old blood splattered across the purple drapes that enveloped the French style glass doors that led to the veranda. This was the last place she had seen her father, Xenus. Even though he wasn't her birth father, he had loved her as much as any parent would. Loyalty dictated that she avenge his death, but it was too late for that. Astrid smiled as she skipped around the room, swooping around as if she were dancing.

Matthew looked on in confusion. "So, what is your plan now, my lady? He will surely know you have returned."

Astrid shook her head as she poured herself some wine. "Evynloth will not bother with me. Not right now, at least," she said as she gulped down her wine before throwing the glass into the fireplace. "I will reveal all, my dear, but for now, we must rest and gather our strength."

EVYNLOTH'S AWAKENING

Evynloth awoke, dazed. *That was some crack on the head,* he thought to himself.

Opening his eyes, Evynloth came face to face with a man tending to his wound. "I am sorry about that crack on the noggin. The master gave me some Magick to use on you, but I prefer a human touch."

Evynloth looked around the room, trying to figure out where he was. Looking around made him ill. The dizziness overtook him, and he passed out again before he could speak.

Five hours passed before he came round again. As he looked around the room, he screamed without control. He was chained to a bar in the corner of a cell. The cell was the same as the cell he had lived in during his five years of hell.

In the distance, Evynloth heard a click-clack of boots. His head swiveled toward the sound. Footsteps approached his cell in the darkness. Evynloth scrambled to move further from the wall as he squinted, trying to make out his captor.

As the jailer came into view of the light provided by the torch on the wall outside the cell, Evynloth screamed, "No, it cannot be you. They imprisoned you in the Elvish prison of loneliness."

Lord Avestyn bowed as he smirked.

Evynloth kept screaming as he spoke, "No one can escape that place."

As Lord Avestyn came closer, Evynloth witnessed a look of malevolent triumph on his old master's face. "I told you you were staying in that dungeon forever. My slaves leave me when they die, and not before. However, for you I will make an exception."

Evynloth was repelled toward the wall, now lumped up in a ball and crying out in writhing, unbridled agony.

"If you stay with me and help me in my quest to regain my power, then I will have the power to give you the impossible. I can give you back Ericka."

Evynloth stopped crying as he turned to face his old master, shouting out in anger, "How is this possible? There is no way for me to get her back, she is dead."

Lord Avestyn paced the hall as he spoke, "Lord Matthew is my latest apprentice. He and I have traveled extensively since he won me my freedom. We even discovered realms in Tera'Loth that we never knew existed." Lord Avestyn motioned to Matthew.

As Matthew approached his master, he pulled out a large blood red book with black embroidered writing on it. "This, my dear boy, is the Necropedricon. It is a spellbook of wonder."

Lord Avestyn had "negotiated" its possession from some goblins when he had discovered the realm known as Necromancium.

"With this book, we can bring Ericka back, if you help me in my plan."

Evynloth's eyes widened with confusion and hope. "If you do this for me then how do you benefit?" Evynloth asked.

Lord Avestyn grinned in a most sinister manner as he spoke, "I see you have grown wiser since last we met. I have motives of my own, for which I will need your help." As Lord Avestyn tucked the book under his arm, he remarked with spitefulness in his voice, "If you want her back, then no price should be too high."

With that, Lord Avestyn and Matthew walked away, leaving their captive to consider their proposal.

AN AURA IS DETECTED

Lord Evynloth Almackia sat in Lord Avestyn's fortress atop the Cliffs of Mt. Curac in Necromancium. As he mulled over his books and wine, something struck him: it was the Aura, also known as the life force, of Beelay.

Rising from his chair, Lord Evynloth Almackia walked over to the Seer's Stone. As he whispered an incantation, it split the Stone open from the middle to reveal the amethyst Seer's disc. "Show me the master of the Aura I feel," he whispered as he dropped some blood onto the oval slab.

As soon as the image appeared, confusion and intrigue overtook him. The Seer's slab revealed an image of his old friend Beelay and a little humanoid girl. Evynloth, puzzled, pondered over the image. Why would Beelay need to travel to the human realm? Who was the girl?

As he continued to study the image before him, he heard a voice from behind him. "She is your great grandchild. Her name is Imogen Welkin. She doesn't know it yet, but she's come to kill you."

Upon turning, he saw an ailing Lord Avestyn standing in the doorway, hunched over his jewel-encrusted wolf's head staff.

"Master, you are tired and confused. Do you not remember long ago, when my child died?" he said as he led Lord Avestyn to his chair by the fire.

As Evynloth sat beside him, he offered his master wine, which Lord Avestyn happily accepted. "Astrid is still beautiful, even in old age," he said. "If it wasn't for Xenus, she would be living here with us."

A cold look washed over Evynloth's face. How had he not sensed that Astrid was still alive? "Come on now, let's get you to bed," he said. "You are getting confused."

After he put his master back to bed, Evynloth returned to the study. *If this is true, then I need to stop them from getting back into Magicka,* he thought. Evynloth walked to the bookshelf and retrieved an old gray book entitled *The Laws of Realm Travel.*

The book contained, as the title suggested, the laws of realm travel and a few unknown spells, such as how to restrict realm travel. As Evynloth flipped through the book, he could hear his master coughing in the distance. Evynloth wanted Ericka back and revenge upon his master.

Raised as the child of a skilled herbalist, Evynloth was slowly weakening his master's body and magickal abilities with a herbal concoction. This was a mixture that a witch or any other magickal person could ingest if they no longer wished to have magickal abilities. It was a potion originally brewed to take away magick from prisoners and other undesirables, and its development had been perfected during the Djinn Civil War.

However, the use of this drug had ceased when the Elves, who saw it as a gross violation of an individual's Aura and an abuse of the freedom to choose, destroyed the main ingredients for the concoction. After a long, drawn out argument between the Elves and the Djinn, the Elves had set out to rid Tera'Loth of the main ingredient of the potion, known as Dementium. This was a flower that, if ingested, sterilized one of magick and left one with psychotic episodes because of the shock to the brain.

On top of the eradication of the plant, the Elves had also confiscated all copies of the recipe and burned every one of them—or at least, so they had thought. Evynloth had stumbled upon the unknown copy of the spell in his youth.

Once, years ago, after Evynloth had returned to the site of his childhood home to pay homage to his parents. There, he had met an old witch named Giselle who lived a few minutes from the site of Evynloth's childhood home. She said nothing to him placing a small box in his hands; Before she turned to leave, she took Evynloth's hand. "It was her choice. She set the fire before she took the poison."

With that admission, the old lady backed away and returned to her home. Evynloth put the box in his satchel. As he walked back to the university, he cried quietly about his mother's decision to end her own life. He was mad at her for her selfishness. If she'd been lucid, why had she not come to rescue him? When he had returned to his dorm room, Evynloth placed a locking spell on the door to make sure nothing disturbed him when he opened this final, and only, gift from his mother. The contents of the box were a few pieces of gold; an overstuffed satchel of herbs; and a small, brown, leather-bound book. Taped to the lid of the box was a letter addressed to him, which Evynloth wasted no time reading:

MY DEAR CHILD EVYNLOTH,

IF YOU ARE READING THIS, then it means I am gone. I am writing this letter to you so I may remind you of your duties to the house and your mother. As I write this, I am feeling ill. I fear that someone has poisoned me with an herb called Dementium. I am not surprised, because I always knew this may be the way my life ended.

When I was born, many Seers cast their predictions. My grandmother, being a woman of power, influence, and money, demanded the best for her first grandchild, so she ordered all the Seers to her home to see me and tell my fortune. A Seer, Zeeder, came to her home with his daughter, Afloriana. When he touched my hand, he screamed as he received my prophecy. When he broke free of my hand, he refused to stay in the home with me.

My father and grandmother accompanied the man outside to witness his prediction. He told them I would have a child who would be the purest evil in all the realms of Tera'Loth. Zeeder also foretold that my child, who would be a son, would unlock a dangerous place to get back the woman he loved. My grandmother could not understand how someone of pure evil could love anyone at all, and they dismissed Zeeder with only half of what they promised to pay him.

I hope Zeeder was wrong about you, my son. You need to understand, you always have a choice. Even if you don't think you do. When you were born, a Seer came, and she told us you would have a great life full of joy, but that your Aura was once inside of someone who knew nothing but extreme evil and hate. The choice is yours, son.

Please remember that we loved you, even if your mother and I did not show it. I wish I could have spent more time with you, but this was my fate. I won't tell you who poisoned me, because I know he will get the punishment he deserves without you ruining your life. Remember to take care of your mother and do what is right. Even when you think it's wrong.

Your Loving Father,
Ereous Almackia

EVYNLOTH SAT, somber after reading the letter. These words were the only kind thing his father ever offered him. The pair had been so distant that he had gone his whole life without ever knowing his father's name. Evynloth had done nothing but struggle with his past since his exit from the dungeon and had experienced nothing but feelings of hate, anger, and shame. He hated his father for dying, but now he hated whoever had poisoned him. Evynloth flipped through the leather-bound book, skimming over the notes and spells. This was the book in which he had discovered the long-forgotten spell used to rid an individual of their magick.

The spell was known as Deterus-Magicka.

XENUS AND ASTRID

Xenus woke up in the infirmary five days after Ericka's murder. As soon as he could speak to the authorities, Xenus made sure there was no doubt who killed his cousin. Before the murder, he had told his mother that he was on his way to check in on Ericka and that Evynloth was experiencing a bad spell, showing signs of mania because of the stress of his upcoming ceremony. Being of a prominent family, there was no question of Xenus's version of the events. The hunt for Evynloth began.

Evynloth ran that night because he knew, while he was only guilty of self-defense, given Xenus's stature, he would surely see the gallows for a crime he did not commit. Meanwhile, in the years after Ericka's death, Xenus got his coveted seat on the High Council and guardianship over Astrid.

One year into his hunt for Evynloth, Xenus found Beelay and Astrid at their home in the Mountains of Memory.

Xenus thought he was smart and that he knew everything, but Beelay had proved him wrong by hiding in plain sight for the past year.

On the day that Xenus and his men arrived at Beelay's house, Xenus found Astrid playing in a bathtub in the garden. Beelay was playing peek-a-boo with her as she giggled and splashed around in the water.

"Hello, Beelay. It's been too long, old man."

Beelay jumped up as he grabbed his cane.

Alorah, a girl that Beelay had hired to help him with the baby, scooped Astrid up from the tub and ran indoors. She knew who Xenus was and did not trust him at all.

"What are you doing here? Leave us alone, please."

Xenus adjusted his robes as he smirked. "Come now, you knew I'd figure out that Evynloth did not take the child. A child is not the easiest travel companion, especially when you are on the run."

Beelay stepped in front of the doorway. "You are not taking her away from me. Please, Xenus. Astrid's happy here with me."

From behind Beelay, Alorah shouted, "You know the laws, sire. You need to go to the High Council before you can have the girl."

Xenus laughed out loud at the girl's remark. "And how could a small-minded village girl know such?"

Alorah stepped up next to Beelay in the doorway, staring at Xenus as she spoke, "Because, good sir, I am not a small-minded village girl. I am the daughter of the High Councilor Lord Kavron," she said as she showed him her family amulet.

The Kavron amulet was a circle with a ruby carved into the shape of a jagged rock.

Xenus took a step backward. Rumor stated that Alorah had died during the conflict at Dwarven Rock years ago. She was not a conventional woman. At age eleven, she had run off toward the adventure of war.

"This is not over, Beelay," Xenus said as he pointed a finger at him before running to his carriage.

After pleading, blackmailing, and bribing, Xenus persuaded the High Council to issue him a writ that allowed him to take Astrid because they were blood. Xenus could not deliver the child to her grandparents, who had died of grief not long after losing Ericka.

Xenus and the High Council left Beelay with no choice other than to let Astrid go, but he never stopped watching over her. Astrid grew up in Xenus's compound in relative seclusion. When she was fifteen years old, Xenus, who she knew as her father, decided that it was time she started her formal education. He did not want her to go to The Erudition with the common children, so Xenus sent her to train with a High Wizard and the greatest Seer in the land, Prov Welkin.

Prov Welkin lived deep in the Forest of Fortune with his wife Edwina and his son Richard. Most Seers lived in the forest because of its seclusion. It was in a part of Magicka that few visited, allowing the inhabitants peace and privacy to carry out their craft. When Astrid arrived at the Welkin home, Prov's son, Richard, who was a Seer like his father, met her. As soon as they saw each other, their connection was instant. He was the most handsome man she had ever seen.

From the house, Richard's parents emerged to greet their new student. "Welcome, my child, welcome," Prov said, shaking the girl's arm nearly out of its socket.

Xenus stepped forward, looking authoritative as always, before ordering his man to remove Astrid's bags from the carriage. "This looks like a nice secluded place for your studies. I want you to be free of distraction and become the best witch in the land," remarked Xenus as he tried not to cry. "Say your goodbyes to your father, then go inside and get settled."

Astrid kissed her father goodbye then retreated to the doorway, where she waved to his carriage until it was out of sight. Astrid studied with Prov for the next five years. She was a natural witch, and she excelled in her daily lessons. She was a great source of pride to Prov as a student, but she scared him too.

Dark magick flowed through her, as well as the desire to practice it.

Once, after classes, Prov found her in the Library, reading from the books he forbade. "Astrid, have you prepared the herbs for your examinations yet? You're scheduled to meet with the herbologist tomorrow, and I do not want shame brought upon my name."

Astrid ignored her teacher as she read from a book called *The History, Laws, and Rituals of Necromancium.*

Prov took the book from her, slamming it shut. "You shouldn't read this. It is dangerous and above your level." Prov looked at the girl with fear.

Her eyes were black as night. She was in a trance from

what she had read. Necromancy and other dark magick interested her more than any other thing he taught her. Although he was cautious of her, he honored the promise he had made to educate her. Even though he knew she was meant for dark magick, he still sensed a good Aura, which he wanted to bring out into the light.

In between her studies with Prov Welkin, Astrid formed a relationship with Richard. He was ten years her senior, but the love they professed for each other was true. Her love for him was the only stroke of good in Astrid's body.

When Astrid turned twenty, it marked the end of her education. On the eve of her journey home, Richard asked her to be his wife. She agreed giddily, but she worried about her father's reaction to the news, fearing no blessing. Seers were not so popular anymore and did not make the amount of money they had in their heyday.

"Do not worry, my love. Your father will give me his blessing, along with a fine job and a home in the capital."

Xenus arrived early the next morning to collect his daughter.

"Ah, my lord Xenus, wonderful to see you. Please, won't you come in for a cup of tea," Prov said in a most welcoming tone.

"No, thank you. We have no time for delay."

Richard approached the carriage with Astrid and her bags. "Sir, if you please, I seek your audience."

Xenus adjusted his posture as if trying to show his authority. "Well, boy, speak."

Richard bowed his head as he asked for Astrid's hand in marriage.

Xenus's demeanor changed in a flash. "I don't think it wise." The thought of a Seer in his family repulsed him, but he could not disappoint his daughter. "But maybe I could consider it, if..."

Richard's eyes widened. "Yes, sir? If what?"

Xenus looked at the boy with anger and considered walking away before he continued to speak, "You can not afford to give my daughter the life she is accustomed to on a Seer's wage. If you wish to marry, you must get 100,000 gold pieces. If you can do this before her twenty-first birthday, then you may be wed."

The prospect overwhelmed Richard. How would he get that much gold? The thought of this terrified him, but he tried not to show it in his face. "Yes, sir, I will do so."

With a heavy heart, he waved the carriage and his bride-to-be away.

That night as he slept, a very disturbing dream struck him. Xenus was fighting with a couple. Then he saw a girl from a dream he had experienced years ago. She was fighting with someone of pure evil. She was trying to stop him from putting something in a hole.

He woke up with a start. It felt as if someone was standing over him, but when he looked about, no one was there. Upon sitting up, he discovered a bag and a note on his nightstand. Inside the bag, thousands of gold coins piled upon each other.

The note left with it read, "Marry her. Damn him."

Richard, confused and elated, put his hand in the bag to grab a coin to check if they were fake. The second his hand touched a coin, a vision struck him.

He stood in a packed room. It was his wedding day, and everyone grinned with glee. The guests ate and danced.

Suddenly, a dark force entered the room. In a flash of light and smoke, the evil Lord Evynloth appeared before Xenus. Richard could see the two speaking before they fought. The fight finished with the death of Xenus and a strange man whisking the newlyweds from the room before Evynloth could turn on them.

Richard awoke from the vision dripping with sweat. He knew this vision was dire, but he also knew emotions could cloud a Seer, causing inaccurate visions of the future. Richard decided that it was wise to keep this vision to himself, at least for now. He had more pressing issues to attend to—such as getting married.

In the morning, he told his parents he was going to the Elves to get the money to marry Astrid. He didn't think Xenus would believe the money had just appeared. To keep his secret, Richard told people that he was going to work in the Elvish mines for a few months. Richard decided, instead of going into the mines for quick money, he would go to the Elves to learn the magick of healing. Thus, he could continue to keep his wife in the lavish life to which she was accustomed, and he could also help the people of the land.

While in the Elvish realm, he studied with Lord Teymark and learned his trade quicker than any other student. As soon as his studies were complete, he went straight to

Xenus's house. Richard walked into his bride's home with a victorious air about him. Without hesitation, he ran straight to Xenus's study, trying not to slam on the door too hard.

"Enter," Xenus's servant muttered from behind the solid oak door.

Upon entering the study, Richard found Xenus hunched over a medical book, asleep from what must have been very dull content.

"Sir?"

Xenus snorted as he awoke.

"Sir, I have returned with the sum agreed. Now your daughter can marry me."

Xenus could not believe his eyes. Xenus had given the boy what he saw to be an impossible task and was none the wiser of the boy's mysterious benefactor. "Well, Mr. Welkin, I am an honest man who keeps his word. You have completed the task, so go find your bride before I change my mind."

THE REALM OF THE DRUIDS

When Beelay and Imogen emerged from the portal, Beelay panicked. Beelay looked fearfully at the surrounding landscape, realizing that they were in the realm of the Druids, known as Sage to the locals, instead of their desired destination—Magicka.

"How could this happen? I set our destination for Magicka. How did we end up in Sage?"

From the distance, a familiar voice remarked, "Are you not glad to be home, my friend?"

Beelay turned to find his cousin Segion leaning against an elm tree. "Segion," Beelay said gleefully as Segion approached. "Cousin, how have we landed here?"

Segion looked at Imogen with curiosity as he spoke, "Evynloth got his hands on a seeing stone. When he found out that you went to the human realm, he stopped you from traveling to Magicka by rerouting your destination. I think he meant to bring you straight to his fortress, but he is not as skilled with divert-magick as he wants to be," Segion remarked as he looked to the skies. "Best head indoors before someone sees us. Lord Avestyn has spies everywhere."

With that, he led them to a waiting carriage. As the carriage rolled through the forest, Segion continued to tell them of Evynloth and everything else that had transpired in Beelay's absence.

"When you left through the portal to go to the Elvish realm, everything went south. Lord Almackia and Lord Avestyn sensed someone other than the Elves casting magick. Going to the Elvish realm to cross over appeared the wiser choice, and I thought you would go undetected, but I was wrong. But their sensing your magick is the least of our problems. They have a seeing stone, and with it, the upper-hand."

As the carriage rounded a corner, Segion's home came into view. Imogen gasped. The home was so grand that it held the title of the biggest home in the realm. The mansion must have contained over a hundred rooms. The house was a deep red, vine covered, three-story mansion made of solid cement. As the carriage approached the front entrance, a man came out to greet them. *This must be the butler,* she thought, giggling nervously. She'd never met a butler before and wasn't sure how to act.

"Hello, sir. May I take your coat?"

Segion nodded and handed off their coats to his servant. "Imogen, if you'd like, you can freshen up."

Segion's butler, Vorlin, nodded. Motioning for the staircase, he led Imogen upstairs.

After changing, she returned downstairs to meet Beelay and Segion in the study. When Imogen saw Beelay in a better light, she gasped.

He was human, but his ears were different; they were the ears of an Elf.

"Fear not, child. I am no threat to you. I am half Elf and half Druid, but we can talk about that later."

Imogen lowered her head in shame. "I am sorry for my reaction. It's just that I have never seen anything—I mean any*one*—that looked like you."

Beelay smiled as he motioned for her to sit. "I know none of what's happened is making sense right now, but I hope by the end of the evening you will have a better understanding of who you are and why I brought you here." Beelay reached into his coat pocket, retrieving a piece of paper. "First, I want you to see the entire letter that your grandfather wrote you. Your grandmother tried to hide it from you, but I intervened."

With that, Beelay handed Imogen the rest of the letter:

I saw a girl in a room packed with people. They cheered for their hero, but their happiness did not last. You will succumb to death by an evil Wizard who is too powerful to stop. I could not let that happen. I planned to move to the human realm, where you could live in safety, but I was not sure I would move there until the night of my wedding.

That wizard took away my choice on that night. Astrid and I left when the chance arose, and that decision has kept you safe and oblivious until now. Please, do not go to the Magicka realm. Any Seer knows that someone can change their destiny with the smallest or biggest of actions. Please, for everyone's sake, do not go to Magicka. The realm is not safe, and the chance of your death is still probable.

WITH LOVE and warning from the grandfather you never knew,
   Richard Welkin

IMOGEN SAT for a moment in silence as she took the letter in. "Why did Granny hide this from me, and why did you not show me this before I came to Magicka? Don't you think it was my right to read this and ask questions before you dragged me into whatever's going on in this place?"

Beelay looked at her with sadness in his eyes. "I brought you here because only you can stop the Wizard your grandfather speaks of. His name is Evynloth."

Imogen's eyes popped. "Evynloth? As in the Evynloth from grandfather's story?"

Beelay twisted in his seat as he spoke. "It wasn't a story, child. Your grandfather wrote it as a story so that we could preserve the history of our land." Beelay cried as he sat slumped in his chair. "I knew Evynloth well. He lived in that dungeon for five years and it was I who rescued him. When I saw him for the first time, he looked so weak, but I could see a madness brewing in him. The years of seclusion robbed him of his inner peace and he never got that back, even to this day."

Beelay turned his head, trying to conceal his tears. "Imogen, you need to know, he knew happiness for a time. Evynloth knew the joy of someone good in his life, but a cruel and jealous man who desired everything Evynloth possessed in the world robbed him of the happiness he deserved. That man's jealousy shattered Evynloth's world and gave evil an opportunity to seep into his soul."

Imogen shifted in her chair, uncomfortable as she tried to take in what Beelay was saying. Imogen looked downward at the paper in her hands as she spoke, "I have so many questions. I do not know where to begin."

From his pocket, Beelay retrieved his pipe, lighting it as he replied, "Just ask the first question that pops into your head."

Imogen thought for a moment. "What is Evynloth doing, and why do I need to stop him?"

Beelay took in a long puff of smoke, exhaling it slowly as he spoke, "Evynloth has become a cruel Wizard. He has stopped most of us from using magick and is hell bent on revenge for everything that has happened to him in his life. We received a prophecy that he and his master intend to reopen a long dormant realm named Necromancium. If they open the gates of Necromancium, it will be the end of Tera'Loth as we know it."

Imogen looked at Beelay in confusion as she tried to form the strange words with her own tongue. "What is in...*Necromancium*?"

AN INTERRUPTED WEDDING PARTY

After months of planning, the wedding was days away. Astrid was in a nervous flurry, wanting everything to be perfect for her big day. There was a sadness overshadowing the day. Astrid wished her mother could be here to celebrate. Xenus had led Astrid to believe her mother died in childbirth.

Richard and his family arrived by carriage the day before the wedding. Xenus, being a stern traditionalist, made the groom and his family stay in a room at the local inn. The big day was finally upon them.

After Astrid was sure everything was in order, she went up to change into her wedding dress. Xenus had instructed the dressmaker to take measurements but had refused to let Astrid see the dress until her big day. When she entered her room, she found an elegant gown. It was white with a blue sash adorned with little purple butterflies.

"The sash was your mother's. I hope the dress is to your liking."

Astrid cried as she pounced upon her father with the biggest hug she could muster. "I love it, Father. You could not have pleased me more if you tried."

Xenus wiped her tears, clicking his fingers for the maid. "Stop crying so Beatrix can help you with your make-up."

The wedding took place at Xenus's home, in the courtyard. Richard couldn't contain himself as he watched his bride come down the aisle.

After the couple said, "I do," the feast began.

Inside the mansion, the household staff had spent the day before the wedding filling the ballroom with tables in the shape of semicircles, stuffing each of which with many decadent foods. In the corner of the room, a band was playing music. As the wedding party filled the room, many of the guests sat to eat while others grabbed a drink before they dashed to the dance floor.

After hours of merriness and feasting, it was time for the father of the bride to give his speech.

"Quiet, please. I'm ready to make my speech. I promise it won't be too long or embarrassing, my darling," he said with a cheeky smirk. "Years ago, when I sent my gorgeous girl off to study magick, I knew not that I was sending her off to meet her husband. I am a jealous man, but no fool. I knew she wouldn't be with me forever, but I hoped to keep her at home with me until she was forty—or until I was dead."

The room erupted with laughter and cheers.

"Settle," Xenus said as he waved his arms in a downward

motion. "I could not have chosen a more resourceful and dedicated man for my only child. I love you, Astrid, and I wish you every happiness in the world."

As father and daughter embraced, a darkness fell across the room. With a great force of wind, the door to the ballroom burst open, flying off its hinges.

In the doorway stood a large foreboding figure, cloaked in a shimmering dark purple robe. The figure swished their hand toward the band, stopping the music instantly. The guests looked around in worry.

"Who goes there?" Richard said as he stepped in front of his bride and father-in-law.

"What a stunning and ever-so-endearing speech, Xenus, and so full of sentiment. I can see you love my daughter very much, but the show's over now, my dear old friend."

Xenus stood back in horror as Evynloth's head emerged from the shadows of his robe. Evynloth was more formidable than Xenus remembered, appearing not to have aged a bit in twenty years.

"It's not possible. Lord Avestyn promised me you were dead."

A flash of ire swept across Evynloth's eyes. "What did you do, Xenus?"

Astrid looked between the mystery man and her father in confusion. "Father, who is this man?"

A painful wash of sadness crossed Xenus's face. "I never wanted to lie to you. Please don't be angry with me. I love you."

Astrid stepped away from her father, taking Richard's

hand instead of Xenus's. The sight of his daughter seeking safety in the hands of another broke Xenus's heart. Through slow-flowing tears, Xenus unfolded the truth.

"Your mother's name was Ericka, and she and I were cousins. For as long as I understood love, I knew I felt it for Ericka. I wanted to marry her, but she refused me. I left to learn and train with the Elves as a doctor. It was in that year my Ericka met your father. On a fine spring day, he slithered out of a hole in the ground to ruin our lives."

Xenus felt the coldness of an Aura pass through his body, causing him great pain. The room was suddenly filled with the Auras of his dead family members.

"You do not speak her name again. Ericka is mine," yelled Evynloth as he struck Xenus down.

Astrid screamed as Xenus fell into Richard's arms. As he lay there dying, he whispered to Astrid, "I was a jealous man, and I let anger take over my Aura." Grabbing his daughter's hand, he continued, "You were my good in the world. If it was not for you, then I might stand in Evynloth's place right now."

Astrid nodded as she kissed her father, stroking his hand as the light passed out of his eyes. Astrid's sadness, in a flash, turned to anger. "You bastard. I will kill you," she screamed as she reached for her wand, but it turned to sand in her hands before she could cast a spell.

"Astrid, I will only warn you once to never raise a wand in my direction. I am your father, and I came here to avenge you and the life he took from us."

Astrid stepped backwards to the safety behind her

husband. Richard, who was trying to get the words out to fight Evynloth, stopped dead in his tracks. He felt a migraine coming on. This happened when he recalled a past vision. Recalls often happened when someone from his visions was nearby.

With a wail, Richard hit the ground. Through the pain, Richard remembered the dream and vision from the night he received the coins needed to marry Astrid. Pushing his wife —who was now on the ground beside him—to the side, Richard shouted at the man who had ruined the couple's happy day. "You will not kill her. You are a liar, and you have not come to save her."

Evynloth raised his wand. "I must kill her. My master commands me to do so."

Evynloth cast the death spell, and the couple disappeared from the room. Evynloth was silent for a time and did nothing but grin in triumph as he cast his gaze to the rest of the terrified wedding party.

"I am so glad that everyone of importance is here. What a treat for me that every member of the High Council is here today. It makes this next bit of business so much easier." Evynloth summoned the Aura reclaimers, known as death's henchmen or *Awat Albiate* in the old language. As they swooped through the room, the henchmen wrapped themselves around each of the High Council members.

The High Council members screamed in agony, while the Aura reclaimers sucked their souls from their bodies before reducing them to dust.

"My master, Lord Jinn Avestyn, and I are now the rulers

of the Magicka realm and soon-to-be the rulers over every realm in Tera'Loth. I ban the practice of magick for everyone except your new masters and our apprentice, Lord Matthew Teymark. You will surrender to a binding spell and surrender your magickal paraphernalia. I will meet resistance to this new age with death."

The room filled with a quiet panic as Evynloth continued, "Return to your homes and gather up your magickal possessions. You must report to the courtyard outside of the High Council building at midnight to surrender these items."

A few hours later, the High Council courtyard filled up with the residents of the capital. With everyone's magickal possessions surrendered, Evynloth administered the binding spell that restricted anyone from performing magick. Evynloth and his underlings forced the crowd to form a line. The new leadership stood in front of the terrified crowd, raised their collective wands and chanted. A tiny cloud of purple smoke flowed out of every person in the courtyard. Flurries of purple smoke filled a large blood red colored chest.

With every last bit of magickal force in the chest, the underlings sealed the chest and took it with the rest of the magickal possessions to a safe location. Evynloth had taken the piece of an Aura that gives beings their magickal abilities from everyone in the courtyard, thus guaranteeing absolute rule over Magicka for him and his master.

MATTHEW HATCHES A PLAN

As Astrid paced around the room, an idea struck her. She pulled out her wand and walked over to a curious-looking stone.

"Our primary concern is stopping Imogen, but we need to find her first." With that, Astrid waved her wand and spoke the spell to unlock the stone before them.

The stone split in two, revealing a large, flat, oval amethyst. She too possessed a Seer's Stone. Astrid placed three drops of her own blood on the Stone and spoke Imogen's name. As the Stone took in the blood, a whirlpool of sorts appeared on the flat Stone. As it swirled, the Stone absorbed the blood. When the whirlpool stopped, the face of Imogen appeared.

"It appears she is in the Druid realm of Sage with Lord Beelay." Astrid knew that even if she and Matthew got to the Druid realm, they could never get past the spells of protection Beelay would likely have placed on his cousin's home. "We need to think. How can we lure her from the house?"

Matthew thought, skimming the room. On the bookshelf, he spotted a familiar book, titled *Harpies: Volume 1*. With a sinister look, he took the book from the shelf and disclosed his plan to Lady Astrid.

Meanwhile, atop the Black Mountains, Simone awoke from her mother's sleeping spell. She could see nothing around her and could not move, for she found herself chained to a crumbling concrete wall.

Simone shouted, "Hello, can anyone hear me?"

Suddenly, the room flooded with light. "Ah. Our newest guest is awake."

Simone looked up toward the voice, only to find a man in strange clothing standing on a chain link catwalk.

"Confused, my dear? My name is Orvin, and I run this prison."

Simone looked up, squinting toward the ceiling. Through the grate she saw a man dressed in black, with long dark-hazel hair and the blackest, coldest eyes, devoid of humanity.

"Why am I in prison? What prison is this?"

Orvin replied with a cold tone, "You are here because someone you thought you loved needed you out of the way."

Simone's anguish and complete obliviousness grew with every passing second. "Where is my family? Did you take them too?"

As Orvin left his newest prisoner, he said but a single word, "Dead."

With that, he plunged Simone back into the darkness as she screamed out in a sound of everlasting torment.

HARPIES, HARPIES EVERYWHERE

Imogen sat frozen in her chair, a blank look on her face. Beelay's story swam around in her mind. A part of her still couldn't believe this was true. "I don't feel well. I need air," she said as she stood. She felt very dizzy and collapsed into Segion's arms. It was too much to handle.

"I think you should go upstairs and sleep," he said. "Today has been tiring and confusing, and it will not get any better as your quest continues."

Imogen climbed the stairs to bed. She was so tired that she did not even bother getting under the covers, passing out before her head hit the pillow.

A few hours later, she awoke to hear a sharp screeching howl from below. It was the sound of chaos.

"Disengage from my bookshelf, you evil beast. Leave this house now."

The sounds of zapping and swooshing wands echoed

throughout the house. Imogen ran downstairs toward the danger. At the bottom of the stairs, she saw a group of what Beelay later told her were harpies. These magickal beasts could break through any magick and were easy to persuade into wreaking havoc and chaos. Beelay and Segion ran through the house trying to kill them, but more arrived with every passing minute.

"I know they mean to chase us from this house. It is not safe out there, but we have to take a chance before these creatures kill us."

With that, Beelay, Imogen, Segion, and Vorlin fled the house as quickly as they could. As soon as they left the house, the harpies retreated to their lair.

"We need to get away from here. No guessing who sent the harpies. I know a safe place in Impenia—that's the Imp-Pixie realm—but we need to hurry," Beelay said as they headed for the carriage.

When they approached the carriage, a man appeared before them. It was Matthew.

"I should have known you'd be behind this attack," Beelay said. "Does this mean she is here too?"

Matthew pulled out his wand and pointed it toward his captives as he circled them. "When you left the human realm, certain parties detected magick being used in a dormant realm. I mean you no harm, Imogen, but I need you to know that your dear mother Simone is, at this moment, held captive by a man named Orvin. He is the prison-keeper of the Prison of Emotion that sits atop the Black Mountains.

"You see, your mother discovered the truth of her

heritage and came to help you in your quest. Much to her regret, she was unaware of how to use magick, so she—oh, what is that phrase you humans have? That's right. She 'found herself in the wrong place at the wrong time'."

Imogen looked to Beelay for guidance.

"If you come with me," Matthew said, "I can help you save her. I am a powerful man and have many resources at my disposal."

Tension locked Beelay and Matthew's gazes. "Matthew, I know it was you who unleashed those harpies that nearly killed us, but I cannot think why you'd do such a thing. How does this help your cause?"

Matthew took a step toward Beelay and whispered in his ear, "My causes are many, but for now I care only for the safety of my master's apprentice. We will win. Evynloth will survive, and Lord Avestyn will rule over Tera'Loth in darkness."

Imogen looked at Beelay and Segion, searching for an answer in their eyes.

Segion sensed her wish for a dose of Druid wisdom. "Imogen, if you go with this man, we cannot help you any further. He will cut you off from us and the knowledge we have to help you. How do you know it's not a trap?"

Trap or not, Imogen knew she needed to save her mother.

Imogen cried as she spoke, "I am sorry, but it's my mother, and she came here to save me. I have to go with this man—even if it is a trap."

Matthew smiled in triumph as he looked at Beelay, grabbing Imogen by the arm and walking her to the center of the courtyard. Matthew opened a portal, pushing Imogen through it before entering it himself. As the portal disappeared, Beelay stared at the empty spot.

Segion placed a hand on his cousin's shoulder in solidarity. "Maybe this needed to happen so that she can realize her destiny."

The men turned back toward Segion's home. "I guess we better get cleaning?" Beelay said as he followed Vorlin into the house.

"Let's just leave it until the morning. I cannot bear the thought of cleaning up right now," said Segion as he pulled a flask from his pocket.

Beelay shook his head as he stole a swig from the flask. "Don't be lazy, Segion. We have magick to help us. It's not as if it will take long," remarked Beelay as he stepped back outside swooshing his wand toward the house.

Inside, chairs and tables floated through the house. A quick spell called catastrophes-disentangle did the trick and restored the house to its former glory. Off in the distance, a burst of light shot up into the skies of Magicka.

Imogen, now in Magicka, was on her own.

THE AWAKENING

Deep in the Forgotten Wood of the Sage stood a grand house filled with many beautiful rooms. In a quiet room slept the newlyweds, Astrid and Richard. As Astrid awoke, confused, she swept her eyes around a room she did not know.

"Where am I? Is this the land of death?"

In a panic, she shook her husband awake.

Richard groaned then shot up with a start, pointing his wand in the direction Evynloth would have been. "Don't you touch her."

"This is not the land of death, child" replied Vorlin, the butler who was charged with watching over the couple. "This is the house of Segion of the Forgotten Wood."

Meanwhile, downstairs Beelay paced the study in panic. "When he finds out what we did, we're done for."

Segion sat in his chair, swirling his wine without the

slightest hint of fear. "Come now, Beelay, he won't find out. He is far too dense and not as in-tune with his magickal senses as he would have you think. Evynloth is the puppet of Lord Avestyn and filled with bloodlust."

As Vorlin rounded the corner, he gave a slight nod to his master. "Ah. It would seem that our love birds are awake."

Vorlin, being a man of few words, motioned for the pair to enter the study.

Astrid looked at Beelay and Segion in confusion. "Who are you and where am I?"

As Beelay rose from his chair, he offered the newlyweds a drink. As Beelay approached the table, he introduced himself as he poured the drinks. "My name is Beelay, and I have been watching over you since you were a baby, Astrid. It is true, your mother died when you were young, but it didn't happen in childbirth."

Beelay handed out the drinks and returned to his chair.

As the young couple sat down, he continued to speak, "Your mother's name was Ericka, and she was, without question, the most beautiful woman in the land. When she was seventeen years old, she met a man by the name of Evynloth Almackia. He was on track to be a great Wizard, but he was a troubled man.

"Evynloth spent many years held captive and tortured by his master, Lord Jinn Avestyn. I was part of the group of Wizards who helped to free him and the other children locked away by Lord Avestyn. With time, Evynloth made a new life for himself by marrying your mother and having a child who they named Astrid. You were the most beautiful baby my eyes ever laid eyes on. You were such a calm baby, it was as if nothing at all phased you. The only time I ever heard you cry was the night your mother died.

"It was the eve of your father's swearing in ceremony. He was receiving a seat on the High Council of Magicka, in honor of the Kami children harmed by Lord Avestyn. That night, I came over to take your father out to the tavern. When I got to the house, I found Xenus standing over your father. Your mother was lying dead next to your father. Xenus would have killed him if I hadn't knocked him over the head with a rock. Your father knew nobody would believe he was innocent, so we ran.

"He asked me to care for you in his stead, and I did—until you were about two. That was when Xenus found us at my home in the Mountains of Memory. He forced the High Council's hand, and they ordered me to give you up. I did not want to, but I had no other choice."

Astrid sat, stunned, as she looked at her husband in utter disbelief. "What happened to my father? Why did he turn evil?"

Beelay shook his head. "The truth is, I just don't know."

As Richard looked at his new bride, he could see the sadness and fear in her eyes. "Do not worry, my love, I will make sure he never finds out we are alive. He will not hurt you as long as I live."

As Richard turned toward Beelay, he did not have to utter another word. Beelay said, "I will get you two out of here. The safest place for you is a realm not known by many. They call it Earth, and it is the humanoid realm. The rest of

Tera'Loth cut itself off from this realm long ago because they are a selfish race full of greed.

"In their world, they trade almost anything for money. Legend tells us that the humanoids once tried to start a war with Magicka because we refused to teach the humans the art of magick."

Vorlin entered the room with two cloaks, stopping Beelay from a very long tale.

"Quickly, put these on," Beeley said. "We have to be fast. It is not safe to open the gateway to the human realm here."

After a long carriage ride, they reached the border of the pixie realm.

Beelay reached into his pocket to reveal a small box with a single lock. "This is the best place to travel from. Evynloth won't suspect a burst of magick from the pixie realm. They are always up to no good, and they are the only thing he seems to fear."

Beelay slid the key into the lock. As he placed the box on the ground, a beam of light shot out of it and onto the ground in front of the trio. The light turned into an arched tunnel of nothing but darkness.

"All you have to do is step through this portal, and you'll find safety."

Astrid and Richard hugged their new friends.

Vorlin handed Astrid a small satchel. "Just a few things for your journey. There is a book in there that you may find interesting."

Astrid kissed Vorlin and turned to her husband. They began walking hand in hand toward the tunnel.

"*Stop!* I almost forgot. You will need money where you are going." Beelay produced a small sack from his pocket. As he spoke an incantation over the bag, the gold changed into human money. "Here you are, and good luck to you."

The couple hurried into the tunnel. As quickly as Astrid had come back into Beelay's life, she exited it again.

"I wish you both peace and safety, and I hope you never see this realm again," remarked Beelay, looking toward the direction of the now-dissipated portal.

ASTRID'S REVELATIONS

When Imogen arrived in Magicka, she immediately asked Lord Matthew for her mother, desperate to find her, but Matthew said, "We are in the home of the revered Witch, Lady Astrid Alphias."

Imogen's voice raised. She was getting increasingly angered at the total lack of regard she was feeling. "Astrid is my grandmother's name. Where is my *mother*?"

Matthew smirked as he headed for the front door. "I think you had best come inside, where my lady shall reveal all."

Imogen looked around. There was nobody in sight and little option of escape. Besides, she didn't even know where she was, let alone how she would get home.

Reluctantly, Imogen entered the home, gasping as she looked around the foyer. Its richness overwhelmed her. It must have cost a fortune to fill it with all the trinkets she saw. The floor and staircase were adorned with gold-trimmed purple rugs, and the door handles were made of silver and gold.

Matthew led her into a large sitting room decorated with bookshelves as tall as the ceiling and even more expensive-looking furniture. Along the back wall sat a fireplace. It was so enormous that it took up most of the wall. Seated in front of the fire were two large chairs and a coffee table.

Astrid sat by the fire in a luxurious, plush velvet chair with red pillows stuffed with Giberal feathers. As Imogen approached the chair from behind, it met her with a familiar smell. It was Astrid's favorite rose-lavender perfume.

"Granny," she said as she approached the chair.

Astrid rose from the chair.

"Granny, how are you here? Why are you here? Are you here to save mother? Where is she and how do we free her? Is this all a dream? If it is, please wake me up."

Astrid looked Imogen over with the coldest stare imaginable. It was a look of utter imperviousness. "You cannot save your mother. She is in a place where evil people send those whom they no longer wish to deal with but do not have the heart to kill. Simone will never be free again. She will die with or without my help, that much is true."

Imogen's confusion turned to anger, yelling as she spoke, "If you can't help me then why am I here?"

Astrid motioned for Imogen to sit. "Sit down and shut up before you have a nosebleed."

Astrid took a book off of the coffee table in front of her. It was the same tattered book retrieved earlier that day. As she looked down at it, she smiled a little as she wiped it off with her weathered hands.

"I know Beelay has already told you that your grandfather was a Seer, and that he predicted that your destiny was to kill a Wizard named Evynloth. Evynloth was a good man but deeply troubled. There are many things you do not know about your family and our past, but I will try my best to explain them to you now. I want you to know the full story and make your own choice. I only hope you make the right one."

Astrid opened the book that Vorlin had given her all those years ago and read the story of Evynloth's life to her granddaughter. After finishing the story, she looked up to see Imogen sitting frozen in her chair.

"Evynloth is your father?" Imogen said.

Astrid nodded as she carefully closed the book. "Yes, it is true. He is my father. Even though he tried to kill me that day, I saw myself in him. It confused me until I read this book, which helped me understand him. On reflection, I never felt this kind of true love and loyalty for the man I thought was my real father." Astrid rose from her chair and put the book away safely in her drawer.

"In the story, you said he killed you," Imogen said. "How long do you think it will take him to figure out that you did not die?"

Astrid smiled. "I hope he will find me soon, because when he does, he will embrace me as his child and true heir. Especially when he sees the gifts I have for him."

Imogen stood up from her chair, having endured enough of being talked at. "What choice do I have to make? I only want my mother back."

Astrid smiled dementedly. "You need to decide whether you want to die tonight or join your family to reign over Tera'Loth. Your mother has more power than you know, and she is the key we need to secure our legacy and fulfill our master's supreme goal."

Imogen felt a sudden coldness in the room, shaking as she spoke, "I just want to get Mommy and go home. I am sure Daddy is worried about us."

Astrid smirked. "Oh dear, don't concern yourself with your father and siblings. They were spare parts, little more than trash, and I got rid of them as one would trash," she remarked with a wide grin as she swiped her hand across the room to reveal an image of her son-in-law and grandchildren burning alive as they slept.

Imogen tried to scream, but nothing came out. She was trapped in silent agony. It was the type of grief a child should never face, the type that robs one of sound when one tries to scream out. She threw a wine glass from the table into the fire. Imogen made a lunge for Astrid, but Matthew—who dived to pull Imogen back from his mistress—held a wand to Imogen's neck, subduing her attack.

"Let her go, Matthew. You know she won't move a muscle with my wand at the ready," remarked Astrid, aiming her wand at Imogen and chanting under her breath.

"I have nothing but my mother now. I would never sacrifice my mother for anything. I still do not know what is happening, but I know it's not good and I know I won't help you. Even if it means I die."

Astrid turned to Matthew with a nod. "Take her and chain her upstairs until she is ready to join us," she said coldly as she looked past her grandchild. "You need more time to make your decision. I think after tonight's journey you will change your mind."

Imogen tried to run but found herself stuck in place.

Astrid laughed as she poured herself another glass of wine. "Did you really think I would let you leave here? My house is a magickal fortress from which you will not leave, dead or alive."

Imogen screamed as Astrid waved her wand, allowing Matthew to drag her from the room.

Astrid watched her granddaughter fight Matthew on her way out of the room, sipping her wine as if nothing out of the ordinary was happening.

Imogen fought all the way up the stairs. "You two won't get away with this. You will pay for this," she screamed as she spat at Matthew.

When they finally reached a small closet altered to double as Imogen's prison, Matthew chained her up to a bar mounted to the wall.

"You cannot see the benefit now, but you will join us, I am sure. This is your baptism in fire, child," Matthew said in a low voice as he threw the door closed, plunging Imogen into darkness.

Imogen sat in the dark, crying out for her family. This

was too much to handle. Crying too much, Imogen hyper-ventilated, passing out into darkness.

From the darkness, Imogen awoke with a scream.

"Sylinah!"

The door was thrown open, and with a howl matching a banshee, Astrid aimed her wand at Imogen, casting the seizure spell. Through shudders, drool, and puke, Imogen still tried to fight, her little body pressed up hard against the wall.

"This will all end if you join us, my child. I am being a merciful ruler and giving you a chance to join us," screeched Astrid as she rose her grandchild toward to ceiling. "Eludius," she screamed.

Imogen, now plastered with her back to the ceiling, looked down to the floor beneath her. It transformed into a sea packed full of crazed undead manatees ready for feeding.

Astrid taunted her prey in a rhyming fashion. "They are hungry, Imogen, darling. It's them or me, dear child."

Imogen shook her head, fighting and calling out to Beelay and Segion.

Astrid, acting like a child, mimicked her agony and struck her grandchild.

Astrid yelped, "Beelay? Segion? Where are you? Help."

With maniacal laughter, Astrid flung Imogen toward the water, and straight into the illusion. Through muffled screams, Imogen took in water as she thrashed around, trying to fight off the manatees, who were tearing at her clothes.

Just as the largest manatee in the group was inches from having her head in his mouth, Imogen emerged from the water, only to find herself thrown back against the wall, the chain magically back on her arm.

"Come on now, child. That's enough. Join us, damn it."

Imogen, now spitting blood, choked out a single word, "Never."

Astrid screamed, almost breaking her wand, before she left the room.

Matthew, standing in the doorway, powerless to stop Astrid's torture, looked at Imogen, shaking his head as he threw her a towel. "Just give up before she kills you, child. This is not worth your life, and Lady Astrid can give you a better life. It is killing me to see this happen, but she is too dangerous. I thought she would just scare you, but I was wrong. You have the power to stop this, just join us, and take your rightful place with our lords."

Imogen said nothing, opting to spit at Matthew before closing her eyes.

"Fine, child," said Matthew as he wiped off his face with a monogrammed handkerchief before throwing it at Imogen. "Your chance to join us has passed. Good luck not dying tonight." Matthew left the room, plunging Imogen back into darkness.

IMOGEN CURLED IN A BALL, humming to herself, tears streaming down her face as she thought of her family. Was her mother even alive? What was truth and what was falsehood?

From below, Imogen could hear muffled yelling. Matthew and Astrid were yelling from below.

"Astrid, my lady, niece, you need to stop this now."

Astrid paced the room, shaking her head and clutching her amethyst. "No, she has the choice, not me." Astrid stopped mid-thought.

From above, Imogen was banging and wailing.

Astrid grinned sinisterly and transported herself upstairs, appearing before her grandchild. "Are you ready for more punishment, or are you ready to concede?" Astrid was now on the ground, nose to nose with her grandchild.

Imogen, with a voice lost from screaming and crying, said nothing before spitting in Astrid's face.

"Very well, dear. I have a lot more where that came from," bellowed Astrid as she raised Imogen up to the ceiling before throwing her into a large chasm filled with Giberals and fire ants. The fire ants and Giberals tortured Imogen at once. They bit and pecked at Imogen uncontrollably. Astrid punched Imogen in the face and left her in torture for the rest of the night.

BEELAY'S REGRET

After cleaning up his cousin's home, Beelay sat by the fire, shaking his head and muttering to himself. He could not stop thinking about Imogen. He knew he should not have let her go with Matthew, but what choice did he have?

This wasn't his destiny, it was hers. Still, he could not stop thinking about her being alone with Astrid. Not when he knew what Astrid was truly like. She wasn't stable.

"Segion, we have to get her away from Astrid. She is far too dangerous to be alone with Imogen."

Segion, who was in the middle of making a list of new security measures for his home, said, "If you were so worried about what Astrid would do, then why did you bring Imogen from the human realm in the first place?"

"It's just a good thing I came to meet you in the woods

when I did. If I hadn't, then who knows where you would be right now." Beelay stopped thinking about Imogen as he looked at his cousin with suspicion. He had not intended to enter the Druid realm, and only Afloriana had known he went to get Imogen.

"Cousin, how did you know I would arrive in the Druid realm?" he said as he pulled a rock from the fireplace, slipping it up his sleeve.

"For someone as bright as you, stupidity seems to run rampant. I have been spying on Evynloth and his forces for weeks. I received a message from the pixies telling me of Evynloth's doing, so please put down the rock. I swear you are part Dwarf sometimes."

Embarrassment washed Beelay's face as he let the rock drop to the floor. "I am sorry, cousin. I am just cautious right now. So much has changed in Tera'Loth, and I feel like I do not know who to trust."

Segion could do nothing but pat his cousin on the back. "If you really want to go after her then we can, but it will take a while. Most of the realms are closed off from each other."

Beelay picked up his bag and sword. "If we are going to do this, we better hurry. I do not trust Astrid. She is not above hurting the people she loves to get the job done."

Segion nodded in agreement. "The safest place for us to cross over right now would be the Elvish realm. Come, let's go."

The pair rushed to the carriage that lay in wait to take them to the realm of the Elves.

"If we are too late, then I will never forgive myself, Segion, because you have no idea what Astrid is capable of."

Segion looked outside the carriage with caution. "I am sure she would not go farther than a good scare."

Beelay shook his head as he looked down at his lap. "Tell that to her husband."

THE DEATH OF RICHARD WELKIN

Astrid and Richard were living happily together in the human realm. Sometimes they missed their home in the Magicka realm, but mostly they were content. Not long after they arrived in the human realm, Astrid became pregnant.

Elated at the prospect of motherhood, she contracted baby fever, dressing up rooms and practicing diaper changes on baby dolls. In contrast to her happiness, vivid nightmares plagued her. In her dreams, she would see her wedding day replayed again and again, reliving the pain of Xenus's death and the confusion she felt for the man who was her true father.

On another restless night, she experienced a different nightmare. She saw herself back in her childhood home, laying in her bed and screaming through labor. With the child barely out of her, Evynloth arrived in the room and swooped down to steal the child from her. Richard, having stepped between his wife and child, was struck down by Evynloth without a second thought.

Astrid awoke with a start and dripping with sweat, turning over to find Richard completely still in his slumber.

The next morning, she told Richard about her dream, which he dismissed as a side effect of the pregnancy. Inside, however, it concerned him. All he could think about was the future he had seen in his vision. Finally, after months of patiently waiting, their baby was born. It was a girl, and they named her Simone. With her arrival, the nightmares stopped.

The trio lived happily together for the next five years. Richard, having nothing more to do than farm all day, became quite good at cultivating vegetables. After a long day in the fields, he retired to his study to work on another passion, writing. He thought his visions and prophecies could serve their purpose in the human realm as fables, allowing him to make a little extra money for the family. They were not without money, but their circumstances forced them to keep up appearances in the human realm so as not to arouse suspicions as to their true identity.

On a cloudy day, Richard was under the trance of writing when a presence stopped him in his tracks. Without looking up from his work, he spoke, "Beelay, it has been too long, my old friend." With a smile, he threw down his pen and jumped up to greet his old friend. "Why are you here? Isn't it dangerous to cross over? I mean won't he detect magick being used?"

Beelay looked rather nervous as he spoke, "I crossed over in Impenia. He doesn't bother with pixies. They are too mischievous for his magickal abilities."

Richard, having reseated himself, offered Beelay a chair.

"I have come with bad news, I'm afraid. I did not want to see you and Astrid only to bring bad news. I, I..."

Richard sat up in his chair with alarm. "Please, Beelay, tell me what has happened."

Beelay took a gulp of air and spoke, "After we transported you two to the human realm, Evynloth began his master's campaign to confiscate all magickal instruments and books. He also made all the people submit to a binding spell. Some resisted and were met with death. Others, not entirely believing in his abilities, fled to the other realms and under ground. When the leaders of the other realms realized what was happening, they closed themselves off from Magicka. They bound the realms with all the magick they could muster.

"Your mother and father refused to leave the Forest of Fortune. Your father and the other Seers used their combined magick to seal the forest off from Evynloth. After years of seclusion, Evynloth found a way past the barrier.

"I am sorry, Richard, but he killed your parents last night. He murdered them because they would not give him the location of a magickal object."

Richard was in disbelief. "Why didn't I feel it? I should have felt a pull in my Aura when they died."

Beelay leaned forward to take Richard's hand. "Your father, being a Seer, did not want you to know. He placed a spell over your Aura so that you would not sense when they were in danger. He knew you were not dead, but he did not want you to feel the temptation to return to the Magicka realm."

Richard, overcome with anger, tossed anything he could find. Beelay ducked to avoid a coffee mug as he fought to subdue him. Finally tackling his friend, they both fell to the floor. Tears, curses, and agony flowed from Richard.

Astrid, unaware of what was going on until she heard the commotion, ran into the room. Shocked to see Beelay, she ran to her husband's side.

"What are you doing here, Beelay? Richard, what has happened? Please speak to me."

Richard fought through the tears long enough to tell her his parents were dead. Beelay told Astrid the rest as Richard sobbed. After Richard calmed down, Astrid insisted he lie down for a while.

As she exited their bedroom, she went back to the study, where Beelay was doing his best to clean up and fix what Richard had broken. Astrid found him trying to figure out how glue worked in order to fix a mug. "Just leave it. Things are cheap enough in this realm... Listen to me. I am even speaking as if I am humanoid."

Beelay was about to say something when they heard the gentle whines of the baby.

"I guess it's dinnertime for her," Astrid said.

Beelay slumped down into the chair by the fire. "Leave the baby for a minute. We need to talk," he said as he swished his wand toward the baby's room, silencing her instantly.

Astrid chuckled. "I wish I knew that trick," she told him before joining him by the fire with a bottle of spirits.

"A few of the Seers fled to the other realms before they were closed off from Evynloth. About a week ago, a Seer and Spell-Caster named Afloriana visited me. She foretold the murder of Richard's parents and she also foretold that Richard would go back to the Magicka realm and attempt to kill Evynloth. I tried to reach Richard's parents in time, but with Evynloth and the army he has amassed, any form of travel is difficult. When I finally arrived at their home, it was too late."

As Astrid listened, she found herself lost in the flames of the fire. She did not mean to seem closed off, but it was a trait she had unknowingly inherited from Evynloth. "What if Richard goes back to avenge his parents? It is a dangerous game you played, coming here to tell him what happened."

Beelay leaned forward in his chair. "That's just it. I don't know if he will try to go back to Magicka, but he needed to know about his parents. You would have done the same."

Astrid's gaze returned to the flames. "I don't know if I would have done the same." Astrid got up from her chair by the fire, handing the bottle of spirits to Beelay. "It's been a long time since we have shared dinner with a guest. Let me go kill a chicken."

As Astrid worked her magick in the kitchen, the sound of stirring came from above. Richard descended the staircase with

Simone in tow. When Beelay saw the pair coming down the stairs, sadness washed over him as he thought, *That little girl is the only family he's got left other than Astrid.* His sadness turned to glee as soon as Simone made eye contact with him. She was taken with him instantly. As her father sat slumped in his grief on the sofa, Simone prattled along, showing Beelay all her toys and telling him all about her own strange little world, blissfully unaware of the even darker shadow now cast over her family.

After they cleared dinner away, Astrid put Simone in front of a magick box the humans called a television while the adults talked. Richard hardly ate but was agreeable to a nightcap after the day's events. "I don't know what to do or say. I cannot believe my parents are gone. I am angry and all I want is revenge."

Beelay looked at Richard with concern. "You know what will happen if you return to Magicka. Evynloth will finish a job he thought was complete. Promise me you will not go there?" Beelay said before he choked down his nightcap with a large gulp.

Richard nodded gingerly as he stared into the flames as Beelay said, "Alright, I best be leaving now. I can't be away from my home for too long. We have wild harpies in the area, and if they sense a home is empty, they will overrun the place."

Beelay exited the living room and bid Astrid goodnight as he headed for the front door. "You take care of him now, young Astrid," Beelay said as they hugged goodbye.

Astrid stood in the farmhouse's doorway, watching Beelay walk off into the night. After a few moments, she saw a flash of light in the night's darkness. Astrid closed the front door and made her way to the living room. Richard was no longer seated by the fire.

As she searched the house for him, she heard a commotion coming from upstairs. It was coming from the attic. Entering the attic, she found Richard digging through a deep red wooden chest.

"What are you doing up here at this hour? What is important enough for you to be looking for it at this time of night?"

Richard would neither look at her nor acknowledge her questions.

Astrid placed herself between the chest and her husband. "Richard, what are you doing?"

Richard now possessed a determined look in his eyes, the kind of determination a person exhibited when they were hellbent on finding something.

Astrid placed a hand on his cheek, locking eyes with him as she spoke, "Please speak to me, darling."

Richard cried a little as he spoke, "I left everything I knew to keep you and my parents safe, and it was all for nothing."

Astrid took his hand in hers as she listened to him. He said, "We cannot be safe until Evynloth is dead. I am going back to Magicka, and I will kill him. It is the only way to keep our family and all of Tera'Loth safe from the hell the Seers destined him to unleash."

Astrid's expression changed from sympathy to an odd sense of loyalty. "But he is my father. I know he tried to hurt us, but he is not a bad man. Why do you want to kill the only family I have left in Magicka?"

Richard looked at his wife as if she was a stranger. "How can you say these things after what has happened to us? I do not understand where this is coming from." As he turned to keep packing up his things, Astrid ran to a small case hidden in the back of the room behind a mirror.

"Please, I have this book," she said. "Vorlin gave it to me before we left Magicka. It tells the story of my father. If you read it, then you will see he is a good man. He was just badly hurt by someone evil."

Richard stepped back in shock. "How can you defend him when he killed my parents and tried to kill us?" he screamed as he ran downstairs toward the front door. "If I hurry, I may catch up to Beelay."

Astrid ran down the staircase after him. She grabbed his arm. The couple struggled.

"Let go of me, Astrid. I have to do this whether you like it or not."

Astrid lunged forward with all her might, but Richard pushed her down.

"Think of our child. Please, Richard. She needs both of us."

Richard screamed over his wife as she lay on the staircase. "I am doing this for Simone. So she can be safe."

Richard turned away, crying as he ran down the stairs.

Seeing her husband running away from her and toward her father sent Astrid into a blind rage. In her anger, she clutched her Amethyst necklace and chanted.

Richard, having already left the house, was halfway across the field. When he was in a clear enough area, he stopped. From his bag he produced a realm travel box. After he placed it on the ground, he felt a pain in his chest. He clutched his chest as he tried to put the key into the lock, but he was unsuccessful as he fell to the ground. Astrid, his true love and bride, killed him, twisting his heart until he breathed no more.

Astrid walked outside, toward the field where her husband's lifeless body lay. As she stood over his body, staring down at him, she was devoid of emotion. "He is my father, and you cannot kill someone like him."

Astrid left her husband's body in the field and returned to the house. She sat in front of the fireplace, dumbstruck with the realization that she needed to get rid of his body but did not know how she would do it on her own. Crying by the fire, she stopped in her tracks as she heard a man's voice say to her, "I will help you, my lady. I am only sorry I did not get here sooner."

Confused, Astrid turned around to find a tall, thin man with long hair standing in her doorway. "Who are you and what do you want?"

Matthew stepped into the room. "My name is Lord Matthew Teymark-Alphias, and I am your uncle. I am your mother's half brother and a product of indiscretion, but we can discuss that later."

Astrid rose and stepped toward Matthew. "I have often felt a familiar Aura in this house, but I could not place it."

Matthew looked down at Astrid. "I have been watching

over you for years. I felt it was my duty to your mother to watch over you." Matthew turned toward the front door, looking out toward Richard's lifeless body. "We need to erase all traces of Richard from this house. It may not seem right to you now, but you have helped your father more than you know. If we can keep all of this hidden from Simone, then your father will live on forever. Praise Lord Evynloth."

Astrid looked at her uncle blankly as she repeated the praise.

"There is a prophecy foretold that your grandchild will kill your father to save our world from the clutches of evil," Matthew said.

Astrid looked past Matthew and out toward the field, crying as reality set in.

"Come now, child, dry your tears and see to your baby while I clean this up. In the morning when you wake up, I will have set everything right. It will be as if Richard never existed."

Astrid nodded as she retired upstairs, leaving her uncle to clean up.

Matthew swept the house, looking for anything that belonged to the late Lord Welkin. After gathering up all his possessions, he placed them in Richard's chest in the attic, casting a spell over the chest before hiding it under a velvet throw. He decided it would be easier to hide the chest here rather than transport a chest and a body.

When he was sure there was no trace of Richard left, he went down to the field. Astrid watched from the window as he opened a portal to the Magicka realm, callously pushing Richard's lifeless body through the portal.

When Matthew arrived back in the Magicka realm, he panicked.

Richard was lying on the ground, moaning.

"How are you alive?" Matthew demanded. "I saw her kill you."

Richard looked around in confusion. "Astrid, why?" he shouted as he looked around.

In a panic, Matthew hit Richard over the head with the end of his cane. "What am I going to do with him now?" he muttered to himself as he looked across the horizon. The sun was rising behind the Black Mountains. Looking toward the mountaintop, he knew what to do.

"Emotion is a dangerous thing," he remarked as he threw Richard in the luggage compartment of his carriage.

"Where to, Lord Matthew, sir?" asked his driver, Bern, a good man who knew how to keep his mouth and eyes shut while on his master's escapades.

"Onward, to the Black Mountains."

With a nod, Bern made his way to the base of the mountains.

THE EDGE OF THE ELVISH REALM

As Beelay and Segion approached the edge of the Elvish realm, a Watch-Keeper of the Elvish realm met them.

"Halt, who goes there?" shouted the guard as he stood in the road's middle.

"It is Beelay and Segion of the Druid realm. Please grant us a passage through these woods and into your realm so that we may save a friend from harm."

The Watch-Keeper was young, full of zeal and oblivious to whom he was speaking. "Who is the friend in question, my liege?"

Beelay tried very hard to maintain his composure as he spoke, "Her name is Imogen Welkin and it is her destiny to save us from Evynloth."

The Watch-Keeper looked Beelay up and down. In the distance, a woman's voice broke the silence. "Let them through, men. The king knows of these travelers. We owe it to all of Tera'Loth to save that little girl."

As the Elvish guard made a pathway, a cloaked figure walked up to Beelay, who exited the carriage to speak to the young guard. As the hood fell, Beelay met the face of an angel.

It was Afloriana.

"It is you? What are you doing here with the Elvish guard? I thought you would wait at your estate."

Afloriana bowed. "I was waiting for you. You were a fool to let her go on her own. Why didn't you put up more of a fight?"

Beelay looked stunned as he spoke, "But how do you know?"

Afloriana looked sideways at Beelay. "You did not think I would let you go without sending my own spies along with you, did you?"

Beelay jumped as two little pixies jumped out of his pocket. Frowning at the pixies, he continued to speak, "I know, but what could I do? You know how powerful Astrid is. I rolled the dice. The situation dictated it."

Afloriana nodded as she lifted her hood. "Well, let's not dwell on that now. It's best we focus on getting her back into our care."

Beelay was lost in Afloriana's gaze. Afloriana was the greatest Witch in all the lands. She was a High Seer and lived in a beautiful two-story cottage in the realm of Impenia. She was born in the Magicka realm but preferred the mostly peaceful life she lived among the pixies and Imps. While they were mischievous, they left her in peace most of the time. Rumors swirled that Lord Avestyn wanted to kill her and take her magick, which only made her more determined to leave Magicka to seek somewhere safe to call home.

"Afloriana, how are we going to get through into the Elvish realm? Won't Evynloth detect us?"

Afloriana shook her head. "Not if you have this," she said as she held up a vial of strange, dark blue liquid.

"Is that what I think it is?" Beelay said as he raised an eyebrow.

"Yes it is, and it is my best brew yet."

Afloriana often used her famed abilities to produce a potion from a powerful rock, whose location was a closely-guarded secret. The potion, named Driftus-Cloak, allowed the person who drank it to become like air and flow from place to place without detection. "We will flow through the barrier and he will never detect that we have entered the realm. This potion masks our Auras and leaves a hint in the place we last were, thus tricking him into thinking we are still in the Druid realm. I don't want to take any chances, so we will do it this way. I don't sense that he is bothered with you right now anyhow. By now he will know that Astrid is alive and that she has the girl. Matthew is working for both Astrid and Lord Avestyn, and he can only play both sides against the middle for so long, but that is not our concern right now. Matthew made his bed in that regard. Alright, bottoms up, men," she said as she gave them each a vial.

Beelay and Segion swallowed the potion in single gulps.

"How long will this last before we are back to normal?" Beelay said as he handed off the empty vials.

"Long enough to get us to the Elvish capital and into the palace's safety. It is cloaked by the old magick that Evynloth and his master would kill to learn. Once we are in the palace, we will be undetected. When the potion wears off, the little piece of our energy will leave the Druid realm and return to us. Evynloth will know we are gone, but he won't be able to detect where we are. Now hurry men, we must make haste."

The drink took effect, allowing them to disappear into the night.

As they passed through the realm barrier, Afloriana said a few magickal words, transporting them right into the middle of the great hall in the palace of Lord Teymark, King of the Elves.

"Ah, Afloriana, my dear. I see you still like to make an entrance—as always."

With a nod and a smirk, Afloriana bowed to the king.

"Well, these must be our weary travelers," Lord Teymark said. "Beelay and I need no introduction. We met many years ago, when the trade delegation came to Magicka. However, I see the girl is not with you. Is all hope lost?"

Afloriana looked at the ground before she locked eyes with Beelay. "If we are to rescue Imogen, it has to be now. Lord Teymark can help transport us straight into Astrid's home without detection. Who knows what she might do to the child?"

Beelay, now showing more fear than ever before, shouted, "What if Evynloth detects us before we can get to Imogen?"

Afloriana moved forward to take Beelay's hand as she spoke, "Stop worrying about what Evynloth will do and focus on that poor girl. Here, I made us each a pack with some necessities for the journey, and I suggest we all be armed with something other than a rock," she said as she looked at Beelay with a hint of a smirk. "I do not know which way Astrid will try to hinder our efforts. She is very unstable and is as unpredictable as Xenus ever was."

Without wasting any more time, the party made their way to the center of the great hall. It was there, in the room's center, that a portal opened, Elves fostered the magick needed to open portals without realm travel boxes. After Lord Teymark wished them luck, the three entered the portal.

After they exited the portal, the trio found themselves in the courtyard of Astrid's home.

"Oh well, there is only one way through this," Afloriana said as she walked straight up to the front door.

From her pocket, she produced a wand. "I need to make sure she hasn't got a protection spell over the door." As she waved her wand over the door, she saw a purple, water-like haze over the door. "Yes, she's got this place locked down."

Segion sighed as he rested against the fence.

"There is another way inside," Beelay said with a nervous smile.

"Well, don't keep us waiting," Afloriana said.

Beelay looked toward the sewers. "Did you keep your home here, dear?" he said, looking in Afloriana's direction.

"Yes I did, but how does that help us?"

Beelay said nothing, but he pointed to the ground below. "Oh yes. Why didn't I think of that?"

With haste, they traveled to Afloriana's home.

As they entered the grand residence, it met them with the unwelcoming smell of a home closed up for too many years. As they made their way down to the basement, Afloriana complained, "I cannot believe that even with all the magick, we still must dive into the sewers. Furthermore, why did we have to do this at my house?"

Beelay took her hand and patted it. "You have been away from Magicka too long, dear. You are not inhabiting the house, so there won't be a rat-trapper standing guard. Those rat-trappers are loyal only to coin and would turn me in without a blink. Remember, I am not a popular man here anymore. Not since Ericka died. Oh well, ladies first."

Afloriana grumbled under her breath as she descended the ladder into the sewers. Segion, being the last to enter, closed the grate before jumping most fashionably into the sewers. The trio waited for a few moments, allowing their eyes to adjust to the light. Afloriana lit the torches, handing them to the men.

"Well," Beelay sighed as he spoke, "at least there are pathways down here, that way we need not wade through the filth."

Afloriana shook her head as she searched her bag. "Here, take these bags. At least I can help us with the smell," remarked Afloriana as she handed out lavender bags. "How will we know which ladder leads to Astrid's home?"

Segion chimed in, "Moreover, how will we get past any rat-trappers?"

Beelay shook his head as he looked at the pair of over thinkers. "My dear, we will, quite simply, use magick. I think sweeping-mystia should do the trick."

Afloriana grinned. "Excellent plan Beelay." She whispered the spell and blew out a gentle breath.

From the distance, they heard a choir of men snoring, who at this point were sliding off their chairs in the deepest of slumbers.

"Okay, that is one problem down, but how do we know which is Astrid's sewer entrance?" Afloriana said.

Beelay tapped a metal plate mounted on the wall as they passed a sewer exit. "Simple. We look for the house number next to the ladder. There should be a map on the rat-trapper to show us how to get to her house."

Segion ran toward a rat-trapper in the distance, only to return a few minutes later. "She is house number twenty-one," Beelay said Segion opened the map. "According to this, the houses in the twenties are along the blue line."

At the end of the pathway, in front of them stood three passageways, one with a green line, one with a blue line, and one with a black line drawn above the archway.

Afloriana said, "I guess it's door number two then?"

As each member of the party entered the passageway, they readied themselves with a wand, a sword, and a rock. It was not long until they found the ladder they were looking for. As they entered the basement of Astrid's home, a sudden draft blew their torches out. Afloriana relit them before anyone hurt themselves.

When the room was illuminated again, they found themselves in a large cluttered basement full of dust and memory. Eventually, they made their way through the remnants of the Alphias family and toward the staircase. As they ascended the staircase, they walked straight through a door, only to come face to face with Astrid, who was pointing her wand in their direction.

"I will admit that it was amusing to see you having to sludge around in the sewers. I thought about coming down to greet you, but there is a vicious monster loose down in the sewers, so I let the fates decide." Astrid fixed her hair, seeing its unkemptness in the mirror next to the door. "Obviously I allowed you to enter my home alive," she continued to speak as she fixed her waistcoat with the aid of the mirror. "I know you have come for the girl, but it is useless now. She has joined the fight to aid my father in his goal."

Beelay shook his head, torn at the sight of what was before him. To him, she was still the gentle little girl who he remembered playing in the tub in his garden. "Look what you have become, Astrid."

Astrid did not respond to Beelay. "It is her destiny to help restore our family to its former glory."

Beelay scoffed. "What former glory? Your father was born as poor as they come."

Astrid raised her neck along with her voice. "Yes, that is true, but he is from a strong magickal line, once a rich and great family."

Beelay stepped a little closer to Astrid. "I don't know what you think you know, Astrid, but you have this all wrong."

Astrid stepped back as she tilted her nose upward. "I need not hear anything you have to say, Beelay. In fact, I am sick of hearing you speak." Astrid attempted to cast the spell of Speechectomus on Beelay, only to find it thwarted by Afloriana.

A flash of insanity washed over Astrid's face. "You think you are more powerful than me? Well, you are wrong," Astrid bellowed as she threw all her magickal force at Afloriana.

The women dueled, allowing a distraction. Beelay and Segion ran to find Imogen. The Alphias mansion was among the biggest houses in all the capital. As they ran upstairs, they could hear gentle moaning, but they could not be sure from where it was coming.

"Beelay, let's split up and find her."

Beelay ran left while Segion ran right. Beelay looked toward a door at the end of the hallway. It looked heavy and old. He ran straight for the door and put his ear up to it. The moaning got louder.

"Imogen, if you can hear me, I am here to save you."

Beelay stepped back a few feet before he charged the door. After breaking the door down, he found Imogen chained up and barely breathing.

"What did they do to you, my girl?" Beelay said as he freed the child from her chains. There were signs of extreme torture. Imogen's head was split open and her left eye was swollen shut from a good punch. Astrid had broken her arm.

There were bruises all over her torso and welts across her back. Her captors had cruelly and degradingly stripped Imogen down to her underclothes. There she lay, urine soaked through her underwear. Even though she was in an awful state, it looked as if Imogen had put up a hell of a fight.

Imogen was weak, but she whispered Beelay and Segion's names as she stirred in and out of consciousness. "I am sorry I did not listen to you...Mother...a trap..."

Beelay picked her up off the floor. "Just save your strength, poppet. We will get you out of here."

A voice came from behind them. "Oh, I don't think so. You are not going anywhere with her."

Beelay turned to find Matthew standing in the doorway.

"We need that girl to make Tera'Loth right again. I cannot let you leave with her. Now put her down before I wipe the floor with you, old—"

Matthew hit the floor mid-sentence.

Behind him stood Segion with a rock in his hand. "I can see why you use this, cousin. It has a personal touch, doesn't it?" he said with a smirk.

"Really, Segion. Only you could find humor in a time like this."

Segion said nothing as he bowed with a grin.

"Come on, Jester," Beelay said, "let's get the hell out of here before he wakes up."

The trio descended the staircase with haste.

Meanwhile, Astrid and Afloriana were still battling down below.

"We need to get to Afloriana quickly. I don't know how powerful Astrid has become."

Rounding a corner, Beelay and Segion witnessed Afloriana and Astrid hurling spells at each other, furniture and artwork destroyed at their feet.

"You think you can win, girl? I am younger than you and I —" Astrid's concentration broke as she saw Beelay from the corner of her eye. Her focus and wrath shifted toward Beelay, who was holding Imogen in his arms. "No, you cannot take her. I won't let it happen," she said as she lunged her magick toward Beelay.

Beelay jumped behind a door with Imogen still in his arms. Trying to cast her magick through the door, Astrid was stopped in her tracks by an Aura wrapping itself around her. She could not move as she screamed out in agony.

"What is that," yelled Segion.

"I don't know," Afloriana said, "but we need to get out of here while it has her disabled."

Beelay and the others ran from the home into the dead of night. Once they had made it back to Afloriana's home, they quickly realized that even with Afloriana's magick, it was too dangerous to stay in Magicka.

"Between the three of us, our magick is strong, but I don't know what Astrid has up her sleeve," Afloriana said as she grabbed bandages.

"Where can we possibly take her that will be safe? Everyone in Tera'Loth is after her," Segion said as he held Imogen's hand.

"We will take her to my home in Impenia. It is the safest

place for her, I assure you. The safest way for us to travel would be through the Forgotten Sea, entering through the Viking realm. Our informants tell us that they have spotted Evynloth around the Mountains of Memory, so we need to avoid that area as much as we can."

Segion gathered up supplies before walking outside to fetch the carriage. "Come, let's get her into the carriage and head for the docks. We will have to travel the backroads to avoid Evynloth's men."

After what seemed like the tensest ride of their lives, they could finally breathe when they arrived at the Moorish docks. There were no boats or people in sight, and it was a cloudy night. On the horizon was nothing but water.

"What are we going to do, Afloriana?" Beelay said.

Segion agreed, "We are sitting ducks."

Afloriana raised her hand as she spoke, "Do not worry yourselves. I have planned for every eventuality," she said as she produced a horn from her bag, blowing on it three long times before waiting in silence.

After a few moments, she heard four long blows of a horn in return. In the distance, they could see flames. As the light came closer, the party met with the largest viking ship in all the realms. As the ship docked, a tall, well-built, middle-aged man with long light brown hair and brown eyes met the party. His name was Av'Dah he was the son of Vi'Lah, who was the Grand-High Master of the Vikings.

Av'Dah jumped down to meet the weary travelers. "I thought you must have perished. We were about to return to our village."

Beelay and Segion looked on as Afloriana spoke, "Well,I am glad you did not." She lost formality and hugged him in a very familiar manner. "Come now, we better get out of here before someone sees us."

After everyone finished piling into the boat, they made their way through the Forgotten Sea.

"Do you know why it is called the Forgotten Sea, child?" asked Beelay as he tried to distract Imogen from her pain. "It is because the Vikings made a deal with the Elves to use their magick," he continued. "They wanted everyone to forget their realm was there so they could live in peace, with none of the other realms interfering with their way of life. It was the best trick they could have thought up, because they have all but been forgotten by most of Tera'Loth. No one knows what they are capable of, and that makes Evynloth too afraid to fight them. The Vikings have a protection spell over them from their ancient ancestors. Magick doesn't work on them at all, and Evynloth is no match for their strength."

Av'Dah patted Beelay on the shoulder before returning to the helm.

Beelay sat against the side of the ship with Imogen in his arms. Looking out on the horizon, Beelay rubbed her shoulder as he hugged Imogen tightly, who had fallen asleep while he was talking.

"I hope you wake up soon so that you can see the beauty of the Viking realm," he said. "It's lush and looks just like your home in the country. I am so sorry I let you go out there by yourself. I brought you into this mess when I should have been firmer with you."

Beelay cried a little. The guilt was seeping into his Aura.

Segion, now at Beelay's side, covered Imogen with another blanket.

"Don't worry, cousin," said Segion as he put a hand on Beelay's shoulder. "She is only resting. She will come out of this."

THE ALMACKIAS MEET IN NECROMANCIUM

When Matthew finally woke up from his knock on the head, he mustered all the strength he could to perform a healing spell on himself. Once healed enough to stand, he went in search of Astrid. As he descended the staircase, he looked around at the path of destruction.

After reaching the bottom of the stairs, he rounded the corner to find Astrid standing with an Aura wrapped around her, struggling to be free of it. Whoever was doing this invoked more powerful magick than she did. Matthew watched in horror before snapping back into reality.

"Disengage," he yelled as he pushed all his magick toward Astrid. The spell would not work. After trying two more times, the Aura let go of Astrid, dropping her to the ground before sweeping itself through Matthew. As the Aura passed through him, it confused him. The Aura was not of malice but of good.

Turning around, Matthew watched the Aura travel out through a broken window like a thief in the night. "What *was* that?" he asked as he looked on at Astrid, who coughed as she lay on the ground.

"I do not know... Please, get me to the living room."

Matthew nodded as he helped Astrid up off the floor, taking her to the living room to nurse her wounds.

"I can't believe she got away from us, Matthew."

Matthew said nothing, nor did he look his niece in the eye, as he poured her a glass of wine.

Handing her the wine, he remarked, "Perhaps this is more fortunate for us?" Sitting in the chair next to Astrid, he continued to speak, "She is more valuable away from us. They will be more willing to give up the Stone's location to the hero from the prophecy."

Astrid scowled, but she could see the obvious benefit of this new arrangement.

Matthew took Astrid's hand as he continued to speak, "But we must talk of other pressing matters now. Don't you think it is time you met with Lord Evynloth?"

Astrid pondered this as she rubbed her head, trying to mask her nerves about meeting her father.

"You must tell him of your loyalty and plans."

Astrid was evidently a fearless woman, but when it came to her real father, she was weak. The thought of contact with him brought with it a flurry of emotions. She had idolized him for years and feared he might reject her for the thousands of reasons she had worried about over the years. She felt he had not been in his right mind when he had tried to kill her. What parent would want to kill their child? She was sure he had not meant to do it. Everything happened so quickly the night of her wedding, leaving her little time to process the situation. The events of that night and the knowledge she had gained after it had left her mad at Xenus for many years following his death.

"I suppose you are right, uncle. It is time to meet my father. Have the carriage brought around and we shall leave at once. Do you know where we can find him?" Astrid said as she hauled herself up off the chair.

"Yes, child, I do," said Matthew as he helped his niece into her coat.

Once they were comfortably in their seats, the carriage set out toward Lord Avestyn's fortress atop the cliffs of Mt. Curac in Necromancium.

After an hour in the carriage, Matthew asked, "My lady and dearest niece, why are we traveling by carriage and not by realm travel box?"

Astrid was staring out the window, responding to Matthew without even looking up. "I have not seen these lands in over thirty years, and I don't know where we would end up if we were to step through a portal. Evynloth has been tampering with the laws of realm travel. How else do you think Imogen ended up in the Druid realm?"

Matthew nodded in agreement as the carriage rolled on toward the Cliffs of Mt. Curac. "I understand the desire, my lady, but if you would allow me, I can use magick to get us there quicker."

Astrid wanted to see the countryside but thought it better to arrive as soon as she could. "Very well, please do so."

Matthew halted the carriage and disembarked. As he stood in front of the horse, he rubbed its face and fed it some strange fruit. "We will be with your father within the hour," he said as he motioned for the driver to walk on, but magick turned the carriage toward the sky. The horse and carriage ascended into the sky, flying the rest of the way to Necromancium. As Matthew had promised, they were in Necromancium within the hour.

"Bring us down, driver," Matthew said as they approached the top of the cliffs.

When Astrid's carriage approached the house, she experienced a flash of anger mixed with anticipation. She was angry at her father for what he had done, but she thought she could bring the family back together, with her daughter as a peace offering.

When Astrid saw Lord Avestyn's new home, she was in awe. It was the biggest, darkest home she'd ever seen. It was crumbling in some spots and appeared to have suffered a fire at some point, but it was still livable. As she looked over the realm from the cliffs above, she noticed instantly that the realm lacked any vegetation and that it was pitch dark even at dawn. She had dark tastes, but this was a little much even by her standards.

Before the carriage even approached the fortress, the butler was waiting for them. It was as if they knew Astrid was coming. After Astrid collected herself, the butler escorted her and Matthew to the study. Astrid's heart was in her throat as she followed Matthew. *Will he think I am here to blackmail him?* she thought as she continued down what seemed an endless hall devoid of life.

As she entered the room behind her guide, Astrid felt herself stop in her tracks. From the corner of the room, Lord Avestyn's wand was directed at Astrid, holding her in place. As Evynloth rose from his chair, he walked toward his daughter in silence.

"I know you and I know your Aura, but you should be dead," he said as he removed Astrid's hood.

When Evynloth saw the woman standing before him, he took a step back and looked at her in confusion.

"Ericka? But how?" Evynloth muttered incoherent words, grief stricken, touching Astrid's face as he wept.

"No, Father, it is me, Astrid. The daughter you thought you murdered."

Evynloth's hand slipped off of her face as his mood changed in an instant. "I thought you were dead, daughter. How did you deceive me?"

Astrid smiled as she stood still under Lord Avestyn's spell. "You thought you killed me that day, but Beelay saved me, leading my husband and me to a life of peace in the human realm."

Evynloth's temper grew increasingly as he turned his back on his master's captive. "How could he betray me? He was my friend. I thought of him as my father."

Astrid smirked at her father's back, overcome with the

desire to taunt him. "Well, doesn't love hurt? It comes with sacrifice. If you only knew what I have done for your sake and the sake of our family name and reputation."

Evynloth whirled to face his child, now seeing her as his prey. "Well then, if that was the truth why have you come here now, after so many years of living hidden in obscurity?"

They locked eyes as Astrid spoke, "I am here to bring you a peace offering. I know you seek a Stone and the blood to go with it."

Evynloth's curiosity was piqued. He knew Matthew would not remain silent about the Stones or the overall plan.

"I can help you fulfill your destiny, Father. I have bought you a direct descendant of the Kami—my own daughter—for the blood sacrifice, but we still need to find the Stone."

Lord Avestyn and Evynloth exchanged cautious glances, nodding at each other.

Lord Avestyn lowered his wand, freeing their new ally from the spell. "Anyone willing to sacrifice their family is accepted by us."

Astrid's emotions eased. He had not rejected her. Free from danger and the freezing spell, she proceeded to walk toward the chairs by the fire. "I am glad you have accepted me, Father. You will find with time that you have made a wise choice," she said as she sat down.

"We have not fully accepted you yet, child. You must prove your usefulness to us if you wish to stay within the fold," Lord Avestyn piped up as he sipped his wine.

Astrid thought he looked ill, but she did not dare bring it up. Instead she steered the conversation back to the matter at hand. "Father, do you have any clue as to where the Stone is?"

Evynloth nodded as he walked toward the bookshelf to retrieve a book titled *The History of Tera'Loth* by Syron Almackia. "This will lead us to the Stone's location."

Matthew emerged from the shadows after observing the exchange, stepping forward into the light of the fire. "Where will we be traveling to, my lord?" Matthew said as he bowed.

Evynloth looked around the room at the expectant faces before carefully placing the old book on the table. "We will journey to Vinlahg, the realm of the Vikings."

THE REALM OF THE VIKINGS

As the ship approached the Shores of Vinlahg, the dock slowly came into sight. A rather tall and commanding man stood dockside with an entourage of men. His name was Vi'Lah, and he was the Grand High Master of Vinlahg. Vi'Lah was a tall and stocky man of about forty years, dressed in clothes made from the hides of many animals. On his hip was a saber and in his boot was a knife. His face was weathered, for his life consisted of much battle and drink. Vi'Lah approached the ship as it docked. As the party disembarked, Vi'Lah hugged everyone, even if the hug wasn't welcome.

"Welcome. We are glad you made the journey safely and could get to the child in time."

Beelay stood holding Imogen with his head toward the ground in shame.

"Don't worry, Lord Beelay. She will heal quickly. We will take her to the healer Marag."

Beelay nodded, still looking at the ground. "Come now, the horses await."

While their guests made their way to the horses, Vi'Lah and Av'Dah remained dockside to speak in private.

"We have a problem, son. Not long after you left, Evynloth swept through the capital city. I do not know how he found out about the Stones' location, but Evynloth is now holding us to ransom. He broke into our home and kidnapped your mother and sister. He says if we do not hand over the Stone then he will kill them."

Av'Dah stood back in anger. "How can we give him the Stone of Auras Reclaim? There is nobody left alive who knows its location, and many believe it to be a myth."

Vi'Lah walked toward the edge of the dock, sitting down on a rock as he sighed, "It is no myth, child. They— the Kami—tasked us of Vinlahg with keeping the Stone hidden and protected many years ago. Until now, there has only ever been one person at a time who knows of its location, but now there will be two. In the Valley of Greengarth is a cave that houses the Stone, but I cannot open the cave."

From a distance, the head guard yelled to his master that they were ready to leave.

"Come, we can discuss this further back at the mead hall."

As the pair approached the horses, their exchange did not go unnoticed by Afloriana, who gave them a suspicious look but did not vocalize her concern. As dawn broke, the party made their way into Ba-er, capital of Vinlahg.

As they approached Ba-er, set up much like a traditional round-style village, many curious faces met them. As soon as the children saw their leader, they cheered as they descended toward him. It was clear that everyone revered Vi'Lah, even the children, and he was not above mixing with his subjects. He had once lived in a lowly place before the clan wars, but his father, being the leader of the victor clan, had taken the seat in the mead hall when Vi'Lah was ten years old.

The mead hall sat in the village center. It was a grand wooden building, adorned with carvings and runes that ran down the support beams and around the trim of the room. Each beam held a piece of important history, from the creation myth to the last clan war. The hall was full of large, long tables and benches.

At the front of the hall sat the High Master's table, and behind it sat a large chair upholstered with deer hides. The arms and legs of the chair were adorned with bear claws. The hall smelt stale and was illuminated by candlelight. The bottom level of the hall lacked windows, which created a sense of eternal night.

Vi'Lah and the rest of the party handed the horses off to the horse keepers and stable boys before taking refuge in the mead hall. Vi'Lah ordered that his men lead Beelay, Segion, and Imogen to Marag's home, which sat right next to the mead hall. Its location was practical, as most of Marag's customers suffered from sore heads and nausea. The house was of modest size, but she was a single woman, needing only a little space.

Marag was a beautiful woman and the youngest healer to grace the village in all its history. She was a short, slender woman with honey-colored hair and deep brown eyes. As Beelay and Segion approached the house, Marag was already opening the door to greet them.

"Please come in, I saw your party arrive," she said as she put a hand on Imogen's head and then her cheeks. "This child is ice cold. I am a great healer, but I can make you no promises. Come, let's get inside."

Beelay placed Imogen on a waiting table, leaving her in the hands of the healer. Marag covered Imogen with a heavy blanket made from goat's wool before she dashed around the room collecting herbs and implements. After Marag brewed a herb drink, she sat Imogen upright and massaged her neck to force a swallow.

"This herb drink will help the girl find her way out of the dark sleep she is in and bring her back to us."

Beelay looked at Marag in suspicion. "What did you give her?"

Marag adjusted Imogen's blanket as she spoke, "It is a root called black-weed mixed with some other herbs. Her body is badly damaged and her Aura is not sure if it wants to stay in her. These herbs are the strongest in Tera'Loth. I hope she lives."

As Imogen lay on the table, Beelay's guilt shifted to anger. "I could kill Astrid for what she has done to you, but I don't know if I have it in me. I'm so sorry, my girl."

Four hours passed before Imogen shifted under the hide. "Beelay, where are we?"

Beelay jumped up from his chair. "Oh my. She's awake. She's awake."

Marag and Segion ran into the room. As Imogen sat up, she looked around the room in confusion. This was not her Granny's house. The last thing she remembered was being tortured by the woman she had spent her life loving and admiring. Imogen locked eyes with Beelay and cried.

"It's alright, child," Beelay said. "It is over. I promise you, she will not hurt you again."

After Imogen calmed down, Marag ushered everyone out of the room. "I know she has just woken up, but we should let her recover a little more in peace."

Beelay and Segion nodded in agreement.

"We will be right outside if you need us," said Beelay as Segion pulled him from the room.

After a good sleep, Imogen was ready to meet with her party of friends. Imogen walked over to the mead hall, healed as if the abuse and torture had never happened. Along the short journey, a boy jumped out in front of her, nearly scaring her to death. The boy was about her age and named Oron. Olive skinned with brown shoulder-length hair and green eyes, Oron towered over her by at least a foot.

"Welcome, my name is Oron Magna, and I would like to be your guide in this realm," he said as he bowed.

Imogen blushed. She was not used to all the attention she was getting, and this boy was very handsome. "Do you usually jump out in front of girls at nighttime?"

Oron grinned. "Only the pretty girls."

Imogen looked at him sideways. "Well I would like that very much. This has been my greatest adventure to date. Before today, the furthest place I had adventured to was the broken fence in the backwoods."

The pair giggled a little as Beelay approached from the front of the mead hall. "Oh, Imogen, I am so glad you are up and awake."

Hugging Imogen, he looked at Oron with suspicion. "And who is this?" Beelay stepped in front of Imogen.

Oron introduced himself with a bow. "I am Oron Magna, nephew of the Grand-High Master."

After a nod and a few seconds spent staring in silence, Beelay suggested that they go for dinner. "Come, let's go get food before the horde leaves us nothing."

Av'Dah met Imogen as she entered the mead hall and led her to sit up front at the Grand-High Master's table. Imogen was glad to see so many happy people. No one bothered her as she made her way to the front, dodging full mugs of mead that were being swung to the tune of a song. Imogen sat down at the table with wide eyes as she scanned the feast. There were many types of food, most of which Imogen could not identify, but they still smelled delectable. From the other side of the table, a girl stood with a plate.

"What would you like to eat, my lady?"

Imogen scanned the table before Vi'Lah suggested she try a little of everything.

"Would our honored guest have a drink with her dinner?"

Imogen opened her mouth to speak before being stopped by Beelay. "No, she will take water."

Imogen looked annoyed at Beelay. She did not want a drink, but she would have liked to have spoken for herself. Beelay did not want to seem overbearing, but he was still wracked with guilt over what happened and wanted only to protect her.

After the meal, Vi'Lah invited Imogen and everyone else for a nightcap in the Grand-High Master's private quarters, the room filled with an uneasy air as Vi'Lah rose to speak. "My friends and guests. These are troubling times. Evynloth and his master are further down the path of insanity then we first thought. When you were away rescuing Imogen, something transpired here in Vinlahg.

"Evynloth crossed over into the realm in search of something he needs complete his quest to dominate the realms. He kidnapped my wife and daughter, and he advised me that if I do not give him what he wants by sunset tomorrow, he will throw my wife and daughter into the Mountain of Flames."

Vi'Lah sighed as he sat back down. Imogen did not understand how he could be so calm at a time like this.

"What does he want, and why can you not give it to him?" Imogen said as she stood to speak.

"What he wants is hidden, and only someone who has pixie dust and Kami blood can open the cave they sealed it in. Evynloth is hunting for a Stone called the Stone of Auras Reclaim. I do not know what it does or why he wants it. The Stone's protection is our only charge."

Afloriana and Beelay exchanged knowing glances before breaking the silence.

"I do not have what you need on hand, but I can have dust sent here," Afloriana said. "All I need is a guide to the border of Impenia. If I use magick, then Evynloth will surely be alerted."

Vi'Lah's spirits rose instantly. "Good woman, anything you need, you shall have."

With a nod from his father, Av'Dah rose. "Good woman, I will take you and lead you to the border at once."

Afloriana nodded in thanks, and the two made haste to the border, leaving the others to wait in the mead hall.

Afloriana and Av'Dah made the journey on horseback. The night was still, with no rain in sight. The couple rode slowly so as not to arouse suspicion. Lord Avestyn and Lord Evynloth had amassed a great number of highly-motivated spies, who were all too willing to give up those acting suspiciously.

"Do you really think Lord Evynloth will hurt my family?" asked Av'Dah quietly. "He is a very sick man, filled with great vengeance and rage. He has not been normal for many years now."

Afloriana turned her head toward the landscape ahead of them, scanning for any sight of danger as she spoke, "I only hope we save your family and end this chaos soon."

After a few hours' journey, Afloriana and her guide reached the border of Impenia. "Wait here, boy. I will return in a moment with the dust we need."

As Afloriana crossed over into the realm, she sent a telepathic message to the other Seers to tell them what she needed. She did not want to leave her guide too long in case Lord Evynloth arrived unexpectedly. After what seemed like an eternity, an Imp appeared before her. Afloriana looked a little surprised to see the Imp King. "Your Majesty, I did not expect you to come and deliver this," she said with her head bowed.

"Well, child, it is not every day we get to save someone's life or have the chance to stop Evynloth in his dark quest," the king remarked as he handed over a deer hide pouch of pixie dust. "Go, child, we cannot waste any more time. We can talk more when you return home victorious," he said with a wink as he disappeared in a flash.

Afloriana wasted no time in returning to the Viking realm, pouch in hand.

Av'Dah and Afloriana threw caution to the wind as they raced the horses back to the mead hall. When they returned to the capital, Vi'Lah and the rest of the party met them.

"Did you get it?" he said as he extended a hand to Afloriana, who was still on horseback.

"Yes, here it is," she said as she handed the pouch to Vi'Lah.

"Right, we have the dust, so how do we get to the Valley of Greengarth?" remarked Imogen, still eager to finish this journey.

Vi'Lah turned to face the little adventurer. "You know, child, you could be mistaken for a young Viking girl. It is a half day's journey from here. I have arranged for Oron to guide you to your destination."

Oron rounded the corner with two horses packed and ready for the journey.

"Imogen is not going without all of us to protect her," said Beelay as sternly as he could.

"I understand that, Lord Beelay, but I need all the help I can get to protect the capital."

Segion interjected, "My lord, if it is agreeable, I can send for some troops. I am on good terms with the Elves, and I am sure they will be agreeable to helping you."

Vi'Lah nodded in agreement. "Very well. Send word to them, please. I fear Lord Evynloth means to carry out his plan for my family and more."

After Segion contacted the Elves, the horses were readied for the party to set out on their journey.

"Is it wise to travel at night in this realm, Av'Dah?" Segion asked.

Av'Dah chuckled a little as he reassured them that they were in the most boring realm in Tera'Loth.

After an uneventful journey, they arrived at the base of the Valley of Greengarth. Before them lay a vast valley filled with twists and turns. Along each side of a crudely fashioned pathway, cave entrances sat every ten feet. Imogen gave up counting them after the fortieth. The Vikings used most of the caves as family crypts or storage.

"Now, which is the cave we need? There must be hundreds. And they all look the same," Imogen said as she looked toward what seemed like an endless row of caves.

"Fear not, my lady," said Oron as he reached into his pocket, producing a map that the Grand-High Master had given him. "This will lead us to the cave—and to the Stone."

Oron handed the map around for the group to study. Afloriana was becoming very nervous, feeling a dark presence in the valley. She was uneasy with this presence because all she felt was death.

As soon as Beelay saw the look on her face, he led her quietly away from the rest of the group. "I know that look. I have seen it before. What is wrong?"

Afloriana looked around before she spoke, "I feel a dark presence on the horizon, but I cannot sense its intent. I do not know if it is the evil of Evynloth or of another, but it is danger nonetheless."

Beelay looked around the wooded area that guarded the valley. "What do you think we should do?"

Afloriana's eyes rolled before they closed. She was seeing. After a moment, she opened her eyes as she woke up. "I do not want to leave you alone, but I think I should go to the border and form a back-up plan. In my vision, I saw all of you being chased by the Vikings we are trying to help, and they did not look happy. I will meet you at the border when you have the Stone. I will have the back-up plan ready if you need it, but I hope it won't be necessary."

The conversation was cut short by the approach of Imogen.

"What is wrong?" Imogen said bluntly with her arms folded.

Beelay and Afloriana smiled at Imogen, trying to look as reassuring as they could. "It concerns Afloriana that we do not have enough security around you, so she will rally us some support."

As Afloriana was about to leave, she kissed Imogen on the forehead as she whispered, "Remember that you are a magickal person, and that your thoughts can be actions if you want them to be. If you are ever in danger, think of ways to protect yourself, and they will come true—if you believe in the visions and in yourself."

With that, Afloriana jumped on a horse, disappearing into the night. Imogen looked on into the distance until Afloriana was out of sight.

I wonder what she meant by that, Imogen thought as she turned and walked back to the campsite, Beelay at her side.

With dawn breaking, the group journeyed into the Valley of Greengarth. As they slowly and carefully made their way through the valley, they heard strange noises coming from all around them. Segion froze instantly. He remembered this sound from a few nights back.

"Harpies," he said in a hushed tone.

"Do not worry, sir. The valley holds nothing but their sound. It is an Imp trick to ward off potential thieves. There is no danger here."

Segion eased a little but still found his eyes darting all over the valley. As the group approached the end of the path, they came to a fork in the road. Oron studied the map for a moment before leading the group down the path on the left. This pathway was short, and after a few moments' walk they found the cave they were looking for.

It looked like an ordinary cave entrance but for a tiny

difference, and that was a tiny "X" that marked the entrance way.

"This is it," said Av'Dah as he looked at the map over Oron's shoulder.

"Alright Imogen, all you have to do is sprinkle the pixie dust over the threshold to the cave and we will be safe to enter. The pixie dust disarms any traps and locks in the cave." Oron stepped up next to Imogen. "Cousin Av'Dah, your father told me that the cave is narrow, and that there is only room for two. I promised to act as a guide to Imogen, so I think it is wise that the two of us enter the cave alone."

Beelay did not like this idea, but he also did not want to starve Imogen of air. "Alright, we shall stay out here, but if I hear any commotion, I will be in there to save you without question."

Imogen hugged Beelay—he was good to her—and she was glad to have him as her friend. Wasting no further time, Imogen sprinkled pixie dust over the threshold. As soon as the dust hit the ground, she heard some strange noises. When the noises stopped, the pixie dust on the ground floated around and formed the words, "Enter At Will."

Imogen looked at the words, then back to Beelay. "Don't worry Beelay, I'll be right back."

With a deep breath and a torch in hand, the pair stepped into the dark cave.

The cave itself was not big. In the cave's center lay a rock fashioned as a table. Atop the rock lay a pouch.

"Well, I guess this is it then," Imogen said as she picked up the pouch, which weighed more than she thought it would. "I think I will open it in front of everyone else. It seems only fair."

Oron was quiet with his eyes fixed on the pouch. "If you want me to carry it, I can do that for you. I am your humble servant."

Imogen giggled a little then shook her head. "No, thank you. The task is mine, but thank you."

Oron's emotions changed quickly, bringing more tension into the cave. "I really need to hold onto that Stone. I suggest you give it to me now, before you get hurt," he said, brandishing a knife in her direction.

"Oron, what's going on? I'm confused."

Oron sniggered as he circled Imogen. "Well then, let me simplify it for you, girl. Before you arrived here, the great Lord Evynloth visited me, and he promised me something I wanted if I got this Stone for him."

Imogen, scared and enraged, screamed, "What could be so important that it is worth making a deal with an evil man?"

Oron grinned as he said, "Power. All I have ever wanted is to be the Grand-High Master of Vinlahg, but my father was the second-born. Evynloth promised to murder my uncle and his entire family so that I may take up the Grand-High Master's chair and lord over the lands until my dying breath. All I have to do is give him that Stone."

Imogen tried to run, but Oron lunged forward, pushing Imogen to the ground. She screamed at the top of her lungs. Oron was on top of her as the pair wrestled with the knife. In the frenzy, Imogen heard Afloriana's voice in her head.

If you believe it, then it will happen.

Imogen thought quickly, conjuring up the image of a snake.

As she opened her eyes, she saw Oron being bitten again and again by a snake that had replaced the knife in his hands. Imogen ran for the exit with the Stone in hand, leaving Oron to his fate.

"Imogen."

She heard Oron screaming her name as she exited the cave. Imogen exited the cave quickly, running straight toward Beelay, who had been pacing back and forth, mumbling toward the cave.

"Beelay, help."

Beelay snapped out of his pacing. "Imogen, what happened? We heard your screams, but we could not get into the cave to save you. The protective barrier returned after you entered the cave. Where is Oron?"

Imogen cried as she held up the pouch. "I have the Stone, but he tried to kill me for it. Evynloth got to him before we arrived in the realm."

Beelay turned his anger toward Av'Dah, throwing him to the ground as he yelled over a terrified Av'Dah. "Did you know about this? Has your whole family been working with Evynloth to set us up?"

Av'Dah looked scared and utterly confused. "I do not know what you are speaking of. Afloriana is my friend and asked me to help you. If my cousin has done wrong, then he has surely acted alone. All I want is my family back together, safely in the mead hall."

Segion came behind Beelay and pulled him away. Beelay snapped back to reality, apologizing quickly for his actions. Segion dragged Av'Dah up off the ground, standing between the two men. "We better leave before Oron gets out of that cave or Evynloth shows up," Segion said as he jumped onto his horse.

"Very well, cousin. Let's get out of here."

The party raced out of the valley and into the woods.

Back in the cave, Oron lay injured from snake bites. As he regained consciousness, he whispered Imogen's name through labored breathing as he crawled out of the cave. In their haste, the party left a horse behind.

After climbing atop the horse, Oron made his way back to the capital. Along the way, Oron, barely breathing, met his uncle flanked by guards. Vi'Lah had decided that he could not sit around and wait for the adventurers to return, so he had followed them. When Vi'Lah saw the state his nephew was in, shock overtook him.

"What happened, my child? Who has done this to you?"

Still being under the spell of Evynloth's promise, Oron told a lie. "Av'Dah has turned on you. He has left with the traitors, and they are taking the Stone for themselves. Av'Dah is sacrificing his own mother and sister for that whore who calls herself a Seer. I always knew outsiders like Afloriana were bad for our realm. Now look what has happened to us—and to me."

Vi'Lah was struck with rage as Oron collapsed off of the horse and into his arms. "We will chase them down, men. They will not leave Vinlahg alive."

The men roared as they took off in search of the party and the Stone.

As the horses dashed through the mountain range of Vinlahg, Imogen held onto Beelay as her eyes welled with tears. She had thought she could trust Oron, but she had been wrong.

"We will never make it to the border," Segion shouted to Beelay.

"Afloriana won't let us down," Beelay yelled back.

Imogen turned to look at the road behind them, trying to hide her tears from Beelay. In the distance, she spotted Oron and a group of Vikings approaching them with great speed.

"Beelay, we have trouble. It is Oron and some men who don't look particularly happy."

Beelay stole a quick glance behind them as the horses continued to gallop toward the border. "Imogen, if you think you can stop them, you need to do it now."

Imogen closed her eyes, took a deep breath, and cleared her mind. After a few moments of silence, she heard the men behind her scream. The men, thrown from their horses, were struggling under a massive tidal wave that had sprung forth over the mountain range. Leaving the Vikings to their fate, the horses galloped into the woods ahead.

Upon reaching the border, Afloriana and the Watch-Keepers met them. As the horses slowed, the Elvish guard quickly formed a line of protection in front of the party.

Afloriana smiled gleefully with a look of pride on her face. "I guess you didn't need my help after all," she said as she helped Imogen from the horse. "Come, let's leave here at once," said Afloriana as she and the rest of the party passed into Impenia.

"Will we be safe where we are going? I am so tired," remarked Imogen.

Afloriana smiled, taking Imogen's hand. "Trust me, my darling. Where we are going, Evynloth would not dare follow."

A NEW PLAN

As dusk set over Tera'Loth, Evynloth transported himself to the mead hall, intending to collect the Stone. When he arrived in the rooms of the Grand-High Master, something replaced anticipation with anger. Before him lay a dozen men who were either dead or wounded.

Having spotted Vi'Lah slumped in his chair, he charged toward a wounded Vi'Lah, greeting him with a palm outstretched. "I hope that the scene before me shows that you put up a great fight to claim my prize," remarked Lord Evynloth with an expectant tone. "I do not think I should have to remind you of your predicament or what is at stake here?"

Vi'Lah looked at the amulet that hung from his own neck. His wife was very rich, and the amulet had been part of her wedding dowry, given to him on their wedding night.

With tears in his eyes, he looked at Evynloth, saying nothing but the words, "Valhalla awaits my wife and child, for we have failed in our quest to save them."

After breathing a large sigh, Vi'Lah dropped his head, sobbing for his wife and child. Lord Evynloth's face became flushed with fury as he lunged forward, placing his hands around Vi'Lah's throat. "You will be joining her soon, old man."

In the frenzy, a young guard, not knowing of Lord Evynloth's power, lunged forward to aid the Grand-High Master. He did not get very far before being thrown against the wall without the slightest touch by Lord Evynloth. Evynloth would have killed Vi'Lah if not for Lord Avestyn's interruption in his mind.

"Stop trying to kill him and get back here. We must find the Stone."

Lord Evynloth released his grip, throwing Vi'Lah back against the chair. "You are lucky that my master has called me back," Lord Evynloth said as he dusted himself off. "Oh, and do not attempt to save your family, for they are already dead. I threw them into the lava pits in Necromancium."

As he walked away, the sound of Vi'Lah's screams echoed throughout the mead hall.

When Evynloth got back to the fortress, he flew around the study in a fit of rage. "How could Oron let her get away with that Stone? After all my careful planning. That useless little Viking will pay for this."

Matthew edged gently toward his crazed master. "My lord, I am sure if you would permit me, I could track the girl with Lady Astrid's help. I am sure we could find an opportune time to retrieve the Stone."

Lord Evynloth looked to his master for guidance. "Let the children go. They will be successful in such an undertaking, I am sure," Lord Avestyn said through choking coughs.

Evynloth turned back toward Matthew, giving a nod. "Very well. Get out of my sight until you have the Stone."

Matthew and Astrid bowed halfheartedly as they left the room.

"My lady, may I suggest we return to your childhood home? It is closer to the realms where I think the girl may seek shelter. I would hazard a guess that she is with Afloriana. She is the only Seer brave enough to stick her nose into our business."

Astrid was in agreement.

As the carriage left the fortress, Matthew smiled at the vain efforts of the two old men below. They were blind fools and out of touch with reality, their minds consumed so much by their end goal that they were blind to anything else happening around them.

"We need to lure her back to the Magicka realm," Astrid said with a raised voice as she scowled at Matthew. "You better have a plan. We will feel a great deal of pain—and possibly death—if we do not return with the Stone."

Matthew smiled at his niece, ignoring her scowl. "Trust me, my darling. They will be in Magicka before you know it."

SANCTUARY FOR A TIME

After the party crossed over the border into Impenia, they quickly transported themselves to Afloriana's home. Imogen was hungry and exhausted. Sensing this, Afloriana led her up to a room to sleep. "I will wake you when we have the food ready, child." Afloriana closed the door, allowing Imogen to lie down and experience some much-needed peace and calm.

As Imogen lay sleeping, she dreamed of home.

She was sitting with her mother at the kitchen table. Simone was looking at a picture of Jonas and the other children as she cried. Imogen tried to touch her mother and talk to her, but it was as if Simone could neither hear nor see her. The room blackened, the face of her mother dimming as she woke up. Imogen lay there with tears in her eyes, feeling ashamed, for during the chaos of the last few days, she had completely forgotten about her mother.

Hauling herself from the bed, Imogen made her way to the bathroom. Upon entering, she found a set of clean clothes laid out for her, along with some toiletries. The sight of soap invoked her desire for a much-needed shower. After Imogen dressed, she heard Afloriana's voice in her head, beckoning her to descend the staircase. Imogen found her way downstairs and into the living room of Afloriana's home. In the living room, Afloriana, Beelay, Segion, and the last of the Seers in Tera'Loth met her.

Afloriana rose to greet Imogen. "These men and women have come a long way and traveled through danger to speak with you. I know you still have many questions, and they are here to answer them."

Imogen walked toward Beelay and Segion. Beelay nodded toward a chair placed before the Seers. "Come, child, please sit with us. I know the journey has been hard, but it is far from over. You have heard many people tell you a lot about the prophecy and why you are here, but we feel you need to hear the full story from us," said the Seer named Zarnus, who appeared to be in charge, and who Imogen would later learn was the Imp King.

Imogen sat down as Zarnus continued to speak, "Yes, it is true that Richard foretold you would be the sorceress to stop Evynloth, but there was nothing that clearly stated you must kill him. Stopping a person doesn't mean you have to kill them. We all know how powerful Evynloth has become. Lord Avestyn is nothing but a relic, and he doesn't even realize he is now the puppet instead of Evynloth. Your great-grandfather did truly have a hard life, but he was saved and given a choice for how he wished to live the rest of his life.

"Now perhaps it is your duty to remind him of that. Evynloth is hellbent on unlocking Necromancium, and he thinks that he will not allow a thing to stand in his way, but he has a weakness, and that is love. Love is the reason he has done all of this. Lord Avestyn offered him something he could not resist: the chance to right his wrongs and change the past. Lord Avestyn told him he could bring Ericka, your great-grandmother, back from the dead with a book he stole from the Necromancium realm. On the night your great-grandmother was killed, she was trying to defend Evynloth from her cousin Xenus. He came to their home intending to kill Evynloth out of a one-sided feud, fueled by jealousy that festered inside him for years.

"Unfortunately, Ericka got caught in the crossfire. Beelay came to the defense of Evynloth and Astrid, although this did not make Evynloth look like the innocent party. Your great-grandfather ran away because he knew that the odds were stacked against him, and he only wanted to live and try to find a way to clear his name. He did not get far from the home he had built with his wife before bad fortune found him. Lord Avestyn got his hands on his former apprentice-turned-slave, but we were unclear as to how Lord Avestyn was set free.

"On the night of Ericka's death, Alumina was visited in her dreams by Ericka's Aura, which told her what had happened. Ericka and Alumina were friends in childhood and trusted each other. We thought of hiding Beelay and the child, but Lord Beelay was already on the run from the capital. We were successful in keeping Beelay and the child hidden for a time, but eventually Xenus found Astrid."

Imogen was listening intently. She seemed overcome by this new understanding of her family and their situation.

"I know this is a lot to take in, but the thing we need for you to understand is that you are the only person who can choose how we handle the situation we find ourselves in, and we will honor your decision. None of us can influence you, but believe me now: we will do everything that is within our power to protect you and see you through the trials you will face in the coming days. For now, child, we will guard this place with all the magickal force we have so that you can rest easy. Do not worry. Nobody will hurt you here in this house."

"Thank you all. I cannot tell you how grateful I am for what everyone here has done for me, but I am still confused about what my choice *is*."

Afloriana looked toward Beelay for a confirmation. He nodded before she spoke, "Imogen, you need to stop your grandfather from unlocking Necromancium. If he is successful in unlocking that realm then he will unleash the dead to spread across all of Tera'Loth. If that happens, he will take over, and most of us will surely be dead. It has always been Lord Avestyn's goal to have revenge on Magicka and on all of Tera'Loth for what he saw as the treasonous act of imprisoning him for his crimes against children—among other things."

Imogen was suddenly overcome with the realization that all the realms were relying on a thirteen-year-old girl for their survival. Imogen felt dizzy. "I am sorry. This is a lot to take in. I don't feel well." Imogen slurred her mother's name as she fainted.

Beelay and Segion ran to Imogen's side as they tried to wake her.

Afloriana shooed them away. "Come, let's carry her back to bed. This has been too much too fast."

In the morning, Imogen joined the Seers again. They all inquired as to how she felt. Embarrassed by fainting, she brushed it aside as she sat down at the table, barely in her chair before Segion was pushing a plate of food piled high in front of her. Upon seeing the mountain of food, Imogen realized how hungry she was, lunging forward to devour her food as she spoke through mouthfuls. "I know I have many trials ahead of me, but I cannot do anything until I know my mother is safe. I know I am in the safest place I can be at the moment, but I cannot leave my mother alone and scared in that prison. I have to save her, and I am going with or without your help."

Segion chuckled at the sight of this little girl devouring her food in between her war cries. "You know Beelay and I will help you, but are you sure you know what you're getting yourself into? I hear the prison is full of traps," Segion chimed in as he carefully put more bacon on her plate, trying not to lose a finger as Imogen continued to shovel the food into her mouth.

"I can help you with that, child," replied King Zarnus as he stole bacon from Imogen's plate. "The people of Impenia built that prison. It was our job to make sure it was rigged with more traps and beasts than any other prison we had previously built. It is a prison from which nobody escapes. We know it as the Prison of Emotion. It is a place that someone sends people they hate or no longer need or want to forget."

Imogen suddenly felt guilty as she looked at her plate. How could she eat at a time like this? Before she asked any more questions, the king grabbed her hand, leading her to the door. "Come with me to the palace so that we can make a plan to get you into that prison."

Imogen turned to look at Beelay, who nodded his head, answering her before she spoke. "You go on ahead," he said. "Segion and I will be along soon."

SIMONE'S PURPOSE

Simone lay in the dark, curled up in a ball on the cold floor, listening to the water drip from the pipes above. "The man said my family is dead, and I am here to be forgotten. I don't understand. Why do I need to be forgotten or imprisoned?"

From the distance, Simone heard a voice say, "You are here as an insurance policy, my darling."

Simone jumped up in fear. "Who said that?" she yelped as she tried to make out the shadow flowing toward her.

From the darkness emerged the ghost of Ericka Almackia. "You look so beautiful. I wish I could have known you in my lifetime."

As soon as Simone saw the woman, she was so enchanted with her beauty that she could barely speak.

"My name is Ericka Almackia, and I am your grandmother. It seems strange to think of myself as someone's grandmother. I was barely a mother before I died."

Ericka sighed as her spirit passed through the bars of Simone's prison cell. "I know you must have many questions and are terrified right now, so let me tell you a story to try to set your mind at ease," she said as she floated beside Simone. "The world you think you live in is not as it seems. You grew up in the human realm thinking there was nothing more out there than what surrounded you, but in truth you were born in a realm known crudely as the humanoid realm, which is one of the many realms that makes up the world of Tera'Loth.

"My husband's name was Evynloth Almackia, and it truly was love at first sight, even with all of his problems. He was strange, mysterious, and completely broken when I met him. We lived together in the Magicka realm once known as Djinn, but they erased that name after an evil man did some terrible things. I married Evynloth after we finished our studies, and we settled into a happy life together as quickly as we fell in love.

"But where pleasure looms, a snag of pain can be found, and that pain came in the form of my cousin Xenus. Xenus was in love with me all of his life, but I did not know if I really felt the same way. He asked me for my hand, but I rejected him, choosing Evynloth instead. This choice only exacerbated the anger and jealousy that was already growing in Xenus's heart. Meanwhile, your grandfather slowly rose the ranks, to the point of being appointed a chair on the High Council.

"Upon learning this, Xenus came to our home on the night I died, intending to kill Evynloth. There was a fight, and Xenus accidentally killed me. Xenus lied about this, which caused Evynloth to run away. Your mother's care was entrusted to a Druid-Elf named Beelay. He was our best friend, but Xenus, in his quest to ruin Evynloth's life, tracked Beelay down and took Astrid from him. I often wonder what her life would have been like if she'd stayed with Beelay.

"After events that were set in motion by Xenus, Evynloth's old master captured him and returned him to the slavery he had escaped years before. With his recapture, Evynloth's metamorphosis into evil was completed. The man who was consumed with making life better for everyone was now hell-bent on avenging me. In cold calculation, he waited until the day of your mother's wedding to exact his vengeance on Xenus.

"After murdering Xenus, he turned on your mother and father. If it was not for Beelay, they would have died at the hands of my husband. With the realization that they would not be safe in the Magicka realm, they moved the couple to the humanoid realm to live in peace and safety. The humanoids, being devoid of any magick, guaranteed them safety from Evynloth. Astrid lived with her small family in peace for about five years before things changed for the worse.

"Beelay traveled to the realm to tell Richard that his mother and father had met their death at the hands of Evyn-loth. In his grief, your father tried to return to the Magicka realm to kill Evynloth. Astrid fought him over the matter, and in the frenzy, darkness overcame her, and she killed her husband. I cannot know if she did this on purpose or by accident, but after that night she covered up all traces of her life before Richard's death, after which she lived a life of normalcy—until your daughter found a chest of Richard's that was supposed to be hidden somewhere very far away.

"When Imogen found that chest, she started down her path of destiny, which had been deliberately concealed. Your mother has been doing everything she can to protect her father from Imogen. That is the first reason you are here in this prison."

Simone's face was awash with emotion. She looked bewildered and hurt by this woman's revelations. "How could my mother do this to me? And what is the other reason I am here?"

As Ericka stood up, she moved to kiss her granddaughter, but being a ghost, she could not. "Your mother is an evil soul, and she sides with your grandfather. They desire to unlock a realm known as Necromancium, and they believe you are the key."

Simone stood up to face her grandmother. "What do they want? What do they seek? I'll give them anything they want, so long as they don't hurt my baby."

As Ericka floated away, she said, "Power."

As Simone watched her grandmother float away, she cried, "Please, do not leave me here."

From the distance, Ericka remarked, "Do not worry. Help is on the way."

Back in Impenia, Imogen and the king made their way to

the castle. Upon arriving, King Zarnus lost no time in making his way to his study, Imogen hurrying along behind him. Imogen stood before the king, her head darting back and forth as she watched the king pile his desk with book after book. As he opened the map-book to study it, he seemed to have an argument with himself. "We could follow the direct path, but it might be dangerous. This is the Giberals' mating season, and you know how they get."

The king thought for a moment, then he pulled out a map from the back of the book. "There is a safer way, but if you are afraid of enclosed spaces, you won't like this option."

The king rolled the map out across the table. "The pixies and Imps made every trap, trick, or maze in Tera'Loth. They call this cave route the Twists of Craze. It is a maze of caves so elaborate that many people have died trying to navigate it."

Imogen gasped.

"Oh, do not worry, dear girl. I will help you make it through with as many limbs as you can save," he said as he chuckled at a less-than-pleased Imogen.

"What's this talk about lost limbs," Beelay said with as he and Segion entered the room.

"Why would you build such a cave in that mountain, Your Majesty?" Imogen asked as the king muddled through his papers before giving a response that was short and to the point.

"We did it to make sure the prisoners did not leave alive."

Imogen could not believe how coldly he was admitting that fact, but he continued to speak, "My people, at a time, were enslaved by the Dwarfs, so we did what we needed to do. I cannot destroy the prison, but I can protect you on your journey."

The king handed Imogen a map. "This is a safe route used by prison guards and other staff. You will be safe if you take this path."

Imogen gave the map to Beelay for safekeeping. "I want to go now. My mother has been in that prison for too long already."

King Zarnus nodded in agreement. "Very well. I will have the stable boy ready the horses."

The king summoned his servant, relayed his orders, then retired to his quarters. After a few moments, the stable boy— a Magicka boy named Ilam—entered the room. In silence, he beckoned for them to follow. Outside in the courtyard, the horses lay in wait, with saddle bags overstuffed with provisions. The party mounted the horses and set out toward the Black Mountains.

From the balcony above the courtyard, King Zarnus waved Imogen and her companions off. "Good luck, my child. You are the best and only hope Tera'Loth has for survival."

THE BLACK MOUNTAINS

The road to the Black Mountains was easy and not at all scenic. At the base of the mountains were two pathways. There was a path leading up the mountains and a path leading into a cave at the base of the mountains.

"I guess this is our pathway up," Beelay said as he arched his neck, looking up at the mountains.

Imogen took a moment to get off her horse and walk for a while as Segion studied the map.

"I am afraid we will have to leave the horses here," Segion said. "These tunnels are too narrow, and I don't hold out too much hope for the quality of the air."

Imogen was not sure she liked the prospect of climbing through the narrow, dark, and stuffy tunnels, but she would bear it for her mother. "Oh, well, girl," she said to her horse, "I guess this is where we part ways. Thank you for the ride this far," she said as she got her pack and other supplies from the horse, kissing it before she left.

Beelay unearthed the torches, leaving Segion to shoo the horses back to the palace stables.

"Torches at the ready," Segion remarked as he lit his first.

"I am scared, Beelay. What if my mother is not there at all?"

Beelay squeezed her hand in assurance as they stepped into the cave.

The caves smelled damp, and its walls were covered with moss.

"Which way do we go, then?" Beelay said as he retrieved the map from Segion.

"According to this, it is a straight shot up through the middle tunnel. There is a system of ladders and tunnels. Judging by this map, it should take us about five hours to reach the top."

Imogen waved her torch over the walls, looking for any signs of life before the sound of Segion's voice snapped her back to reality.

"Come now, chaps. There is no time like the present. Big smiles, for today we are someone's hero."

Imogen made a face at Segion. "How can you always be so cheery, even in a moment like this?"

Segion's grin widened as he remarked, "Sometimes in life, humor is the only thing that keeps you sane. Take, for instance, the fact that my home was nearly destroyed by harpies, and I was taken from my quiet life and thrust into a quest to stop a madman whose reign of terror I thought would never end."

Imogen looked at Segion blankly as she replied, "I guess when you put it that way, I need to laugh all day every day."

Beelay coughed in interruption. "I wonder if you two philosophers could continue this conversation another time? The air is thin, and we don't know how much time we have before Astrid figures out what we are up to."

With that, the trio began their journey up the ladders, thrusting themselves into the depths of the Black Mountains. After about a half an hour of climbing, the party reached the first rest stop.

"Oh, thank goodness. I don't think I could have climbed a second longer," Imogen said as she flopped herself over a rock.

Beelay and Segion reached into their packs for something to eat and drink.

"We should rest here, but only for a short while," Beelay said. "We do not know what may lurk in the shadows. Here in this cave, we are on borrowed time."

Imogen and Segion nodded in agreement. After a few moments' rest and some sustenance, they were back on their way. They walked through some caves to get to the next network of ladders. As they entered the next cave in the network, they heard strange moaning sounds.

"Beelay, what is that noise?"

Beelay looked around, trying not to seem worried as he reassured her, "It must be the wind coming through the tunnels. There are many entrances into the mountains along the pathway."

As they continued through the cave, the sound got louder. When they rounded a corner, a pack of strange-looking beasts were waiting to greet them. As soon as the creatures sensed their presence, they were ready to eat.

"Berserk Goblins. Ready your weapons," Beelay yelled as he darted into the pack of what Imogen thought must have been at least two dozen hungry-looking Goblins. "I will fight them off. Just get Imogen to the ladders."

Segion was torn between helping Imogen over Beelay, but he conceded to lead Imogen through the chaos and up the ladders.

When they arrived at the next network of ladders, Segion hoisted Imogen up to the ladder. In the distance, they could hear Beelay yelling as his sword and wand clinked and zapped. Segion looked up to Imogen with a long face.

"Climb, child. I will help Beelay. Just get to the top and we won't be far behind, I promise," Segion said as he ran back to aid his cousin.

Imogen climbed the ladder, tears welling in her eyes as she listened to the sound of her friends fighting for their lives.

Meanwhile, Beelay and Segion fended off the Berserk Goblins as quickly as they could, but the slew was endless. In their exhaustion, they were nearly ready to give up and drop their swords, if it were not for the light that washed over the room. With the light obscuring their vision, all they could hear was the sound of

Goblins screaming. After a few moments passed, the light dissipated, and the sound of deafening silence filled the mountain. When their eyes finally adjusted to the light, they found themselves surrounded by dead Goblins.

In the middle of the bodies stood a woman of average height, with black hair and brown eyes that could be mistaken for red. Her name was Drayah. She was a Witch who had been in high standing until Lord Evynloth and Lord Avestyn's reign of terror began.

"Drayah, is that you?" Beelay could not believe his eyes, for he had thought she had died in the Forest of Fortune years before.

"Yes, it is me. I know people think I am dead, but for all his charm, Evynloth is not the smartest Wizard who ever lived. I have been living under ground ever since the night he took over. Do not think me a coward for running. My reasons were my own."

Beelay ran toward Drayah, hugging her harder than he had hugged anyone for a long time. He was never a person for absolutes, but he was quite sure that Drayah had just saved them from death.

"Come, we have to get to Imogen at once," he said. "Who knows what else lurks in this mountain."

Drayah looked at the sorry men before her, shaking her head. "Come now, we will have to transport up there, because I don't think you two will make it up those ladders in this state."

They each took one of Drayah's hands as she whispered

some magickal words and transported them to the place in the caves where Imogen was.

Imogen, who was waiting at the top of the ladder for her friends, panicked, realizing that in the frenzy she hadn't taken the map and was at a loss to figure out where to go next. Looking down toward the bottom of the ladder, she heard a voice behind her, "Come now, you don't want to fall and have to climb that again. It's murder on the body, and I don't feel like any more exercise today."

Imogen jumped around in fright to see Beelay and Segion looking half-dead but happy to be alive. Her eyes quickly diverted from them and over to the stranger standing between them.

"Who are you?" Imogen said with caution.

"My name is Drayah, and I am—or I *was*—the Highest Witch in Magicka. Do not fear me, for I am on your side."

Imogen's mind eased a little. "Thank you so much for saving my friends."

Drayah responded with a slight bow of her head. "I don't mean to be rude, but I think we need to get out of here now. I want my mother out of this place and safe with me."

The party wasted no more time with pleasantries as they hurried toward the Prison of Emotion.

After a long journey through the pixies' secret caves, they arrived at the top of the mountains. Before them stood a dilapidated building made of brick surrounded by metal fencing, which stretched eighteen feet into the air. The front gate was open, but given the location of the prison and its extensive security, there was not much need for a locked gate.

Drayah stepped ahead of the group to check for any locking spells or curses. Luckily, she found neither. Satisfied, she led the group into the Prison of Emotion. As soon as they entered the foyer, they were met by Orvin the prison master.

"Hello, friends. It's not every day that fresh bodies come crawling into my prison. It must be my birthday," he said with a laugh that made Imogen's skin crawl.

"We are here for her mother and nothing more, you inhuman beast." Beelay stood instinctively between Imogen and Orvin, eyeballing Orvin as he spoke. "I don't know why you didn't leave Tera'Loth when all the other pirates and lowlife scum did."

Orvin chuckled even louder. "Ah, but you see, I was gifted with a lucrative business and a good return on my investments."

Imogen walked around Beelay. "It's okay, Beelay. I can do this."

Orvin's ears pricked up. "Beelay, you say? As in Beelay, the Druid-Elf from the Mountains of Memory?"

Before Beelay could answer, he was in shackles. "What is this? Let me go now."

Orvin sauntered down the staircase. "Oh no, friend. You are on the inter-realm bounty list, and I am collecting it."

Beelay struggled in his shackles. "Who put a bounty on me? Is this a game?"

Orvin, who was now standing face to face with Beelay, shook his head as he looked his new captive up and down. "Why, it was Xenus Alphias, of course."

Beelay shook his head, looking to his friends for help. "He

said that was void because I gave him Astrid, and he is dead, so who will pay you?"

Orvin bellowed as he laughed harder still. "I was not aware of his death, and I am not always out to seek monetary payment. What I have planned for you is payment tenfold," said Orvin with a crazed look. "I hope you will enjoy your stay with me."

Beelay struggled in place and felt an odd sensation come over him. Before he knew it, he was being pulled toward the center of the room. There in the room's center lay what looked like a mat in the shape of a barrel top.

"Enjoy your induction ceremony," said Orvin as the floor beneath Beelay made its descent.

"No. Beelay." Imogen tried to run toward him, but Segion held her back.

"Just save your mother, Imogen. I will be fine, I promise. Just get Simone."

As Beelay's head disappeared, another barrel-shaped mat slid across the opening.

"Well now, poppet. I guess it is just the four of us—or should I say three," Orvin remarked as he lunged toward Segion.

As the two wrestled and fought, Segion got the keys from Orvin. throwing them to Drayah. "Let's split up and look for your mother. I will try to find a log book or something to help us figure this prison out."

Drayah and Imogen ran in opposite directions. During the fight, Orvin managed to get loose from Segion's grasp, picking himself up off the floor, running for the staircase.

Before he made it two steps, Segion lunged forward, grabbing Orvin by the legs, thrusting him toward the ground. Orvin struggled to turn over to face Segion but was struck over the head with the butt of his own knife, which Segion had pried from the sheath on Orvin's hip. Segion looked down in victory.

"Now where should I tuck you away?" Segion spoke over a comatose Orvin.

Segion looked around the room, trying to formulate a plan, when he spotted a closet at the top of the stairs. "Oh well, let's keep this simple," he said as he hoisted Orvin over his shoulder.

Once Orvin was tucked away in the closet, Segion made sure the door to the closet was jammed shut before running off to aid his friends.

Meanwhile, while Imogen ran down the hallway, she was struck by a thought. *I have no idea where my mother is, or what key will fit the door to her cell. I could search for days to find her in this prison.*

It was at that moment she heard someone yelling from a cell behind her, "Child, I can help you."

Stopping dead in her tracks, she turned and walked in the voice's direction. "How can you help me locked in a cell?"

The figure got up from their makeshift bed to approach the light of the torches that were burning along the hall. From the shadows emerged none other than Richard Welkin.

Imogen gasped, recognizing him instantly. "Richard? I mean, Grandfather, is that you?" she said, taking a few steps back.

"Yes, child, it is me. I know you must be very confused. I know they told you I was dead, but obviously I am not."

Imogen was confused and scared, her eyes darted around her as she waited for someone to spring a trap.

"Imogen, we do not have time, but I promise it is me. Let me out now and I will explain it all to you as soon as we are safe."

Imogen was about to poke Richard when she was interrupted by Drayah, who rounded the corner with a look of determination. "We need to find the main switch that opens these doors."

From the distance, they heard Segion yell, "I think I have it."

Segion was on the catwalk above. As he pulled the switch, the gates to every cell opened.

In a frenzy, prisoners emerged from their cells en masse.

"Please don't run. You are safe now. Just follow me to the exit," Drayah yelled as she tried to maintain some order.

Imogen's eyes quickly scanned the hall, searching for her mother in the crowd. *Where are you, Mother, and where is Beelay?*

Beelay rounded a corner, dodging a strangely fit old man who was running for freedom.

"I am here, girl," Beelay said as he hobbled toward her, having gone toe-to-toe with a Berserk Goblin down in the initiation room, where the prisoners went to have their minds broken by Orvin and his "Tools".

Imogen hugged Beelay, tears in her eyes as she looked at the sorry state before her.

"I am alright, child. I am just glad our man on the catwalk got those doors open in time," Beelay said as he hugged Imogen harder.

"I am sorry to break this up, but we need to get out of here." Drayah took Imogen by the hand and led her to the exit.

Along the way, they spotted a cell door that hadn't opened. "I wonder why that cell did not open?" Drayah shook her head as she pulled Imogen along, casting a spell over the cell to check for signs of life. "Don't worry. It's empty."

As they exited the prison, Imogen felt an ache in her heart. Her mother was not where Astrid had said she was being kept. Imogen kicked herself for believing Astrid would have been truthful. Upon exiting the prison, Imogen and the freed prisoners were met by none other than King Zarnus and nearly thirty carriages.

"I hope I am not too late," King Zarnus chuckled as he jumped out of his carriage.

"Your Majesty, how are you up here when you said we could only travel safely through the mountain itself?"

The king grinned as he told the group how he had persuaded the Dwarfs to help lift the spells around the mountain for a while so that he could aid in the rescue. "Dwarfs can be exceptionally amenable when it comes to the safety of their precious treasures," remarked King Zarnus with a wink. "Come now, child. We need to get everyone to the Elvish realm. We do not have enough medicine to help everyone, and the Elves have been kind enough to extend us help."

Drayah extended her hand to help Imogen into a carriage. As the carriage pulled away from the mountains, Imogen sobbed uncontrollably for her mother.

AID FROM THE ELVES

Upon the party's arrival in the Elvish realm, there was a flurry of people running from place to place. Many of the prisoners were severely wounded, and the Elves ran this way and that throughout the makeshift hospital they had prepared.

Imogen walked around in a daze. When she saw Richard, she collapsed, but a young Elvish girl caught her before she fell to the ground.

"Here, let me take her to a room," Beelay said with his arms outstretched.

"Yes, we should let her sleep. The poor child has been through a lot."

A young Elvish girl led Imogen and Beelay toward a room that the Elves had prepared for her. Once she was tucked into bed, Beelay went back to the courtyard to help with the wounded. As Imogen lay sleeping, someone visited her in her dreams. Whoever it was possessed a warm and safe Aura. She could not see who was speaking to her, but she felt safe as the Aura began to speak, "My name is Ericka Alphias-Almackia. I am your great-grandmother, and my husband was accused of killing me when I was twenty-three. He did not do it, but it happened all the same. All of what you have been through so far is because he wants to fix the past. I know in my heart something or someone overcame him with the power of evil, and there is no coming back for him.

"I am sad for the life I lost, but I do not want other people to suffer so that I may return to my Loth. Imogen, I come to you now because I want you to free my Aura. There is an ancient ceremony that can stop Evynloth from bringing me back, but it is dangerous. You will have to go into the lion's den.

"In the High Council storage yards, beneath the High Council halls, there is a spell and a magick knife that are needed to perform the ceremony. They call the ceremony the Ceremony of Auras-Separation. My family should have performed it after my death to allow my Aura to be given to another, but in their grief my family neglected to perform it before they buried my body.

"If you do this, my child, it will set everything right. In the Elvish realm there are those who know how to perform the ceremony. I love you, my child. Be strong and brave, for this will all be over soon."

Imogen opened her eyes in tears. The Aura she felt was the most loving spirit she had ever experienced. When she turned her head, she saw Richard was sitting watching over her as he wrote in a notebook.

"Oh, thank goodness you are awake. I was worried. You have been asleep for a whole day now. I suppose you needed it after all you have endured."

Imogen sat up, still groggy from sleep. "Mother?"

Richard shook his head. "We will find her, dear, don't you worry."

Imogen could not get over how well-spirited he was even after being locked up by Orvin for twenty-five years. "You seem like nothing has happened to you at all, Grandfather."

Richard chuckled a little as he produced a flask. "The Elves give you the best cure for a quarter-century imprisonment."

Imogen grinned as she hauled herself out of bed.

"Where do you think you are going, child?"

Imogen looked at her grandfather with determination as she remarked, "I have to find something to eat, and then I will continue to search for my mother."

Richard nodded in agreement as they left the room.

In the courtyard, Imogen smelled her way to the food, only to find Beelay and Segion devouring plates piled high. Imogen was barely seated at the table when a plate piled high with food appeared before her. Without a word to her friends, she devoured her plate. After subduing her hunger, she told her friends about the visitor in her dreams.

Beelay nodded as he got up from the table. "Well, it sounds like we are not stopping to rest for too long."

Imogen nodded in agreement. "If we are successful in this then Evynloth may not carry out his master's plan."

Beelay hugged Imogen, smiling as he spoke, "You are so full of hope. Don't ever lose that."

Imogen nodded in agreement. "Come, let's walk off a little of that food."

At the end of the courtyard, Imogen took a seat on a bench, looking around at the beauty of the realm. Off to the side of the courtyard, Imogen caught a glimpse of some Elvish children that were taking lessons in the art of magick.

"Beelay, I just thought of something. If I am to be successful in this quest, then I think I need some help learning how to fight—in case I have to battle with Granny again. Or Lord Evynloth for that matter."

Beelay looked over at the Elvish children, giggling as they attempted spells on the flower buds in front of them. "Yes, it is a possibility, but I do not know how we can teach you everything you need to know. We are on borrowed time as it is. I don't know if Evynloth can get into the Elvish realm, but if he gets the chance, he will take it."

Lord Teymark, being close by, appeared before Imogen and Beelay.

Imogen jumped a little, for she had not sensed Lord Teymark's approach.

"Please, allow me to introduce myself. My name is Lord Teymark, and I am the King of the Elves."

Imogen looked him up and down before extending a handshake.

"Forgive my impertinence for eavesdropping, but I think I

can help you. If you are willing, everyone here can teach you all we know about magick to aid you in your journey, but I would be remiss if I did not remind you of how much you have already done on your own, with little magick and a lot of brawn."

Imogen shied away from the complement, feeling it undeserved in the failure of saving her mother. Her accomplishments were vast, but she did not want to go any further in this quest without a better arsenal. Lord Teymark, sensing Imogen was ready to train, extended his hand to her.

"Well, there is no time like the present," said Lord Teymark as he led Imogen off for a crash-course in magick.

Imogen spent the next two weeks learning everything she could, from spell-casting to lock picking. Lord Teymark was a hard task-master and did not allow Imogen to quit or fail at anything he taught her. The hardest lesson for her was blocking others' telekinesis. Her mind was young, but if she wanted to save Tera'Loth, she had to get her head around it.

During the last days of her training, Imogen was forced to go into the Forest of Fates for her last test. The test was to make it through the forest alive. On the dawn of her trip through the forest, Beelay and Segion prepared a small pack with food, and they gave her nothing but a wand for protection.

After readying herself, Lord Teymark led Imogen to the edge of the forest. "This, child, is the final test. This forest is four acres long. I will wait for you on the other side. Oh, and please try to survive," remarked Teymark as he turned to walk away.

"Is that all the advice you have for me? You haven't even told me what is in there."

Lord Teymark turned. "No questions, just survive."

With a deep breath, Imogen entered the Forest of Fates.

Upon entering the forest, Imogen turned, wanting to leave as quickly as she had entered. As she walked back toward the entrance, she found herself falling to the ground. Someone had placed a magickal barrier around the entrance, forcing her to continue. There was only one way out, and that was forward. Slumped on the ground, Imogen, who was fearful of what she was about to encounter, screamed and hit herself.

She was being attacked by fire ants.

They were all over her body, jumping up. Imogen swatted at her entire body, but to no avail. The fire ants let out a scent and attracted more and more to her body.

In her mind, she heard the voice of Lord Teymark yelling, "Use your spells, girl."

At that moment, Imogen screamed at the top of her lungs, "Pyrobeltus!"

From the sky, firebolts lunged across her back, dispelling the ants as quickly as they had crawled onto her body. With a deep breath, Imogen watched the ants run away toward the entrance of the forest.

How were they able to get through the barrier? thought Imogen to herself.

With herself collected, Imogen took in her surroundings. Before her lay the thick forest, with tall elms and lush bushes. There wasn't much of a path before her. With a deep breath, she charged full steam ahead, into the brush. After clearing a pathway with her wand, she embarked deeper into the woods. After walking for ten minutes, she heard a man's voice calling her name. It was the voice of her father, Jonas.

"Imogen, come over here. This way is quicker, for the path is straight through."

The sound of her father confused Imogen. How was father here? Realizing it was a trick to distract her from the path, Imogen kept her linear route, ignoring the pleading of her father. After a few more feet down the road, she heard the voice of her sister Vivian.

"Last scalawag to the tree's a rotten egg."

Imogen shook her head. "No, you are not here. This is not real."

Imogen stopped for a second and closed her eyes while she chanted a spell of dissipation. The spell did not work, and Imogen was dragged against her will off the path. Fighting this unknown force was hard. Who or whatever it was, it was very strong.

Opening her eyes, she did her best to remember her way back to the path, but the forest was dark, disorientating, and every bush looked the same. Continuing to fight the presence, she came to a halt in midair. Below her was a deep hole with spikes in the ground below. Held in midair, she fought and pushed, trying to will herself to fly forward, escaping the grip of this great force.

"Please, Imogen, come and live with us again. It is so nice in this place, and they allow us anything we want for dinner.

There is no bedtime and Dad never has to leave to go to work."

The force was Vivian, but Imogen remembered that her sister was dead. "Vivian, please. I have to make it through this forest so I can defeat Granny. Please let me go."

Vivian shouted, "*No!*"

As she bellowed, Imogen dropped to within an inch of the spikes. With all her strength, Imogen held herself in levitation above the spikes. "Please, Vivy, I have to save the people of this land. I can't die. I can't be with you."

With a loud, banshee-like scream, Vivian wailed, "Fine. I don't want to play with you anyway. I am going to find John."

With great force, Imogen hit the ground, and the spikes disappeared with the ghost of Vivian. With a great deal of effort, Imogen hauled herself out of the hole and back toward the path. Once back on the path, Imogen found a door standing in the middle of the pathway.

It looked just like the door to her home. She tried to walk around it, fearing it was another distraction or test. She could not walk past it, for a magickal forcefield blocked each side. She tried to backtrack down the path, but she was blocked off that way too. There was only one way through the path, and that was through the door.

With a deep breath, Imogen opened the door and walked into the darkness. Walking through the door, she found herself back in her home in the humanoid realm. It was as if the family had abandoned the house years ago. A thick layer of dust covered the contents of the house, and it was eerily quiet.

Instinctively, Imogen climbed the stairs, heading for the playroom. When she tried to open the door, she found it locked. All the other doors were also locked, all except for Granny's room. With a deep breath, Imogen opened the door and walked in. The room looked just as it had the last time she was in it. Astrid had filled the nightstand and coffee table with trashy novels and crossword books. Everything was in its place, just as Granny liked it.

Imogen shivered. It was cold, so Imogen lit the fire. As Imogen struck the first match, it blew out instantly. With the light from the match being blown out, the whole room plunged into darkness. With clenched fists and wand at the ready, Imogen turned around, only to find a familiar face sitting in the chair behind her. It was Astrid, lost in a trashy novel.

From her novel, Astrid looked up. "Oh, hello, dear child. Are you cold?" remarked Astrid as the fire was lit behind Imogen.

"Granny, what are you doing here?" said Imogen as she stood up from the floor.

"Why, dear, I am here to see you through this task. I know we have been at odds, but I want you to come out of these woods alive so that we can be a family again. What do you say? Why don't we leave it all in the past?"

Imogen fought back the tears as she spoke, "You killed my family. Why would I want to play happy families with you? I would rather kill you than get out of here alive."

Astrid smirked. "I was hoping you would say that. If you kill me, then I will succeed."

Imogen ran for the door, rethinking her choice of words. All she wanted now was to be free of Astrid, but before Imogen could make it to the door, Astrid swooped in front of her, locking the door and sending the key into the flames of the fireplace.

"Oh no, you are not getting away that easily. If you want to be free of this forest, then you will have to kill me. For me to die, you must die as well."

Imogen shouted and squirmed. She was being gripped by Astrid, and there was no way she was getting away from her Granny.

"Come now, let's drink a potion together. We can be free and live with my father forever. All you have to do is drink this potion."

Imogen was torn. She looked around the room for any escape.

"Oh no, dear, don't bother. There is no way out of here."

Imogen tried the door to the bathroom. It wouldn't budge. She tried the windows only to find them sealed shut. Anything she used to try to break the glass turned to dust when she touched it. From the corner of her eye she noticed the key. Having shot through the flames, it was on the edge of the fireplace. Imogen looked between the key and Astrid, before the pair made a run for the fireplace.

Imogen dove over the coffee table and reached for the key. Her whole body was engulfed in flames, but she managed to teleport herself across the room, opening the door before Astrid could make a move. With the door unlocked, Imogen found herself plunged back into darkness.

In shock, Imogen ran into the darkness and as far away from the door as she could. In the distance, Imogen could see a light and hear the sounds of people clapping. As she edged closer to the light, she found a ladder. With little thought, she climbed the ladder to the top. At the top of the ladder she found a hatch. As she opened the hatch, she found two hands waiting to help her up. It was Beelay. She had made it out of the forest.

"Well done, child. You did it. You're officially a Witch."

Beelay hoisted Imogen out of the hole, where she was met by all of her friends cheering for her. Lord Teymark hugged and congratulated her. "Well done, dear. I am glad you did not succumb to those spikes, and the fire ants were a nice touch, don't you think?"

Imogen stepped back, enraged at his tricks but happy to be alive. Looking back, she saw the forest behind her. She knew in that minute that she could carry out this fight, no matter the outcome.

On the last night of her rushed training, Beelay and Segion prepared a celebration for her. After a much-needed shower to wash off the smell of bog water, Imogen got dressed and headed toward the courtyard.

Opening the door to her room, her grandfather met her. He was dressed in the most handsome outfit, his hair was combed, and he smiled as he presented her with a rose and a card. The card was an invitation to her very own graduation party. "May I escort you to dinner, my lady?" said Richard.

"Just a minute," Imogen said as she slammed the door in his face. She hurried to the closet to search for something to wear. To her great fortune, she found a beautiful light gray satin dress with thousands of tiny amethysts on it and slippers to match. The dress was a perfect fit.

Reopening the door, she continued the halted conversation with, "Yes, sir, it would delight me."

The pair walked arm-in-arm slowly toward the courtyard. When they arrived at one of the many great halls, Imogen found the room filled with more food than she could eat in a lifetime. The room was decorated with beautiful mesh curtains and many vases filled with flowers.

At the front of the hall sat the main table, reserved for Imogen and her companions. Segion was the first to spot Imogen's arrival in the hall and nudged Beelay to attention. Beelay and the others grinned happily as they complimented Imogen on the dress and her crash-course in magick.

As soon as they seated Imogen, Lord Teymark rose to give a speech. "I am always glad when we have cause to celebrate. As you all know, we have lived for many years under a shadow of uncertainty and very much on borrowed time."

Lord Teymark turned to face Imogen as he continued, "I know that you are about to set out toward the face of danger, and we together have taught you as much as we could with the time we have had. I know that everyone here would gladly offer you their lives for this cause, and they may have to in the coming days." Lord Teymark raised his glass as he toasted Imogen. "To Imogen. May those who came before us protect her and guide her through the coming storm."

The night rolled on, and people drank and ate and danced as if they did not have a care in the world. Richard and Segion were off to the side with serious looks on their faces as they spoke, but Imogen did not think much of this, for everyone was under a lot of pressure right now. Imogen was trying to have fun but could not stop thinking about her mother. Beelay, sensing this, led Imogen away from the party and out to the courtyard. "If you want to leave now, we will. It might be best if we slip off without a fuss."

Imogen nodded as she looked out across the night sky.

"Collect your things, and I will find us a ride," Beelay said as the pair hurried off to prepare for the journey ahead.

THE QUEST FOR ERICKA'S SEPARATION

Back in Magicka, Matthew and Lady Astrid sat in the study, sipping wine as they played a hand of Khan'asta.

Matthew sighed as he spoke, "I feel a tad guilty to be playing and drinking when we should concern ourselves with thoughts of how to lure the girl here to Magicka."

Astrid smirked a little as she pulled another card from the stack. "Do not worry, dear uncle. I know that eventually she will come here. The prophecies dictate it," she said absentmindedly as she lay her cards on the table with a look of victory. "I believe I have won."

Matthew slammed the table with his fist. "Ugh, I've lost again. Another round?"

Astrid nodded as she slung her cards across the table. "Fear not. My father and his keeper have magickal detectors everywhere. This will alert us the second she crosses into

Magicka." Astrid looked down toward her chest. "Do not forget, dear uncle, that my necklace also glows when it senses magick. We will make it to our guests before those Raze Goblins get here to warn—"

Astrid stopped mid-sentence, looking down toward her necklace, which was now glowing. "It would appear we have company. Come, Matthew, let's get to the carriage."

Just as the pair exited the house, a Raze Goblin swooped down to meet them. It screeched and howled in front of Lord Matthew.

"My Goblin is rusty, but I think he is trying to tell us that our guests were heading toward the Old Council district of the capital."

Astrid threw the Raze Goblin a pheasantine before climbing into the carriage. "Come now, they should be easy to spot. Our masters allow nobody who is still living in this realm out after dark."

Meanwhile, as Lord Teymark's carriage trundled through the streets of Magicka, Imogen could do nothing but stare out the window in silence. In her daze, she spoke without even looking in Beelay's direction, "Do you think we can see Evynloth's old home along the way to the High Council tower? I want to see where he lived, how he lived. If I can see it, then maybe I can make sense of this whole thing."

Beelay looked in her direction for a few moments before he agreed. He was nervous, but he had not brought her this far just to hide things from her. This was the place where Evynloth's dreams were made a reality—if only for a short while.

"Very well. Let's go there now, but we must be quick. It is dangerous enough being in Astrid's domain."

Eventually, the carriage was halted by Beelay as they pulled up to a line of modest brick houses. Evynloth's house was just a few streets away from the High Council and barely a stone's throw from Ericka's childhood home.

"Well, this is the place, sweetheart," remarked Beelay as he opened the door.

The trio exited the carriage as quietly as they could.

"Which is it? They all look the same?" Imogen whispered as she followed Beelay.

"It's over here."

The door in front of them was adorned with an old and faded plaque with the words "Home of E and E Almackia" written on it. Above it was the number two. Imogen was the first to pass through the front entryway.

Beelay produced a large iron key from his pocket, handing it to Imogen. Wasting no time, Imogen turned the key in the lock. The door was heavy, but they found the strength to push it open with little noise before allowing Imogen to creep inside. Beelay and Segion followed behind her but did not explore the house.

Instead, they stood guard near the front and back doors while Imogen explored the house. It was a house locked in time. From floor to ceiling, there was layer upon layer of dust. Not to mention the cobwebs in every corner of the room. Everything was still laying as it had been arranged all those years ago. In the corner of the room sat Evynloth's desk with all its papers still arranged. Ericka's family had not been able to bear entering the home after the murder, leaving it as a shrine to their daughter.

Imogen heard a floorboard creak behind her.

"Hello, my child. Fancy seeing you here."

Imogen knew the voice instantly, turning to find Astrid standing in the room with Matthew at her side. Imogen screamed, causing Beelay and Segion to run to her aid.

"Astrid, how did you get in here?" yelled Beelay as he edged toward Imogen.

"Come now, you know you are no match for me," she said as she moved toward Imogen, who was now backing toward Segion, whose hands were at the ready to spell-cast.

"If you touch her, I'll—" Beelay was cut off by a sword aimed at his neck.

Matthew was skilled in the art of swordplay, having trained with a ranger in his early years. Segion made a move toward Imogen, standing behind her with his hands still at the ready.

"Now, Beelay, I only want to talk with Imogen. I would not intentionally hurt her. I am her granny, after all." Astrid's evil gaze switched to Imogen.

"You are deranged, Astrid," Beelay said. "Do you not remember what you did to this child a few nights ago?"

Astrid ignored Beelay, keeping her eyes on Imogen. "Now, I do not want to kill you, my child, so please give me the Stone. I know you have it. You must have it, because it was not in the Valley of Greengarth. Not to mention Oron and the other Vikings say you took it."

Imogen stood red-faced with clenched fists. She was

shaking a little, but she maintained her ground. "If you know I have it then why don't you just take it from me?"

Astrid gritted her teeth and screamed a little. "Give it now, child. No more questions."

Imogen stood steadfast. "I will never give that to you if it means you, your father, and his master get to rule these lands."

Astrid raised her wand in Imogen's direction, but Imogen continued, "You won't get the Stone, and he won't get Ericka back. I will stop you even if it's the last thing I do."

Astrid's voice rose as quickly as her demeanor changed, showing a side of herself rarely seen. "What do you know about Auras and Stones? You are just a child who does not know of the subtle art that is magick."

Imogen raised an eyebrow as she produced a wand from her pocket, aiming it at her grandmother without a second thought. "Afloriana, the Seers, and the Elves have trained me. I do not know everything, but I know enough to protect myself. If I have to fight you, then I will," said Imogen as she planted herself in place, trying to look as steadfast as possible.

Astrid took another step closer without the slightest regard for the threats made to her, grinning in amusement as she continued to speak coldly to her grandchild. "Would you really, my dear? And what if I told you that if you killed me, you would kill your mother?"

Beelay and Segion looked at each other in confusion.

"Yes, that is right. I have what the humans refer to as 'insurance'. If you kill me, then you will kill her. There are only two ways out of the prison. Release by Orvin, or release by the death of the person who put you there. So long as I am alive, she will be too."

Imogen kept her wand pointed in her grandmother's direction as she continued to fight her. "You are a liar. We rescued everyone from that prison, and mother was not there."

Astrid's grin widened. "You silly girl. Did you think I would not have extra security there? Tell me, did every cell door open?"

Imogen's face dropped as Astrid continued, "She is still in that prison, under a cloaking spell, waiting to be rescued."

Teary eyed and confused, Imogen looked to Beelay for help. "Beelay, help me. I do not know what to do."

Beelay turned slowly toward Imogen so as not to be cut by Matthew's blade. Matthew stepped out of Beelay's way, keeping a sword on him as he bent down to Imogen's height, taking her little hand as he tried his hardest not to show fear. "I know this woman, and I know she is not above lying to get what she wants. Just give her the Stone, because if you don't, she will kill all of us."

Imogen looked around the room at everyone before throwing the pouch at her grandmother. "I am disgusted to be your family," she said as she spat on the floor.

Astrid ignored everything else as she clicked at Matthew then pointed to the ground.

On command, Matthew bent down and picked up the pouch. "I will gladly hold this for you, my lady," he said as he placed the pouch in his pocket.

With the Stone in their possession, the pair hurried to a carriage that lay in wait.

As soon as her grandmother was out of sight, Imogen threw herself around Beelay as she wept. Looking down toward her shoes, she yelped as she ran into the other room, embarrassed. With the tension, nobody had noticed that Imogen had wet her pants in fear of being in the same room as her grandmother. Beelay ran after her, assuring her not to worry about the accident.

Imogen cried, throwing herself into Beelay's arms. "What are we going to do now? How will we save everyone from this evil?"

As Beelay hugged Imogen, he thought of the prison in the mountains. "Well, I don't know about everyone else, but I think it would be a good idea if we moved on to the High Council. If we can get the knife and spell, we might be able to stop Evynloth from helping his old master. The Elves may have a solution to the problem of your mother. Segion sent a message to the Elves. I am sure they can help get Simone to safety." He said all of this as he dried her tears. "Come now, we need to focus on Ericka now," he said as they hopped into the carriage bound for the High Council.

The High Council sat dead in the capital's center. Its halls and offices had been closed up since Lord Avestyn's coup d'état on Magicka and were now guarded by some of Lord Avestyn's prized possessions: his Raze Goblins, a mutation of his very own. The last time anyone had tried to take back the High Council was fifteen years ago. It had been a battle quickly lost. There had been, according to Beelay, a short-lived attempt to overthrow Lord Avestyn's rule. As they approached the High Council building, they stopped the carriage at the edge of the woods that lay near to the building.

Upon seeing the Goblins who were standing guard, Beelay scoffed, "Goblins? This must be a trick. Why would Lord Avestyn use half-wits like that to guard such an important target?"

Segion shook his head as he looked on, counting the Goblins that lay in wait. "Those, my dear cousin, are no ordinary Goblins," remarked Segion as he rummaged around in his bag. "Cousin, you need to trust me. I will get you two inside there, but you have to trust me."

Beelay looked at him with suspicion. Segion was known for his antics and was somewhat of a legend in Sageland. "Why don't I like the sound of this?"

Segion ignored him as he continued to fish in his bag. "These are Raze Goblins. They are a berserk spliced curiosity of Lord Avestyn and take no prisoners. Meat is their sole desire and they will stop at nothing to get it."

Beelay was not amused by his cousin's candor in front of Imogen.

"How do you know they are Raze Goblins, Lord Segion?" Imogen asked.

"You see those big black holes on their backs? That is where their spikes shoot from when they sense danger or when they are hunting for meat. Their range is not that far, so they will not have detected us yet."

Beelay's face was getting redder with the further information that Segion was offering. "There is no way we are going in through the front door," snapped Beelay as he put himself in front of Imogen.

"Well, I am most certainly not roaming around in the sewers again," Segion remarked with an absolute tone before pulling a bundle of pheasantines from his bag.

"I have a plan. I will throw these pheasantines out to lure the Goblins away from the front entrance. I will use myself as bait to get them away from their guard posts."

Imogen objected strongly but tried not to raise her voice. "You can't do this. They will kill you, and I do not want any more deaths on my hands."

Segion smiled and kissed Imogen on the head. "Child, it will take a lot more than a pack of Goblins to off me. Now you and Beelay get behind that rock and cover yourselves with this," he said as he passed her a bottle of strange green liquid.

"What is this?" she said, screwing her nose up at the bottle.

"It will disguise your scent so that they won't detect you or your fear. With this, you can hide in plain sight."

Beelay pulled Imogen back into the woods to hide behind a large rock. From experience, Beelay did not trust his cousin's inventions, so he opted for a little cover. "Hold your nose and close your mouth," he said as he doused them both in the liquid, which Segion later told them was a mixture of troll saliva and other ingredients far more disgusting.

Once he knew his companions were safe, Segion stepped

out from the wooded area to face the enemy. "Hello, old chaps," he taunted as he strolled toward the Raze Goblins, slinging the bundle of pheasantines as he walked. "Nice night for it," he said as he lunged a pheasantine covered with extra blood toward the Goblins.

The Raze Goblins' demeanors shifted instantaneously from those of guards to hunters. Collectively, the Raze Goblins howled, having sensed the meat that had volunteered itself to them. The Goblins' howling was earsplitting and echoed through the center of the capital. Imogen, being unable to bear their current plight, covered her ears and held her eyes closed as tightly as she could. Meanwhile, the Goblins ran toward Segion and the pheasantines. Segion dashed away into the woods with lightning speed, dropping pheasantines every few yards as he disappeared deep into the woods.

After the howls subsided, Beelay and Imogen took their chance to gain access to the High Council. As they stepped through the main doors, being back in the foyer struck Beelay with many emotions, but he buried them instantly for the sake of their mission.

"Okay, we're in," Imogen said. "Now what?"

Beelay scanned the foyer as he tried to get his bearings after so long away from the High Council halls. "This way," he said as he pointed toward a passageway behind the stairs. "This will lead us to a hidden staircase. If the knife and spell are anywhere, they will be in the cellar. We cannot know if there is more security than the Raze Goblins, so we need to be as safe as we can."

Imogen and Beelay made for the staircase. When they reached the bottom of the staircase, they found a single door with no locks, bolts, or even a handle.

"What game is Evynloth playing, Beelay?"

Beelay looked utterly confused. "I don't know, child. Let's see if we can find a lever or a secret hiding place for a key."

Just as Beelay ran his hands across the wood, the floor shook.

"Who goes there?" bellowed a deep and loud voice.

"Imogen Welkin and Beelay Sageland of Druidonia," Beelay said.

The voice continued to speak, "Only a person of a pure Aura with truth in their heart may enter these chambers. If you wish to enter, then place your hands on the door. It will open for you if your Aura is pure."

Beelay and Imogen placed their hands on the door.

After a few seconds, the door made a shifting sound.

"Enter, friends," said the voice from behind the door.

With that the door pushed inward, revealing nothing but darkness, Beelay lit a torch and entered after Imogen.

"It is so dark. Why does everything in this place have to be so dark?" Imogen said in frustration.

"Do not worry, child. As soon as we get what we came for, we can help Ericka be free and stop Evynloth in his tracks."

As they descended the single narrow passageway, they finally came to a wooden door with a tiny barred window like one would find in a prison.

"Well now, I hope they did not lock this door, too," Beelay said with a hint of a chuckle. He knew Imogen was not in the best of spirits, so he tried to keep the mood as light as he could.

"Well there is only one way to tell," Imogen said as she pushed on the door.

The door opened without hindrance. This time, there was light behind the door. Beelay and Imogen stepped into a very large room. This was the grand cellar of the High Council. For miles, all she could see were wondrous trinkets, fine carpets and gold coins, among other things.

"Beelay, how will we ever find what we are looking for? We might be down here for days," Imogen said as they walked deeper into the room.

"Stop right where you are and turn around slowly," commanded a voice from behind them.

The pair stopped dead in their tracks, raised their hands, and turned around slowly, as commanded. Who could be down here with them? All of Lord Avestyn's recruits were far from human. Beelay looked forward and began to smile with relief.

"Zaygarth, is that you?" Beelay said in elation.

"Beelay. How are you here? I thought you died," said Zaygarth as he hugged Beelay.

"No, I ran away after that night. I am sorry, I was a coward, but I needed to help get someone away from Evynloth."

Zaygarth did not seem to mind as he looked his old friend over. "And who might this be?" he said, looking at Imogen.

"This is Imogen Welkin," Beelay said, "and she is here to save us all."

Zaygarth dropped to his knees in front of Imogen. "The rumors are true. You have come. Please, you must come and meet the others."

Beelay looked confused. "What others?"

Zaygarth grinned as he spoke, "The resistance."

"What resistance?" Beelay said in confusion.

"I will reveal all. Just follow me," Zaygarth said as he led them up a staircase hidden by the door they had just come through. As they climbed the stairs, the sounds of voices came into earshot.

"Where are we, Zaygarth?"

Zaygarth grinned at Beelay as he continued to climb the stairs.

"We are in Old Djinn. This is where our ancestors lived after the great extinction. Many years ago it was not safe for us to live on the surface. Our ancestors were overrun with wild beasts who hunted our kind without mercy, almost to the point of extinction. Each day, brave men and women would use themselves as bait and fight them to create a distraction while the others dug down below their huts in secret. Legend told them that below the surface lay habitable catacombs where they could live in peace and security. Eventually, they built up a bursting metropolis, where they lived in safety.

"About five years after they finished the underground town's construction, the Mountain of Memory erupted, spitting out molten lava. It obliterated everything on the surface of our lands. The lava forced us to live underground until the land settled and cooled.

"It was difficult to live underground after the eruption, and many people died because of food shortages and disease. Eventually, we returned to the surface, and many forgot all of this."

As they walked through Old Magicka, Imogen looked around in awe and fascination at the crumbling brick buildings. In front of the houses lay the remnants of the town's past. Toys and chairs sat on stoops and cats roamed the streets in search of prey. Eventually, they reached the center of the old city.

"Come inside. Everyone will be so excited to meet you," Zaygarth chuckled happily as he ascended the steps.

Before them stood a tall building with a commanding presence. It was devoid of windows and was flanked by two ten-foot doors that looked as if they weighed 10,000 pounds. "This is the old High Council building," Zaygarth said as he banged on the door.

After a few moments, a pair of eyes peeked through a slot.

"Zaygarth has returned," said a voice from behind the door.

The door opened at once, revealing a community of people rushing around in the flurry of their day. Despite having various habitable buildings around them, the townsfolk lived together in the old High Council hall.

A little girl spotted Imogen and squealed as she pointed. "Ooh, pretty hair."

Another woman in the crowd gasped, "People."

As word spread through the crowd, everyone's eyes moved toward the main hall door. As the crowd descended upon the weary travelers, Imogen panicked. "I thought you said we were among friends, Zaygarth?"

Zaygarth laughed as he patted Imogen's hand. "Worry not, child. They are just curious to see a new face."

The crowd before them split as an old man pushed through with the use of his staff, a young boy with him.

"Clear the way, people. Clear the way for our leader," shouted the young boy.

The old man coming toward them was named Kavron. He was once a member of the High Council and was thought to have been lost to Lord Avestyn's guards years before.

"Zaygarth, I see you have returned from your post early. Your watch is not meant to be over for another two days," he said in a scolding manner, looking over his glasses at him.

"I have wonderful news, Lord Kavron. This girl is the one from the prophecies left to us by the Seers. Her name is Imogen Welkin, and she has come to free us from our life below."

Zaygarth turned to face Imogen as he bowed down on the ground in front of her. As the crowd before her saw this happen, they also bowed. Imogen looked around, overwhelmed by the sight of all these people she did not know bowing to her. All of their fates, placed in the hands of a thirteen-year-old girl.

Kavron approached Imogen. "My dear, welcome to our

city. Please, you must be tired and hungry," he said as he clapped his hands.

From the crowd ran two young girls about Imogen's age. "Please come with us, my lady. We will take you to rest while the women make a feast in your honor."

Kavron watched as the girls led Imogen away. When they were out of sight, he turned his gaze to Beelay. "I guess you thought I was dead, didn't you, Lord Beelay?"

Beelay extended his hand to Kavron, and the two men shook hands in silence. "I thought you were dead. I received word that Evynloth killed every High Council member on the night of Astrid's wedding."

Kavron nodded in agreement. "Come, let's go to my rooms. There is much to discuss."

Kavron's rooms were as grand and luxurious as they would have been when he was on the High Council. Kavron was Lord Genoa's second-in-command and had been a trusted adviser for years. Around him was all that was left of his life. Rugs sat rolled up against the walls. His books were piled four feet high and covered with dust.

Lowering himself down into his favorite chair by the fire. Kavron's gaze moved to Beelay. "Come now, man. You look as dumbstruck as the day I told you we elected you to the High Council. Now sit down, because you're making the place look untidy."

Beelay managed a smirk as he looked around the room, the irony of the statement not lost on him. Beelay slumped down in the first chair he could find.

"I imagine that you have many questions for me, and I

would be happy to oblige you," Lord Kavron said. "However, we must discuss more pressing issues," he said as he swallowed down a large gulp of whiskey. "What does she know?"

"What do you mean, Kavron?" Beelay said as he reached for an empty glass and motioned it toward Kavron.

"Please, have you forgotten my abilities? I know you are here for the knife and spell to free Evynloth's bride." He obliged Beelay, and the drink was gulped down just as quickly as Kavron had poured it.

"She knows of the prophecy, and the Stone—which he has probably already placed in his master's shriveled old hands—and she knows how to free Ericka, but that is all."

Kavron stroked his chin as he thought. "The question is, should we tell her everything, or do we dare let her go on as she is right now?"

Beelay pondered the question but stopped at the sound of a familiar voice.

"Tell me what?"

The two men turned to find Imogen standing in the doorway.

"My dear, you should be resting now. Come now, let me have the girls take you to rest," said Kavron at the sight of the ragged and weary traveler before him.

Imogen raised her hand in opposition. "No, thank you." She could not rest, not with her mind so preoccupied. Imogen wandered around Kavron's room a little as she viewed the remnants of what his life had been like before Evynloth and Lord Avestyn's reign of terror. "I know that I am young, sir, but I do not wish to be lied to, and I am sick of nobody giving me the whole story or the truth. Please tell me what I need to know," she said as she locked eyes with Kavron.

"Very well, my dear, but I think you should at least sit down," he remarked as he motioned to a chair that sat beside his own. "I know that you have been through a lot to get here to us, but there are more trials to come, and they will not be without sacrifice."

Kavron rose as he continued to speak, "As you may know already, you are descended from a long line of magickal humanoids, some of which were the kindest people and greatest minds in all Tera'Loth and were responsible for shaping the world we used to know." Kavron reached for a book off a very unstable-looking pile. "There were some, of course, who were not so kind to Tera'Loth in the pursuit of their endeavors," he said as he thumbed through the pages of the book retrieved from the pile. "The Stone you retrieved from the Viking realm is a Stone Evynloth needs to open up the Necromancer realm. I am sure by now it is in his possession."

Imogen looked down in shame. She had sacrificed Tera'Loth for the sake of her mother.

"Come now, child. Hold your head high. You sacrificed for the one you love, and there is no shame in that. Besides, Evynloth does not have everything he needs to enact the spell, and we will make sure he never does."

Imogen and Beelay both leaned in closer, their curiosity piqued.

"He needs the blood of a Seer to open the gates of Necromancium. It cannot be just any Seer. It needs to be the blood of a Seer directly descended from any of the five mages who locked down Necromancium during the Old Kami-Djinn War that took place many hundreds of years ago."

Imogen gasped. "It's Richard, isn't it? My grandfather is the Seer he needs?"

Kavron nodded in silence. "There is a way to stop Lord Evynloth from achieving his master's goal."

Beelay and Imogen looked at each other in hope as Kavron continued to talk, "As with everything in the universe, there are positives and negatives, counter balances or opposites. The Stone you retrieved has a sister Stone named the Stone of Auras Demise. It is a Stone that has the ability to lock down Necromancium forever. That Stone, combined with another element, will shut down Evynloth's plans entirely."

Kavron placed the book on the table next to Imogen. It was a map book of the Elvish realm. "The Stone you seek lies in wait on an altar in the Mountains of Myth. It is our only hope of stopping Lord Avestyn in his attempt to take over completely. That is, if you can get to it, of course. The Moun tain lies on the border between the Dwarf and Elvish realms. They call it the Mountains of Myth because it is hidden due to constant cloud cover."

Kavron walked to his apothecary table to retrieve a small black bag. "This is a powder to help guide you up the moun-tain path. Please take this map book. It will guide you to the bottom of the mountain. After that you are at the mercy of fate. The mountain is dangerous and can be deadly, but with the right guide, you should make it to the top with all of your limbs. When you get to the pathway, sprinkle a little of the powder on the ground and follow it. The powder I have given you will produce a spirit cloud, which will lead you to the doorway of the cave that houses the Stone. I cannot tell you what may lie in wait for you when you get inside, but I wish you all the luck in Tera'Loth."

Imogen exchanged glances with Beelay. There was no question of what needed to be done. "Thank you for the book, sir. We will leave at once to retrieve the Stone."

Kavron nodded in agreement. "I will keep what you came in search of safe until you have the Stone. The focus must be on stopping Evynloth and Avestyn."

Beelay looked at Imogen. She looked so tired, but more determined than ever. "Imogen," he said, "I know you are eager to leave, but if Segion were here, you know he would scold us for not eating and resting first."

Imogen nodded in agreement. She wanted to listen to Beelay, but she was overcome with worry.

"Do not worry, child. Evynloth does not have all the pieces of his puzzle. You still have time to rest." Kavron rose from his chair. "Come now, friends. I am sure that there is a feast waiting for us," he said just as a little girl appeared at the door. "Ah. It would seem my senses have not left me."

The little girl nodded as she moved out of the doorway.

"Thank you, Gerta," Kavron said as he patted her cheek. "Let's make our way to the main dining floor."

Imogen placed the book under her arm as she followed Kavron. She halted in the doorway. Lord Kavron turned around in the hallway to see why she had stopped. "What is it, child?"

Imogen shifted the book under her arm as she edged toward Lord Kavron. "Sir, you said the Stone of Auras Demise needs to join with another element to ensure Necromancium remains permanently closed. What is the other element?"

Lord Kavron tried to look reassuring as he told her to worry about that later.

While Beelay and Imogen freshened up, the people of the underground lined the main dining hall with tables to seat 1,000, although the population was about 600. On the extra tables sat platters of salted meat, fruit, cheeses, breads, bowls piled high with mashed potatoes, and gravy boats to accompany them.

Flora, the head cook, stepped forward to greet the honored guests. "I thank you humbly for gracing us with your presence and further apologize for the state of our feast. Living underground, it is hard to come up with creative or decadent meals."

Imogen tried to make her face look as kind as she could. "My lady, this is the best-looking meal I have seen in a very long time, and I am in awe of how quickly you prepared it for us. I am sure we will enjoy it until the last bite."

Flora's eyes widened as she smiled. "Well, thank you, my lady. Please let me take you to your seat." Flora led them to the front of the hall to sit as guests of honor next to Kavron.

After they had seated everyone, the meal began. Imogen tried to be polite by eating some of everything that was made. However, she looked like a piglet about five minutes into the meal. Undoubtedly, she had underestimated her hunger. Four plates later, she was heavy-eyed and ready for sleep.

"All right, Miss Imogen, I think it is time for bed," said Beelay as he carried her sleepy self to bed.

After a good night's rest, it was time for the pair to set out on their next adventure.

Before the pair left, Lord Kavron approached to bid them farewell. "I know you probably have everything you need already, but I thought you may need a little backup from afar," he grinned as he handed the satchel to Beelay.

Beelay looked inside the satchel to find a large black egg with red spots on it. "Is this what I think it is?"

Kavron grinned as he nodded.

"Now how did you get a Harpy egg?"

Kavron winked. "Ways and means, old chap. Just be sure he sees and smells you and Imogen first, that way he won't turn on you."

Beelay closed the satchel up and put it gently over his shoulder.

Kavron turned his attention to Imogen. "Alright, young champion. We are all behind you and we believe in you. Here, take this book. It will tell you everything you need to know about raising your new companion," he said as he handed her a book titled, *Harpy Cultivating and Birthing, Second Edition.*

"Thank you, sir. Thank you all," she shouted across the hall.

"Good luck," the people of the underground called back.

"Now you best be on your way," Kavron said. "My young apprentice Goren will see you safely to the edge of the Forest of Fortune. After that, you are on your own."

As the large doors opened before them, Imogen grabbed Beelay's arm. "I don't know if we will survive this, but please know how grateful I am to have gone on this journey with you."

Beelay could do nothing more than smile at her as he pushed back his tears.

Lord Kavron stayed by the door and watched as they walked away from the hall, disappearing into the darkness.

After about twenty minutes, the trio arrived at a ladder on the side of the corridor wall. "This ladder will lead us into the sewer system above," Beelay grinned. "Now it's your turn to wade through this filth in aid of me."

Imogen gave him a confused look. Beelay had not told her about his escapades in the sewers in order to rescue her from Astrid.

Quickly, they ascended the ladder behind their guide. When they emerged from the city below, they found themselves hit in the face with the smell of long festering filth. Once they were all out of the hole, they stood for a moment, trying not to heave while Beelay got his bearings. They were in the sewers below the High Council.

"Alright, we best not waste any more time standing around," commanded Beelay as he adjusted his satchel. "Young guide, which way to the exit?"

The young man produced a map from his pocket,

scouring the paper with his finger. "We need to head left, and it's a straight shot to the exit."

Beelay and Imogen exchanged glances. Nothing up to this point had run smoothly, but they still hoped for the best outcome. The trio started off into the darkness with a single light to guide them.

During their walk through the sewers, Imogen could do nothing but think of her family, both those dead and alive. Astrid had taunted her with the news of her mother, but she tried to put the thoughts out of her mind as they approached the exit.

"Here we are. This exit will bring us to the edge of the woods," Goren said as he took a step back away from the ladder. "You must continue on alone from this point. I wish you well," he said.

Without another word, he disappeared off into the darkness of the sewer system.

"What a brave young boy. I wanted to thank him, but I guess he is not much for pleasantries," said Beelay with a sigh. The satchel with its precious cargo was becoming heavy as it continued to grow inside the comfort of the surrounding velvet blankets. "Alright then, let's get out of this stinkhole before I lose my breakfast. After you, Imogen."

Imogen wasted no time as she climbed the ladder. The smell was so repugnant that she thought it would be in her nostrils for a week. Once the pair was safely above ground, Beelay ran over to a patch of pixie flowers. These were groups of pixies disguised as flowers, whose sole purpose was to act as messengers. They inhabited every realm and could send messages to anyone. Once you whispered the message, the flower would morph into a pixie and fly the message to its recipient.

Once he finished whispering his message into the flower, the pixies sent it to Afloriana. He had alerted her to expect them so that the Elvish Watch-Keepers would allow them to travel through the barrier between the two realms.

A MEETING WITH THE DWARF KING

After Imogen and Beelay were safely back in the Elvish realm, they went to the meeting hall at once. As they rode through the capital, they found it eerily quiet. There was nobody in sight, and the markets were closed.

"I don't like this at all," Beelay said. "Where is everyone? Something must have happened when we were gone."

Imogen was a little unnerved but tried not to let the lack of hustle and bustle bother her. "Come on, Beelay, we know nothing yet. Let's just get to the palace meeting hall and go from there."

Beelay smiled at her from his horse. She now possessed the air of a wise woman, yet she was only a child. *I guess change can be an instant thing after all,* he thought to himself.

As they approached the palace gates, they heard voices. Beelay breathed a sigh of relief and kicked himself for worrying. Afloriana would not have let them walk into danger. In fact, the whole capital was gathered to meet the weary travelers with a grand feast, over which they would discuss the issue of Evynloth and Lord Avestyn as a community.

"They have arrived. They have returned," yelled a little Elvish girl at the top of her lungs.

"Yay." The crowd burst into cheers and applause. The people made a path for them as they continued to ride up the street. As they approached the palace steps, they were met by Lord Teymark, The Imp King, Afloriana, and Richard Welkin.

"Welcome back, adventurers. Were you successful in your mission?" Lord Teymark said as he looked at the tired adventurers.

"We discovered the location of the dagger, but Astrid got the Stone from us. We could not stand up to her power."

Lord Teymark's face fell as he looked at Afloriana.

"I am sorry for letting this happen, my lord," she said, "but there may still be a way to stop Evynloth and Lord Avestyn in their plans. I would discuss it with you, but perhaps it is best done in private."

Teymark nodded as he motioned for the pair to come inside.

"Please, my loyal subjects. Our travelers are weary and wish to rest before they feast. Please eat, drink, be merry, and do try to save some food for them," he said with an eyebrow raised, looking toward the Dwarf table.

Imogen and Beelay changed clothes before meeting Lord Teymark in his study. They could not seem to shake the smell of the sewer no matter how much scent they used. On her way to the study, something stopped Imogen dead in her tracks.

She heard a familiar voice—it was Segion. Running toward his familiar chuckle. Imogen burst through the door to Lord Teymark's study. There, before the fire, sat Segion, with Beelay and Lord Teymark in the chairs beside him. She ran up and hugged Segion as hard as she could.

"It's all right, my dear. I am safe. It would take more than a few Razer Goblins to finish me," Segion said with a smile.

Beelay said, "Segion was just telling us how easy it was to get away from that pack of Razor Goblins."

Segion puffed up his chest as he congratulated himself on his triumphant journey back to the Elvish realm. "You see, what the Razor Goblins did not know is that I knew the old woods better than they did. I ran them straight into a trap I found—next to a sewer entrance of all places—while I was scouting the area a few weeks ago. I do not know how long ago someone set the trap, but if those who did so still live, they will feast well tonight."

Beelay chuckled, winking at Imogen as he remarked, "They are nothing but a bunch of lemmings."

Silence fell over the room. Imogen was still sitting next to Segion, who was holding her little hand in his. She felt a strong connection to Segion and Beelay, as if they had been her family from the first day of her life.

"I know you have been through a great ordeal, young Imogen, but I need to know what happened while you were in search of the dagger," remarked Teymark.

Imogen and Beelay looked at each other, trying to decide who would regale the group.

Beelay cleared his throat.

Imogen nodded at him in agreement.

"Well, my lord, it happened like this. Imogen wanted to see where Evynloth lived. We did not know we were being followed. Somehow Astrid figured out where we were. She blackmailed Imogen into giving her the Stone. She told her that her mother is in that prison but hidden. Imogen did not want to take a chance that Astrid was lying, so she gave the Stone up.

"We made our way into the High Council hall courtesy of my dear cousin. When we set out to explore the cellar beneath the hall, we met the survivors of Evynloth's terror. Sir, there is a resistance, and they have given us a way to stop Evynloth once and for all." Beelay paused, opening the book Kavron had given him.

Teymark saw Kavron's name in the book. "You don't mean Kavron is alive?" he said as shock overtook his face.

"Yes, he is, and he told me the best news we have heard in many years. The Stone of Auras Reclaim has a sister Stone. They know it as the Stone of Auras Demise. With it, we can make sure the gates of Necromancium stay sealed shut forever."

Teymark snatched the book from Beelay's hands, flipping through it frantically. "Where is it? How do we get it and destroy it?"

Beelay looked at Teymark with a hint of anger. "I am at a

loss to understand why you, the leader of these lands, do not know about the Stone's existence or its location."

Teymark's temper rose slightly as he continued to speak, "My own father was not a cruel man, but he exhibited no hopes for me as a leader. He refused to train me or give me any of the secret knowledge. When he died, it was found that he did not name me an official heir, thus all of his written knowledge was taken with him to his grave. I have done the best I can to research our history and protect my people, but I am just an Elf at the end of the day. Do not judge me harshly."

Beelay's face dropped. He was overcome with shame and exhausted from the journey thus far. "I am sorry, my lord. I apologize for my behavior."

Teymark nodded as Beelay continued, "Someone hid the Stone inside a cave in the Mountains of Myth."

Teymark's eyebrows rose at the prospect of the Stone's location. "Are you absolutely sure of the Stone's location?" he said, almost shouting. Imogen could see the fear in his eyes.

"Yes, my lord."

Teymark looked at Imogen as he spoke, "Then may the gods help you on your journey, because it may kill you. The Mountains of Myth are the most dangerous mountainous region in all of Tera'Loth. The pixies and Imps changed the mountains to help the Dwarfs hide their gold and other treasures from thieves. The young Elves use it as their initiation challenge to be accepted into adulthood among the Elves. There are traps and tricks at every turn, and many do not make it to the top of the mountains. I cannot help you in getting past any of these traps, because the Dwarves still have treasures hidden within the mountains."

Teymark turned to the Imp King. "Can you be of any help to the child who risks her life to save us?"

The king shook his head. "Not without the Dwarf King's approval, and I do not see that as likely to happen."

Teymark walked to his desk. From the drawer, he brought out a piece of paper and a quill. "I shall write to the Dwarf King and seek his permission. We cannot know what he will say, but he is our only hope of Imogen not dying when she attempts this task."

As soon as he sealed the envelope, he handed it to Afloriana. "My dear, please take this letter to King Oafe. You are a voice of reason, and I know he respects your opinions."

Afloriana nodded as she accepted the letter. "Very well, I will leave at once," she said as she hurried from the palace.

The Dwarf realm was named Hammedge. It was a neighboring realm of the Elvish realm. The Mountains of Myth separated the two realms. Afloriana was friends to all, so her visit was not unwelcome. The King of the Dwarves, King Oafe, met her carriage at the border. King Oafe was three and-a-half feet tall and looked just as one would imagine if they thought of a Dwarf. Dressed for war, with a weathered face and scruffy hair.

"How did you know I was coming to meet with you?" said Afloriana as Oafe helped her from the carriage.

"Your little pixie friends flew ahead. Obviously, they thought I would not want to be surprised, given the current state of Tera'Loth."

Afloriana nodded.

"Well, I am told you have a letter for me from Teymark?"

Afloriana pulled the sealed envelope from her robe's pocket. "Here you are."

Oafe tore the letter open and began to read. After he finished, he looked at Afloriana with a heavy heart. "Should I leave you now, or would you like me to return with your answer?"

King Oafe paced in front of the carriage. "For thousands of years, we Dwarves have protected what is ours over anything else. I know we are a warring kind, but I fear once I lift the magick from the mountains it will leave us with no bargaining power to fend off Evynloth. We have more than just treasure in those mountains."

King Oafe stopped pacing and turned to face Afloriana as he gave her his answer. "I am sorry, my dear, but I cannot allow the Imp King to remove the magick. Our safety is my priority, and besides, many an Elf child has made the journey safely. Can an Elf child not simply accompany the girl?"

Afloriana could do nothing but nod in agreement as she climbed back into her carriage. King Oafe waved at her until the carriage was out of sight. From behind him he heard a voice say, "You have done the right thing, King Oafe. Just make sure you do everything that I ask, and I will leave you in peace when my master and I take over."

King Oafe turned around to meet with the face of the voice. "Yes, my Lord Evynloth. I will keep my promise if you do."

Evynloth nodded as he disappeared before the king's eyes.

Afloriana returned to the Elvish capital with a heavy heart. She was always the voice of reason, but she had been afforded no chance to argue with King Oafe. What would the others think of her failure—and what of Imogen? Could a child so young manage the journey?

As the carriage approached the steps, she found Lord Teymark and Beelay waiting to greet her. As they locked eyes, they knew the answer.

"How could he say no," yelled Teymark. "He knows as well as we do what is at stake. How can he leave us like this?"

Imogen stepped forward. "If he doesn't want to help us, then I will do it on my own. I want no one else hurt, and this is my journey."

Beelay shot up in anger. "You are not going by yourself, not after everything you have been through."

Imogen shook her head at Beelay. "This is my decision, and like Lord Teymark said, others have achieved it, so I can complete the journey as well."

Feeling a tension in the air, Segion interceded, "I think everyone is tired, and it might be best if we eat, sleep, and decide in the morning with clearer heads."

Lord Teymark nodded in agreement. "Yes, let's all freshen up for dinner. Imogen, would you like to accompany me to your grandfather's room? I think it would be nice if you checked in on him. We gave him some medicine, and he almost feels himself again."

Imogen nodded as she took Lord Teymark's arm.

Richard sat alone in his room, writing in a journal as he looked up at the setting sun.

"It is a nice night, isn't it Grandfather?" Imogen said from the doorway. She had tried knocking, but he had not heard her.

"Yes, it is," he said, still looking up at the sunset.

Imogen edged slowly into the room. She turned to Lord Teymark. They both nodded at each other as Teymark left the room.

"I have many things to tell you, but I do not know if you are ready to hear most of them," Imogen said as she sat down on the edge of the bed.

"Nothing to worry about, my darling. I have seen all that can be and all that ever was. If you're going to run, you better do it tonight."

Imogen looked shocked. "How did you know...?"

Richard looked at her over his glasses. "Please, dear girl. Who do you think you are talking to?"

Imogen laughed a little as she breathed a sigh of relief.

"Inside the closet is a bag already packed for you. I would suggest you make your way to the stables before it's too late. If you are successful, you will make it to the top of the mountains by dawn."

Imogen took the bag from the closet. "This is Beelay's. Kavron gave it to him."

Richard grinned as he looked up again at the moon. "That man should learn to keep better track of his things. I think everything you need is in there. Powder? Check. A map to the mountains? Check. Oh, and a Harpy egg that looks ready to crack."

Imogen closed the bag and put it gently on her back. She hugged Richard. Even though he flinched at the slightest touch, she wanted to show him her love and appreciation. She left his room and made off like a thief in the night. As Imogen approached the stables, a cloaked figure met her, standing in the road's middle.

"Who goes there?" she said as she yelled at the cloaked figure.

The unknown figure approached her. When the figure got close enough to be seen properly, the figure lowered their hood to reveal an Elvish girl who looked to be around Imogen's age.

"Hello, my lady. Please forgive my intrusion in your escape, but Richard sent me to help guide you up the mountains. I wasn't sure you would come and was about to return to my home."

Imogen looked at the girl with curiosity. "Who are you? I mean, what is your name?"

The Elvish girl bent down on one knee as she bowed. "My name is Silveen Teymark, and I am most humbly at your service."

Imogen looked at her with suspicion. "Teymark. You don't mean you are...?"

Silveen chuckled. "Yes, Lord Teymark is my father, but I never let that stop me in my adventures."

Imogen was dumbstruck, but she shrugged it off.

"Come now," Silveen said. "I have a horse waiting for us. We need to hurry before the night-watch makes their rounds to the stables," she said as she ran toward the bushes to retrieve the horse. "This is Moonlight. I know it's an odd name for a horse, but she has been with me since I was a child, and back then I did not want to name her anything else."

Imogen smiled as she extended her hand.

Silveen lifted her onto the horse. As they rode off into the night, Imogen looked back toward the palace. "I hope Beelay will forgive me for this someday."

MURDER AND KIDNAPPING

When Astrid and Matthew returned to Avestyn's fortress, it was swarming with Auras, Harpies, Raze Goblins, Magicka people who were loyal to Evynloth, and a few other creatures that Astrid could not identify. There was a flurry of creatures running about, readying for battle and strengthening what was left of the fortress.

"Here is the Stone, my lady," Matthew said as he handed off the pouch to Astrid.

"Thank you, Matthew. Come, let's not waste any more time."

The pair made haste to meet with their masters.

In the study, Evynloth was hunched over a spell book, scouring it for the spell needed to open Necromancium.

"Father, my lord, I found the girl, and I believe I have

gained the Stone in question," Astrid said as she handed the pouch to an eager Evynloth.

"Give it here, boy," yapped Avestyn from his chair by the fire.

Evynloth rushed to his master's side. "We finally have it, my lord. Finally, our desires will be realized."

Avestyn opened the pouch gingerly. As he placed his hand in the pouch, his expression changed quickly to anger. "What game is she playing with us, boy? There is no Stone in this bag."

Astrid looked at her uncle in panic as Evynloth's hate turned towards his daughter. "What game do you think you are playing here? I want Ericka back, and you are standing in my way. I have no time for tricks, so hand the Stone over," he yelled as he choked Astrid.

"Father, it is not a trick, I promise. I put it in my pocket before I got out of the carriage. Matthew handed it to me," Astrid said as she choked. She tried to look in Matthew's direction.

"My lord," Matthew said, "we did not look into the bag before we left the girl. I suggested that we do this, but Lady Astrid dismissed the notion."

Evynloth's eyes went black with rage. "I knew you would not help me. You are as useless as dead herbs, as useless as the useless pig you thought was your father. I was deceived once in your death, but I won't be again," he said as he snapped Astrid's neck.

Releasing his grip, her lifeless body fell to the ground like discarded trash.

As Evynloth stood, grinning over his child's lifeless body, he spotted her Amethyst necklace. Evynloth bent down and yanked the necklace from Astrid's body. "Hello, I thought I lost you," said Evynloth as he stopped dead, clutching the Amethyst as he received a vision.

Evynloth saw Orvin, the prison-keeper in the Black Mountains. He was throwing Simone's body to the feral Harpy Necromancers.

"*Nooo!*"

Evynloth, overcome with blind rage, forgot the key rule of the Prison of Emotion.

Lord Avestyn rose from his chair, leaning on his cane as he walked up behind Evynloth. "Do not worry about the girl in the mountains, Lord Evynloth. We have additional resources," he said as he stepped over Astrid, knocking loose the dirt on his boot as he passed over her.

Evynloth's attention turned to a stunned Matthew, who was now trying to suppress his emotion over Astrid's death. "I only spared you out of need for your services. Think nothing more of it."

Matthew nodded as he looked at Astrid's lifeless body.

"Come, master, let us dine as we discuss our new plans," Evynloth remarked, leading his ailing master from the room.

After Evynloth, Matthew, and his master finished their meal of smoked fish, rice, and lemon root, Evynloth brought the conversation back to the situation they now found themselves in.

"My lord, you said that we have a back-up plan," Evynloth said. "Forgive my impertinence, but who or what would that be? You know we need the blood of the Seer's child to aid us in opening the gates to Necromancium. If the child is dead, then who is left?"

Avestyn grinned as he sipped his wine. "The Seer is still alive."

Evynloth kicked himself for not thinking of this. If he had not killed Astrid, then he had not killed Richard. "My lord, do you know the whereabouts of the Seer?"

Avestyn arose, extending his hand to Evynloth. "I do not know, but the Stone will tell us."

Once the Seeing Stone was activated, an image of Richard appeared sitting next to Lord Teymark.

Avestyn turned to Matthew. "It would appear that you, my young apprentice, are going home."

Matthew looked at the image in horror. This would be his first trip home since they had assigned him to guard duty on the island. He could not bear the shame of his family, so he asked Lord Avestyn to make him appear to have died during Lord Avestyn's escape.

"I suggest you leave at once, my boy. We cannot waste any more time," Lord Avestyn barked as he left the room. "Bring us back the Seer or do not come back at all."

Matthew ran straight for his carriage. After a few minutes' travel, he found himself at the edge of the Elvish realm. The Elvish watch-keeper met him there. As the carriage came to a stop, a young watch-keeper opened the door to the carriage.

"State your business in the Realm of the Elves." The boy

tried to sound commanding, but Matthew could tell he was still a child.

Matthew extended his hand to show his signet ring. The ring was oval in shape and engraved with ripples around a "T" engraved with gold. It was the symbol of the House of Teymark. The watch-keeper stepped back and bowed.

"I am sorry, sir. I did not know who you were. The Teymark family is large, and I have not met every member of the clan. Please forgive me."

Matthew adjusted his posture as he answered the boy. "No matter, child. I forgive you. Now, please do not hold me up any longer. I need to see my uncle at once," he said as he closed the door to the carriage.

The young watch-keeper ran up in front of the carriage and sprinkled powder in front of the barrier to the Elvish realm.

"Please enter, good sir," he yelled as he stepped out of the way of the carriage.

Matthew and his carriage disappeared at once through the magickal barrier, bringing him right into the lion's den.

Lord Teymark sat in his study with Richard. Dinner was running late, so they played a game of chess. Lord Teymark stopped mid-sentence when his amulet lit up. It only did that when someone of his family passed in or out of the realm. He sat in confusion, as he could not think of any who would leave the realm. Nobody was set to leave on a trip or was already out of the realm at present.

"Watch-keeper," he yelled toward the study door.

"Yes, my lord," replied the watch-keeper.

"Please travel to the realm barrier post and make inquiries for me as to who entered or exited the realm a few moments ago."

The watch-keeper nodded as he left the room.

Teymark said, "This is most peculiar, Master Richard."

Richard grinned a little as he made his move. "It is not to a Seer. Checkmate."

Lord Teymark punched the arm of his chair. "Distraction, my lord, is what diverts us from the truth," he said, grinning as he packed the pieces of the chess set away.

As night set in over the Elvish realm, dinner was set out in the usual fashion. More food was being made of late due in part to Lord Teymark's unexpected—but not unwelcome—guests. Lord Teymark was cherry and ate in his usual fashion, but he could not get his mind off of the events of earlier. The watch-keeper could not determine who had entered through the barrier.

All will be revealed, he thought to himself.

After dinner, Lord Teymark retired to his study. He sat at his desk, thumbing through a book as he sipped his wine. From the dark doorway, he heard a familiar voice say, "I would have thought you would have recognized my Aura the second I passed into this realm."

Matthew moved into the room to reveal himself to his uncle.

Lord Teymark turned white. "Impossible. You died when you were on prison duty."

Matthew sat down slowly, trying hard not to look his uncle in the face.

"What happened to you, Matthew? Where have you been? You know the shock of your death killed your mother. She was not the same after we thought you died. We tried to raise her spirits, but eventually she gave herself back to the universe."

Matthew could do nothing but look down as he spoke, "Someone gave me a chance, and I took it. That night, I received word of my sister's death. My father wrote and told me Evynloth killed her in a fit of rage, from which he frequently suffered. I was crippled with grief, weak to the words of Lord Avestyn. He told me that if I helped him escape then he would help me get my revenge for Ericka."

Lord Teymark was visibly angry, but he continued to listen to his nephew's confession. It was the way of their kind to listen without judgment.

"Uncle, I am here because I need the Seer. He is the only hope I have of avenging my sister. Lord Avestyn has promised me Evynloth's head on a spike if I only bring him the Seer."

Lord Teymark's voice rose. "Matthew, this is not our way. We do not sacrifice for vengeance. We are not Vikings. Please, Matthew, you need to understand that you always have a choice. Live here in your home in peace and security. We will help you get better and rid yourself of this evil."

Matthew broke down in tears. "I only ever wanted to avenge my sister, but as the years have gone by, I have developed a taste for power and dark magick."

Lord Teymark stood up to comfort his nephew but was

stopped dead in his tracks. He tried to move, but something froze him.

An ailing Lord Avestyn appeared in the room before them. "Weak," he yelled at Matthew. "I knew you would not stick to the plan. Obviously I have to do everything myself."

Lord Avestyn snapped his fingers, putting the two men under a sleeping spell. Lord Teymark and Matthew fell to the ground. "Now where is that blasted man?" Lord Avestyn barked through coughs as he disappeared into thin air.

Eventually, he found his way to Richard's room.

Richard was sitting on the edge of the bed. "I have been waiting for you, Jinn. I knew once you two realized I was alive that it was only a matter of time before you came here to take me."

Lord Avestyn said nothing as he nodded.

Meanwhile, back in Lord Teymark's study, the two men found themselves revived by Afloriana.

"Richard..." Matthew said. "He came to take him."

Afloriana nodded. "Watch-keepers. Please go to Master Richard's room at once. I fear he is in danger."

The guards nodded and ran down the hall.

"I have to get to Richard's room," Matthew said. "I cannot let it happen..."

Afloriana helped Matthew up. "Please, you are not strong enough yet. Leave this to the guards."

Beelay ran into the room, having been alerted to the commotion. His face was scared as his eyes scanned the room for Imogen. He began to panic. "When I heard what was going on, I went straight to Imogen's room, but she wasn't there, and now I fear she has been taken by Evynloth."

A watch-keeper ran into the room. "My lord, your wife is in a panic. Silveen is missing. I have searched the palace, but she is nowhere to be seen."

Afloriana ran to the window. From her satchel she produced a bag that was full of a purple powder known as Finders Shards. They were made from a piece of the Seer's Stone that lay in the palace hall and were used by the Elves when they wished to find someone who was missing. Afloriana took some powder and blew it onto the wind. "Find the girl known as Imogen."

The Finders Shards flew out into the night in the direction of the Mountains of Myth.

"*No*," shouted Afloriana.

"What is it, my lady?" replied a watch-keeper.

"The Finders Shards are heading in the direction of the Mountains of Myth," Afloriana said. "It is too dangerous for her to go on her own."

Beelay began to panic. "Should we follow her or not? Maybe she is not alone. The Queen told me that Silveen wants to be a watch-keeper, and she knows the area like the back of her hand."

Afloriana took some more of the Finders Shards and whispered Silveen's name over them as she blew them out onto the wind. "They are following in the same direction as Imogen's."

Lord Teymark stood up from his chair as he began to speak, "I am very much worried for the children, but you know our laws, Afloriana. They made the decision to go up the mountains alone, and even if we wanted to help them, we could not, not without more of Kavron's powder. He is the only spell-caster who left the High Council with a stockpile." Lord Teymark looked in the direction of the mountains. "I am afraid they are on their own."

Beelay stepped closer to Lord Teymark as he voiced his disagreement, but Teymark said, "Lord Sageland, you of all people know our laws are absolute. Once they start a journey up the mountains, they cannot be aided. I am sorry."

As Lord Teymark looked toward the mountains, he was struck with a realization, turning to everyone in the room he said with urgency in his voice, "Please, nobody must let my wife know what has happened. She was born of a warring clan and is the best ranger I know. She will try to pursue the children."

Everyone in the room nodded in agreement. Imogen and Silveen were on their own.

"Uncle, my lord," Matthew said, "we cannot follow the girls, but we can at least be waiting for them at the base of the mountains. I fear that Lord Avestyn may try to capture them. He is not in any shape to climb the mountains, but he is not above waiting to hurt the girls in order to get what he wants."

Lord Teymark nodded in agreement. "Very well. Let's get to the carriages. I need everyone's help with this."

A BOX ON THE MOUNTAIN

Imogen, Silveen, and Moonlight continued galloping across the countryside with great speed.

"Silveen, do you know how to get to the mountains?"

Silveen nodded as the horse continued to gallop. Not long after their escape, they came to a fork in the road. Silveen jumped down from Moonlight.

"We must walk from here. Come, follow me," Silveen said as she extended her arm to help Imogen down. "Do you have the powder?"

Imogen nodded as she retrieved the powder from Beelay's satchel.

Silveen pulled powder from the bag and blew it into the air. A cloud formed from the dust and led the way to the Mountains of Myth. "Remember, these mountains are full of tricks and traps. Just follow the cloud and watch your step."

After an hour of walking up the mountains, Imogen felt movement coming from Beelay's satchel. "Silveen, I have something to confess. I did not tell you, but I bought someone with us," she said as she pointed to her bag.

Silveen looked puzzled as Imogen placed the satchel on the ground as carefully as she could.

"We met with a great man when we went to retrieve the knife and spell for Ericka's ceremony, and he gave us a wonderful gift," she said, opening the satchel.

Silveen gasped at the egg. "Is that what I think it is? How did he get an egg without being murdered by the mother?"

Imogen shook her head. "I don't know. Maybe the mother abandoned it."

The egg slowly cracked open.

"Let me get out of its sight. It needs to bond with you," Silveen said as she walked over and hid behind a tree.

As the Harpy fought its way from the egg, it squeaked out what Imogen thought was a little howl. Imogen was a little scared of the newborn for obvious reasons. When the Harpy opened its eyes, it locked its gaze on Imogen. The Harpy, a male, presumed Imogen to be his mother, bonding with her instantly.

"Oh, you are a feisty thing, aren't you?" she said as he snapped at her hands. "I hope it won't turn on us."

Silveen stepped out from the trees. "I am sure he will love us," she said as she offered the newborn a berry from those she had picked while she had lain in wait.

The Harpy snatched it from her and gobbled it up.

"Come on now, we better get moving before the sun rises."

The rest of the journey up the mountains was very dangerous. Every ten feet, the pair met with an avalanche of boulders or water that seemed to come from nowhere. After they finally reached a mountaintop, they came to a cave door.

"This must be it," said Silveen with a slight chuckle. "Well we are at the top of the mountain and there's clearly only one entrance way," Imogen remarked in a sarcastic, yet playful tone.

The pebbles on the ground moved behind them. Silveen swung around, pulling an arrow from her quiver with a single solid motion.

"I would not go in there if I were you."

It was King Oafe, standing behind them propped up on his ax, with two of his trusted guards.

"I cannot let you get the Stone. You do not know the hell you will unleash. Lord Avestyn and Lord Evynloth will do whatever is necessary to get the Stone from you."

Silveen moved in front of Imogen. "Imogen, my lady, please do what you need to do to get into the cave. I will stand guard while you get the Stone."

King Oafe growled out in anger as he ordered his men to seize the girls.

Silveen shot both of the guards with her arrows before they moved even two feet toward them.

King Oafe looked at his slain men in shock and awe. "How dare you kill my children. Come here, you little wench."

Imogen threw down her satchel, forgetting about her new little pet. Imogen readied her wand, but in her terror could not think of the spells that the Elves had taught her. Stepping backwards as the king lunged toward her, Imogen braced for impact, but none came.

Instead, she opened her eyes to a scene of chaos and screams of terror across the mountaintop. During the stand-off, the young Harpy, having sensed its mother's danger, had emerged from the satchel and was attacking King Oafe. During the frenzy, King Oafe dropped his axe to the ground. The strength of her new pet amazed Imogen.

In the chaos, her Harpy picked up the 300-pound Dwarf and threw him off the cliff. King Oafe fell to his death, screaming out in agony while the Harpy sat screeching as he watched his enemy fall to the ground below. The Harpy shifted his attention to the axe behind him.

It was glimmering in the morning sun. Silveen ran to pick up the axe, but the Harpy picked it up first and flew over to sit at his new mother's feet.

"Okay, we should not waste any more time. We need to get into that cave and get the Stone." Imogen turned and walked toward the cave.

The cave itself was so dark that her eyes could not adjust, forcing her to light her way with a torch. Upon entering the cave, Imogen saw a lone bench with a small stone box atop it. As she edged forward to reach out and touch the box, a great breath of wind blew her torch out. Suddenly the room filled with a bright white light.

After a few moments, Imogen's eyes adjusted to the light.

Before her stood a tall bald man dressed in a gray robe. Imogen could do nothing more than look at the man, as she could not move or speak.

"Welcome, my child, please fear not. I am Lynth. We two are some of the last of my line of Kami. I was the first soul carrier, and you are the current. In Tera'Loth, all souls recycle from each generation to the next. I know you are here to collect the Stone to release Ericka's soul. Please, take this Stone and save us from Evynloth and Necromancium. If Evynloth successfully unlocks that realm, then there will be no hope for Tera'Loth. There is an evil locked down in Necromancium that even I would not want to cross paths with." Lynth edged toward Imogen and kissed her on the forehead.

With that, the light dissipated. Imogen opened her eyes to find the Stone in her palm. She wasted no further time in the cave.

When she exited the cave, she found Silveen playing with the Harpy.

"I got it," she said as she held up the box victoriously.

Silveen nodded in approval. "Okay, let's get out of here before anyone else comes to visit."

Imogen looked at her new pet and grinned as she said, "Silveen, can Moonlight get back to the palace on her own?"

Silveen, looking suspiciously at her, replied, "Yes?"

Imogen slung her bag to her back and grabbed the axe before the Harpy's claws yanked them both from the cliff. "Fly us home, baby."

With that, the trio flew off in the palace's direction.

When the girls arrived back in the palace courtyard, there was nobody in sight.

"What time is it? The sun is up and there is nobody around," Silveen said. "Something is not right."

In the distance, a loud scream pierced the area and a purple light shot up toward the sky.

"What was that?" Imogen yelled.

Silveen's face dropped. "That was the death ritual. The Dwarves must have received word of their king's passing. Come, we need to hide. Let's go inside."

As the two girls ran inside, Zaygarth was waiting.

"Zaygarth. What are you doing here, and where is everyone else?" Imogen said as she hugged her new friend.

"I do not know. When I arrived there was nobody in sight. I have come with the tools for the ceremony on behalf of Lord Kavron."

The trio walked toward the seats by the fire in Lord Teymark's study, only to be stopped short of sitting by a crash on the door, which was thrown open to reveal none other than Silveen's mother, Lady Teymark.

"Where have you two been? I demand an explanation at once."

Silveen stood to meet her mother, overcome by fear produced by the wrath in her mother's eyes. She was tongue-tied.

"My lady," interjected Imogen, "we went in search of the Stone of Auras Demise." Imogen pulled the Stone from her pocket. "And we won the Stone from that old Oafe."

Zaygarth gasped, bringing attention to himself.

Lady Teymark, shocked, recognized her old friend. "Zaygarth. Is that you? I thought you were dead."

Zaygarth bowed without words.

Silveen looked at the two adults locking their gazes. This is what she thought must be love.

"I went underground the night Evynloth killed off the High Council," Zaygarth said. "I am sorry that I could not get word to you, but I could not risk Evynloth turning on you in his quest to locate Kavron and myself."

Lady Teymark was crying a little, but she subdued this when she looked at her daughter. "Well you are here now and the girls arrived back safely, so that is the main thing."

Silveen rolled her eyes a little. "Mother, I wish you would not call me a girl. I am nearly 200 years old."

Lady Teymark turned her focus back to Zaygarth. "Why are you here now?"

Zaygarth showed the implements for the ceremony to Lady Teymark, explaining the situation and their purpose.

"Well, it would seem I am very much in the dark about a lot of things lately. I can help you with the preparations for the ceremony. Let me get word to my husband. He will want to know you are here and that the children arrived home safe."

With that, Lady Teymark sent a message on the winds, telling her husband to return to the castle for the ceremony.

DEATH AND SEPARATION

Lord Avestyn arrived back at the fortress with Richard in tow, visibly tired from his journey.

"Young people. They never do a thing right," grumbled Lord Avestyn, dragging himself over to his favorite chair.

After he found his comfortable spot, he could do nothing more than stare at the lump of human that was laying on the cold concrete floor.

"Well, I guess I need to tuck you away somewhere for safekeeping," he muttered under his breath. Lord Avestyn was too old to move him on his own, and his magickal abilities were weak from the journey to the Elvish realm. "Where is that boy when I need him?"

Lord Avestyn clutched his cane as he hauled himself from his chair. He walked over to the Seeing Stone. As he dropped his blood on the Stone, he spoke the words, "Show me the boy."

Evynloth's image appeared. He was in the Elvish realm, walking around in circles and cursing at the sky. "Where is that mountaintop?"

Lord Avestyn hobbled over to his desk. He pulled a handful of powder from a pouch. With the powder in his hands, he whispered over it, "Find Lord Evynloth and tell him to come home. I have the Seer."

He blew the dust into the air.

Evynloth was in a frenzy as he ran in circles looking for the Mountains of Myth. "Where is the pathway? They said it would be visible. That Dwarf better not have lied or else his Queen dies."

Lord Evynloth's head was spinning so badly he found he needed to sit down on a rock and rest a moment. As Evynloth sat rubbing his head, he suddenly felt a presence coming toward him. It was a cloud of Founders Dust. As the dust cloud came to a stop in front of him, he heard a thousand tiny voices relaying the message to him from Lord Avestyn.

"He has the Seer."

Lord Evynloth found himself elated but equally torn between returning to the fortress and kidnapping Imogen. "I will return to the fortress. I will get you in good time, Imogen. All in good time." Evynloth traveled back to the fortress at once.

When he arrived back at the fortress, Lord Avestyn was waiting outside for him. "It's about time, boy. What took you so long?"

Lord Evynloth ran to his master's side. "I am sorry, my lord. I was trying to get the girl, but I have been unsuccessful in finding her. I came as soon as you called me, my lord."

Lord Avestyn scrunched up his face. "No time for apologies, boy. We have the Seer. Now we need the Stone."

Lord Evynloth cleared his throat. "My lord, we have a bigger problem than just the Stone. As you know, I have many informants across the realms, and King Oafe of the Dwarves is also aiding our cause. He told me of a rumor that has swept the lands. It is said that the Stone we seek has a sister Stone, an Anti-Stone. Rumors suggest that the girl is in search of it. If successful, she could seal shut Necromancium —forever."

Lord Avestyn scoffed at his apprentice. "Nonsense, boy. I am the greatest spell-caster in all the lands. I would know of something like this."

Evynloth coughed a little.

"Oh, spit it out, boy. We are long past standing on form."

Evynloth spoke quickly, "The Dwarf King can be very amenable when he needs to be. He told me of a land unknown to the rest of Tera'Loth. It no longer exists, but it was once a bustling realm for mages. They knew it as Old-Kami. They helped Tera'Loth build the foundations for the magick we practice today.

"Records are thin, but from what the Dwarves can piece together, the mages differed with the people of Djinn— which we now know as Magicka—over the fuel used for the realm travel boxes. In their ire, the mages threatened war over the issue. The people of Djinn swore they would open the gates of Necromancium if they did not leave them in peace, to live their lives the way they chose.

"Feeling the pressure of the situation, the mages decided there was no other choice but to make sure this did not happen. They sealed shut the gates to Necromancium. Two Stones were crafted from two large pieces of rock, known as 'Reclaim' and 'Demise'. These Stones were what gave life to all the good—and bad—magick. These Stones were carved as an insurance policy in the event that the mages would need to reopen Necromancium. The only way to open the gates again would be to use the blood of a direct relative of the five mages who sealed the gates of Necromancium paired with the water from the Stone of Auras Reclaim. Blood and life to reopen what should stay sealed forever.

"When the Djinn found out what the mages had done, they waged a great war between the two realms. The Djinn obliterated the mage realm. Those of the Kami left alive fled to the four corners of Tera'Loth, but not before entrusting the Stones to the King of Impenia. The King hid the Stones away with two of his most trusted allies to remain secret until there was nobody left who remembered their purpose or existence. The Djinn turned their bloodlust on the people of upper Necromancium. They saw them as allies of the mages and decided their fate should be death for allowing the mages to close Necromancium.

"Using the combined magick of the armies of Djinn, they unleashed their full force to murder every inhabitant of the realm. Without the power of Necromancium to aid them, the mages were powerless. It took two days to wipe out the mages' realm. Now, we know of the Stone of Auras Reclaim, but the Stone of Auras Demise is a well-guarded secret almost lost to time."

Lord Avestyn's face dropped. "Well where is the Stone? We have to get it before they do."

Lord Evynloth nodded in agreement. "I was trying to get it when you summoned me back to the fortress. The girl is looking for it in the Mountains of Myth as we speak, and she may already have it."

Lord Avestyn shouted with rage, "Of all the places they could have hidden it away. We cannot make the journey. We are too old, and it is full of Imp and pixie magick. Too many traps... No, we must wait for her to descend the mountains, then we shall retrieve the Stone."

Lord Avestyn climbed into the carriage at once. "Come now, boy. No time to waste. She may already be back at the palace."

The carriage flew off with haste, bound for the base of the Mountains of Myth.

As the carriage descended, Lord Teymark and the Elvish guard met them.

"Ah, Teymark, how did I know you would be here?" Lord Evynloth scoffed as he helped his master from the carriage.

Lord Teymark spoke, "I am here to tell you that I have destroyed the Stone, and I hope to bring an end to your reign of terror. Tera'Loth needs to be free again. I will not let my people live in fear of you any longer. The people of Magicka need light in their lives again. Come now, you are old men, and this is a fruitless task."

Lord Avestyn raised his wand and struck down a watch-keeper. "Now who's old, eh?"

Lord Teymark looked at his fallen watch-keeper in horror as he shouted past a deranged Lord Avestyn. "Come now, Lord Evynloth. Did you suffer so much at the hands of this man that you cannot feel compassion for anyone else? Ericka is dead. Please, let her rest. We can perform the Ceremony of Auras Separation and give her the peace her family should have given her fifty years ago".

Lord Evynloth flew up close to strangle Lord Teymark, but someone struck him down. Fear crossed his eyes when he looked up to see who had struck him.

"Drayah? How could you do this? You were down there with us."

Drayah shook her head. "No, Evynloth. We both suffered under this disgusting man's reign of terror. You should count yourself lucky that you did not suffer like us girls did in that dungeon. I thought I would suffer and die down there, but the people of Magicka gave us a second chance at life. I moved on with my life and channeled my anger in a different direction. We always knew there was a choice as to how we lived our lives afterward, Evynloth. You made your choice out of anger and chose the wrong path," Drayah said with her wand still on Evynloth.

"Lord Avestyn, why are you not helping me?" Evynloth said as he turned around to see Lord Avestyn being held under the wands of Beelay, Segion, and Matthew.

"Traitor," shouted Evynloth. "How could you go against our master?"

Matthew looked at his uncle for strength. "I joined Lord Avestyn and helped him escape. For my loyalty, he promised me something I wanted. It would seem that today is the day I cash in on that. You see, in your arrogance, you learned nothing about me.

"My name is Lord Matthew Teymark-Alphias, and Ericka was my sister. My mother was Lord Teymark's beloved sister, Telanar Teymark. She accompanied Lord Teymark on the trade delegation to Djinn that took place before they rescued you. Her beauty took Lord Andreas, and I am the product of that indiscretion. They kept my existence secret, but my father came to visit me as often as he could. He paid for my upbringing, and my mother married a human guard of the Elvish Prison of Loneliness to keep her honor. My stepfather knew of her pregnancy and used it against her until the day she died. After years of physical and mental abuse, she ended her own life. It was my uncle who pulled her from the Lake of Souls."

Drayah struggled and screamed, "Hurry, he is fighting me. I cannot hold him much longer."

Matthew continued, "So you see, I made it my mission to kill Lord Avestyn, you, and Xenus, but you helped me with the latter. I saw all three of you as being equal in the death of my sister."

With that, Lord Teymark started the death rites. "Lord Jinn Avestyn, by the Elvish ways, laws, and reasons, I find you guilty of the death of Lady Ericka Alphias-Almackia. Customary to our ways, her blood relative is here to rid you of your life on Tera'Loth."

With that, Matthew used his wand to draw a magickal line across Lord Avestyn's throat. As the blood drained from his body, Lord Avestyn clutched at his neck, choking on his own blood. Matthew released his lifeless body at once and let it fall to the ground.

"*Noooo*," screamed Evynloth. "He was the only person who knew how to bring my Ericka back. You will pay for this."

Matthew cracked.

With bloodlust, he turned his wrath toward Evynloth. He pointed his wand in Evynloth's direction, only to find himself halted by a flash of light that blinded everyone. When the light dissipated, Evynloth went with it.

"No. How did he get away? What was that light?"

Everyone looked at each other in confusion.

"How did he get away, and who or what helped him?" Matthew yelled, frantic as he searched the skies for Lord Evynloth.

"We cannot worry about that now," Lord Teymark said. "We need a new plan to save Richard. I am sure Evynloth is already back at his fortress."

At that moment, a very strong feeling of his wife came upon Lord Teymark. On the wind, he heard her calling him home, for the girls were back. "Come, let's get back to the palace. The children are already there. Afloriana and Drayah need to get to work on that potion as soon as possible."

Back at Avestyn's fortress, Lord Evynloth sat in his master's chair, pondering his rescue in confusion. How could he have gotten back here? In that instant, he heard a familiar voice in his head.

"It was me, my love. I saved you from yourself."

It was the voice of Ericka.

"My love, is that you? Why have you never shown your-self before?"

Ericka's ghost showed itself to Evynloth. "It is difficult to be in contact. My soul is weakened by being tethered to a dead body. Loth, you need to let me go. It's been fifty years since I died, and you are not a young man anymore. Our daughter is dead. All we have left of us is a good little girl who deserves none of what she has been through. Please, stop hurting people."

Evynloth rose and paced the room, hitting the side of his head frantically. "No, my love. I cannot stop this. Lord Avestyn promised to bring you back to life if I opened Necro-mancium."

Ericka shook her head. "How can he help us now? He is dead, my love. Besides, the only way to bring me back would be to use the souls of those committed to Necromancium. If you bought me back, I would be here in flesh but devoid of my true soul. I would not be your wife."

Ericka floated up to the window. "It is such a nice view from here. You can see the ocean." Ericka turned to face her husband. "I won't let you bring me back, and you need to stop hurting Imogen. She is all we have left of our line, and I will see you fail in this venture—with her help."

Without another word, Ericka came before her husband

and made a motion as if she was touching his face before disappearing from the room.

"No. Ericka, please come back," Evynloth wailed as he fell to the ground, setting free fifty years of subdued grief and pain. In his cantankerous manner, he still plotted his wife's return. With the Seer, he was sure he could still execute the plan.

After Evynloth composed himself, he went down to the dungeon to visit Richard. There, in the cell's corner, lay Richard, curled up in a ball, a nervous wreck with his back facing the wall.

"Well, dear Seer. It would appear that the time for your usefulness has come," Evynloth said as he opened the gate to the cell.

From his robes, Evynloth produced the Necropedricon, placing it gently in front of Richard's curled up body. "As you may already be aware, my master's life has ended, and that puts me in a bind."

Richard reached for the book slowly as Evynloth continued to speak.

"This book will help me open the gates to Necromancium. In it are the spells I need to do that—and to reunite me with my love." Evynloth knelt down beside Richard. "Unfortunately, I cannot read this language, but as I understand it from my late master, all Seers have knowledge of all the languages in Tera'Loth."

Carefully, Evynloth opened the book to show what appeared to be a contents page. "If you help me unlock Necromancium, then you will be free."

Richard looked dead at Evynloth, his eyes widening at the prospect of freedom. "You know why my ancestor and his companions sealed the lower realm shut. You know what lies beneath. If you let it out, then it will be the end of Tera'Loth."

Evynloth smiled as he rose from the ground. "It will surely be a *different* Tera'Loth."

Richard slid the book away from himself. "I will not help you, so just kill me."

Evynloth smiled as he folded his arms. "If you do not help me, then I will kill Imogen. She is easy to get to if I should want to kill her. Until now, I haven't bothered. I have enjoyed the little girl's spirit. I feed off of the hope of people like her. She won't stop me, no matter what."

Through his tears, Richard agreed to help his father-in-law execute his plan.

"I am glad you have come to your senses," Evynloth said. "Let's get to work. I need you to find out what we need to bring my wife back. Those meddling Elves want to separate her Aura from her so that Tera'Loth can reclaim her soul."

Richard thumbed through the pages, trying to prolong finding what Evynloth needed. "Perhaps, my lord, if I might have food, I could think better."

Evynloth grumbled but left the room in search of food. As soon as Evynloth disappeared from sight, Richard attempted to commune with Afloriana, but he could not get through to her. Lord Avestyn had enchanted his fortress with far too many blocking spells. He needed to warn his friends that time was running short.

Lucky for Richard, Ericka was one step ahead of him.

After leaving Evynloth, Ericka's spirit had returned to her grave, knowing Imogen would make sure someone would perform the Ceremony of Auras Separation. Ericka used the last of her strength to cast a spell of protection over her grave to stop Evynloth from digging her up.

"I have done what I can, Imogen. Now the rest is up to you."

With that, Ericka disappeared back into purgatory to await her release.

A CEREMONY OF SEPARATION

When the carriages arrived back in the palace courtyard, Lady Teymark, Zaygarth, and the girls were waiting to greet the party. As the group descended from the carriages, nobody wasted time on anger or scolding. Instead, everyone agreed on a task to complete.

"Zaygarth, please give me the implements for Ericka's separation ceremony. I shall need them to prepare the spell, and Lady Teymark, I need you to read up on all the rituals for Ericka's ceremony," said Afloriana with a commanding tone nobody knew she could muster. "Drayah, you go with Imogen and mix the potion of Auras Demise."

Drayah nodded and ran off quickly, almost dragging Imogen.

"Everyone else is to go with Lord Teymark at once."

Lord Teymark led the rest of the group to his study. Once

inside, they discussed the next steps, while Matthew told them everything he could about their new common enemy. Including the location of a destructive receptacle (called the Receptus-Chaotica) that destroyed anything and everything, while doubling as a guard for the gates to lower-Necromancium.

"With Lord Avestyn gone, that leaves Evynloth weak. If we are to stop him, then it needs to be now," said Lord Teymark before gulping down a glass of whiskey. "More to the point, we need to get Richard out of Evynloth's clutches."

Segion stood up to address the room. "I mean no offense, but I would like to volunteer my services as liaison to the other realms. I am well-loved, and I know I can rally support to take Evynloth out."

Lord Teymark nodded in agreement. "Alright then. Lord Segion, make haste, and when you return, we will have formed a battle plan."

Segion wasted no time in heading out to rally the troops.

Meanwhile, down in the apothecary, Drayah was working in a fury to prepare the potion of Auras Demise. Drayah looked at the Stone, frazzled. In front of them lay all they needed to enact the spell, except for a tiny obstacle. They could not milk the Stone. The pair tried everything they could to break the Stone.

"Ugh, it can't be this hard. We are so close to laying waste to Evynloth. Think, Drayah, think."

Imogen was flipping through the books as quickly as she could, but it was useless. Afloriana was quickly and quietly working in the other corner on the preparations for Ericka's separation ceremony. When she worked, she could be almost in a hypnotic trance, but the extreme tension coming from Drayah broke this.

"Please, Drayah. You are smarter than this. Think hard. What could cut through any material in this world?"

Drayah thought for a moment, then jumped from her chair. "A pickaxe from the Dwarven realm."

Afloriana winked and returned to her work.

"But I have no idea how I am going to get that."

Imogen ran from the room without a word. She returned a few moments later, dragging King Oafe's axe behind her. "Will this work?" she said.

Drayah looked at her, dumbstruck. "Do you have any other tricks up your sleeve?"

Imogen grinned as she bowed. "Come, Afloriana. Help me wield this axe."

The two women walked to the table, ready to conquer the Stone.

"Imogen, please put the Stone in the vice and hold a cup underneath it. And whatever you do, don't let go of the cup."

As Imogen held the cup, the two Witches raised the axe together, throwing it down at the count of three onto the Stone. It worked. The Stone cracked in two, spilling its blue water into the cup that was being held by the shaking hand of Imogen.

"There we go. See, Drayah, we are still in our prime," Afloriana said as they threw the axe down. "You can breathe now, Imogen. Bring me the cup," Afloriana told her, taking the cup from the girl's shaking hands for transfer into a readied vial. "All that's left to do is for us to get some of Richard's blood, which I am sure we will have soon."

Back in Lord Teymark's study, Lady Teymark was reading through books as fast as she could. After a few hours, she sighed and put down a book written in a language Zaygarth could not read.

"This is grimmer than I first thought," Lady Teymark said. "Where is my nephew?"

Zaygarth shook his head. "I don't know, but I shall find him, my lady," he said as he exited the room with haste.

After a little searching, Zaygarth found Matthew by the pond in the family's private garden. "I thought I would find you here. Why did your mother give you a humanoid name? Nobody knows of that world any longer."

Matthew spoke without looking up from the water. "I suppose Mother was a romantic. She never stood on form. If she was a proponent for tradition then she would not have produced me out of wedlock, would she?"

Zaygarth winced at the remark. He had known Matthew's mother all his life, and he had seen her as a best friend.

"Why are you here, my man?" said Matthew as he pulled himself from the ground.

"Your aunt sent me to find you. There is a way to free your sister."

Matthew nodded as he dusted off his clothes. "Very well, bring me to my aunt at once."

Aphorias Teymark sat waiting for her nephew, pretending to thumb through a book on herbs. In reality, thinking of the ceremony tore her and made her wish to leave before her nephew arrived, fearing his reaction. As she went to stand, she saw Matthew walking toward her with a look of determination on his face.

In the fashion of the Elves, Lady Teymark stood to greet her guest, kissing him before they sat down. "I have found a way for you to free your sister of Evynloth once and for all. But you will not like it."

Matthew sat down. Sensing the tension, he kept quiet and heard his aunt out.

"Ericka has been dead for many years. Because of the ceremony not being performed sooner, her Aura will not be strong enough to travel to the seas. There is no other way to say this. We have to dig Ericka up."

A look of shock and anger came over Matthew's face. "I will not do it. You are disgusting for even suggesting that I should do such."

Lady Teymark edged toward her nephew. "Please, son. You need to know that this is the only way, and if someone bought her back, she would be something unnatural."

Matthew fell to the floor, sobbing in quiet acquiescence. "I know, aunt, but I cannot dig up my sister. Please let someone else do it."

Lady Teymark dropped to the floor to embrace her nephew. "I will not let you suffer the task. We will have undertakers to do that part."

Through his tears, Matthew's gaze turned to the window, looking toward Necromancium. He knew in his heart that he could not allow Evynloth to bring his sister back to this world. The Necromancers' magick was dark and filthy and not something he wanted inflicted on the corpse of his sister.

Matthew walked toward the window for air. "I won't allow Lord Evynloth to get his hands on my sister again."

Lady Teymark nodded in agreement as she edged toward Matthew, placing a hand on his shoulder as he looked across the dusk sky. "You know it's for the best, child."

The next morning, Matthew found himself at the grave of his sister in the Magicka realm, joined by Afloriana and Lady Teymark.

"I never knew a purer girl in all the lands. She would have done anything for anyone without question," said Afloriana as she stood next to Ericka's grave. Lady Teymark—with whatever influence her position had left in the realm—had organized Ericka's exhumation with nobody alerting Lord Evynloth.

"Alright, men," she said. "Please load her safely, and with respect, into the carriage I have provided."

The undertakers nodded as they raised up Ericka's coffin onto a gurney so that they could easily place it in the carriage. With the coffin in the carriage, Ericka was finally en route to her journey to the Sea of Souls. As the carriage rocked gently toward the sea, Matthew could do nothing but stare out the window and try not to cry. This moment was painful, and was years in the making. It was the entire focus of his life. He thought of nothing more than revenge for his beloved sister. Even if she had never known he existed.

Lady Teymark sat quietly, clutching her nephew's hand. As she squeezed his hand a little, he turned to look at her.

His eyes darted between her eyes and the book in his hand as he spoke, "Aunt, I do not know the rituals for the Ceremony of Auras Separation."

Lady Teymark sighed as she grabbed her nephew's shoulder. "It is all right, son. Afloriana and I will guide you through it."

As the carriage approached the sea, Matthew's breath quickened, terrified that they could not help Ericka without Lord Evynloth being alerted. Afloriana and Drayah had placed every protection and cloaking spell they could over Matthew, Lady Teymark, and Ericka's grave. As the carriage came to a stop, Matthew took in a deep breath and descended from the carriage. The men slowly edged Ericka's coffin from the carriage, carrying it gently toward the edge of the sea. After carefully placing the coffin down on the shore, the men stood back to let the ritual begin.

Afloriana approached the coffin and whispered a spell of unsealing. As she swooped her hands across the coffin, the noise of a lock disengaging came from inside. Upon hearing this, Afloriana motioned to the men to come forth and remove the lid, sliding it off carefully to reveal a perfectly preserved corpse.

After all this time, Ericka's corpse could have been mistaken for someone who died only yesterday. In reality, Lord Alphias spared no expense in the burial preparations, including the most expensive form of embalming, a solution made of an anti-aging potion mixed with Elvish tears.

The sight of Ericka and her beauty overcame Matthew. He had seen pictures of her, but they had never spent time with each other for obvious reasons. Lady Alphias, Ericka's mother, had gone to her grave none the wiser of her husband's indiscretion.

Afloriana and Lady Teymark arranged the implements needed for the ceremony, allowing Matthew a few moments with his sister.

Matthew stood up from the ground, pulling a piece of paper from his pocket. "Dear sister, I know that you did not know me in life, but we shared a father, and he told me of you so much that I feel I always knew you. On many lonely nights in the Elvish realm, I would dream of a life in Magicka with you. Me, you, and your parents, all living together in happiness. Not that I did not love my mother and family, but I resented her for how she bought me into this world. I spent years in tangled emotions and writhing agony of the relationships denied me.

"Eventually, I joined the Elvish guard, and as luck would have it, I avenged your death. I have killed Lord Jinn Avestyn, and now I only need to set you free to get my revenge on your husband. I know he did not mean what happened, but he still could have chosen to be a good person. He chose evil, and that is why I find myself here over your body. This is the first and last time we will be together as a family. Imogen gave us your message, and now we will set you free of the bindings of an unfinished death."

Drying his eyes, Matthew stepped back from the coffin. Afloriana and Lady Teymark positioned themselves on either side of the coffin. Lady Teymark handed Matthew the knife, motioning him to approach the coffin. "Matthew, please run the knife in an infinity symbol over Ericka's body, but don't let the knife touch her. This is going over her Aura. Without the symbol broken, we cannot release the Aura from Ericka."

As Matthew did this, the women chanted in a strange form of Elvish, which nobody—including Matthew—knew. As they continued to utter the strange words, the infinity symbol glowed. After uttering the words, they instructed Matthew to slice an "X" through the infinity symbol that had appeared. He did so, and jumped back at the sight of a light that shot up from his sister. The light extended to the heavens, shooting up thousands of tiny particles of dust.

As quickly as the light shot up from Ericka's corpse, it disappeared. For a few seconds, the area plunged into darkness. From the darkness came a downpour, drenching Matthew and his companions with rain. After a few minutes, the rain and clouds of darkness cleared to reveal the clearest cloud-free sky they had ever seen.

Matthew cried as he looked to the sky, feeling a sensation engulf his body. He could only guess this was Ericka's Aura. Feeling overwhelmed by emotions, he looked toward the coffin to see that the beauty of his sister was now nothing but bones. Lady Teymark approached Matthew, embracing him as she cast her eyes toward the helpers looking on in awe. The last time anyone had witnessed the ceremony was thirty years ago, and some—including the helpers—were seeing it performed for the first time in their lives.

"Come now," Lady Teymark said. "Let us return her to the cemetery. Ericka is safe now. She is free."

AN ASSAULT ON NECROMANCIUM

Segion arrived at the Hall of the Druids a little before dawn. The hall was known colloquially as The Hall of Foreshadow. The Druid numbers had slowly dwindled over the years. Being a group in tune with nature, they had realized that resources were dwindling. This, paired with the shadow of Lord Avestyn, caused them to encourage population control. The world was always uncertain, but the group collectively was particularly concerned with the path that the Seers had once foretold.

Segion entered the hall to find it empty, which was not uncommon for this time of day, and if he was truthful, to have a few moments alone with the spirits of the fallen was what he needed. On the walls were carved the names of hundreds of his ancestors.

The Druids, although a large population, could trace themselves to a common ancestor known only as "The First."

Once, long ago, they had known their father's name, but that, like many things, was lost to time.

From behind him, Segion heard a floorboard creak.

"I was wondering when you would arrive."

Segion turned to find his mother, Hedra, standing before him.

"Yesterday I heard the celestial scream, but I could not think of who my ancestors were calling. I did not feel the pull of a dead child, and the only other person I know to be left alive is far too powerful to be killed."

Segion saw a look on his mother's face. It was a look of suspended breath.

"Mother, Lord Jinn Avestyn has been executed. You are free."

It had taken Hedra years to get past what had happened to her in her youth. Even now, she could barely believe her cousin was dead. Segion helped his mother to a seat, leaving her to make herself comfortable while he found her something to drink. Hedra shook her head as she looked toward the names of the dead carved on the wall. Segion was always absolutely devoted to his mother and left her wanting for nothing. After hurrying back with her drink, he sat down beside her.

"You are such a good son. I wish I was as good a child as you have been. My mother loved Jinn very much and refused to believe any of what I said." Hedra took a sip before continuing, "You know my mother tried to make me return home many times over the years. Nobody knew she was coming to see me, not even my father. She began visiting me after you were born and always frowned on me for spoiling you. I wanted you to know you to know a mother who loved you no matter what. I wanted to be at home with those I loved, but I was far too afraid of my cousin to return. Besides, I had already made a life for myself, and I could not uproot you like that." Hedra gulped down the rest of her drink. "I have only a few regrets in my life, but if I could have kept what had happened to me a secret from you then I would have."

Segion shook his head, now crying a little as he kissed his mother's hand.

"I fear that it has consumed your life. I know you never sought revenge, but I feel I denied you a proper childhood by making you my confidant."

Segion rubbed his mother's face and smiled at her. "Mother, if you did not tell me then I would have learned it from someone else, and that would have hurt me more, so you know you have nothing to forgive." Segion rose, extending a hand to his mother. "Come, Mother. Let's visit Father. We haven't cleaned the Stone in a while."

Segion and his mother returned to the hall after a few hours to find all the elders in assembly. Their organization needed no explanation. In the back of the room sat Beelay and Imogen. Elder Foran, who was the collective leader, stood to greet Segion.

"Lord Beelay has told us of the perils, but I ask you, why should we involve ourselves in this battle of wills?"

Segion motioned to Beelay to seat his mother as he approached the center of the circle. "My fellow Druids, for many years we have lived in relative seclusion, but the serene lifestyle we live is now under threat. At this moment, Lord Evynloth is working on a way to break the seal to the gates that hold back the horrors of lower Necromancium. The legends of the Kami are true, and the Dwarves and Vikings have known the secrets of the lower realm for generations."

The room erupted with murmurs.

"Lord Foran, you must help us. Without a collective effort, we cannot stop Lord Evynloth. He has amassed a large army backed by the Vikings and all those in Tera'Loth who pledge loyalty to him."

Lord Foran rose to share the floor. "I dislike involving us in the troubles of our neighbors, but if Lord Evynloth successfully completes his task, it will only be a matter of time before the peace we have known for generations disappears forever." Lord Foran slammed his walking stick on the floor three times to call a vote. "We will settle the matter by a secret vote. I want nobody to feel the public weight of their decision."

After the last elder cast their vote, Lady Hedra tallied them up.

The Druids were at war.

"The collective has decided," Lord Foran said. "Druids, we ride to war. Men, please say your goodbyes and prepare yourselves, for we ride at dusk."

From the back of the hall, a docile voice emerged, "If we are a collective group, then why are you only encouraging the men to fight, Lord Foran?" From the crowd emerged Segion's cousin Parilla. She had become a widow early and was childless.

"We need the women here to tend to the homes and the children."

Parilla laughed. "Lord Foran, have you forgotten I am a childless widow? I am sure my Aunt Hedra would not mind tending to my home?"

Hedra nodded in agreement.

"There, the matter is settled, and I am glad, because I need an adventure in my life."

Segion chuckled as he threw an arm around his cousin, patting her on the back before she ran off to pack. After the hall was cleared, Segion, Beelay, and Imogen were alone.

"What are you two doing here? Am I not capable of rallying the troops on my own?"

Beelay chuckled as he threw down a drink. "First, if I did not cast my vote, you may not have the aid of our family, and second, we came to let you know the pixies and Imps are already on their way to Necromancium, along with the Elves."

Segion looked down in shame. "I am sorry, cousin. This is just so very overwhelming, but I am glad we will have the forces we need."

Beelay picked up his bag and headed toward the door. "Come now, we must get back to Lord Teymark at once."

Arriving back in the Elvish realm, Beelay, Imogen, and Segion came upon a barrage of creatures from all across Tera'Loth. In every direction, creatures were readying for battle. Somehow, Afloriana had even found swamp trolls willing to help. The trolls surprised Beelay because he had thought them to be extinct, if not only unwilling to help.

As the trio pushed their way through the crowd, they made it to Lord Teymark's study. Upon entering the room, they found Lord Teymark and his most trusted advisers stooped over a map of Lord Evynloth's fortress, muttering and grumbling as they moved pieces around on the map.

"If we attack from the side of the castle, we may inflict more carnage in a surprise attack."

Imogen approached the table, bringing silence over the room. "I know we all want this man stopped, and I want peace for Tera'Loth. I want him to know fear, so I say let's come right up to the front gate. Let him see us and fear us."

Across the room came a collective nod.

"Very well, Lady Imogen. We shall attack this beast head-on."

Lord Matthew sat at the table looking pensive. "Nephew, so you have more to add?" Lord Teymark inquired cautiously.

"If we are going to do this right, then we need to trick Evynloth into sealing shut the gates to lower-Necromancium himself. Send the pixies to spread rumors to his spies that we have milked the Stone of Aura's Reclaim and make it known that we plan to throw it into the Receptus-Chaotica so he will never be able to unlock the gates of Necromancium."

Matthew looked tired and defeated but he was sure that Evynloth would take the bait and be laying in wait for the vial.

With nods of agreement the plan was set in motion.

After a rushed meal, Imogen and the others went to prepare themselves for battle. Imogen could not sleep and was still awake when someone came to get her at three o'clock in the morning. By the time dawn broke, everyone who could fight was present at the base of Lord Evynloth's castle atop the cliffs of Necromancium. Imogen stood tall on her horse, but inside she was utterly terrified of what was about to happen.

Beelay, sensing this, nudged her as he whispered, "Just remember to focus on getting to Richard and leave Evynloth to us."

Imogen nodded as she looked on at the crumbling fortress. "I have the vial now. All I need is the blood."

Matthew and Beelay sat on horseback beside each other. Matthew was doing everything he could to not cast his eyes toward Lord Evynloth's fortress. Without lifting his head, Matthew spoke to Beelay, "I know that I have done a lot of evil in pursuit of my end goal, and I am sorry for that. I know you may never forgive me, but I want to do a final thing to prove myself to you."

Matthew, who had finally fought through his fear, cast his gaze toward the fortress, continuing to speak, "In the treasure room attached to Lord Avestyn's chambers is something that will restore these lands to their former glory. In that room is the chest that houses all the good and stolen Magick in Tera'Loth. If you help me fight my way to that room, I swear I will release it back to Tera'Loth after this is all over with."

Beelay looked at Matthew with suspicion.

"If you do not believe me, then have Afloriana hold me a prisoner in her home until you return to the Magicka realm, and we will release it together."

With little thought, Beelay nodded in agreement.

In the distance, Imogen could see Lord Evynloth on his balcony, pacing back and forth. Lord Evynloth and his army were not prepared for such an onslaught. He had assumed that Imogen would come for Richard, but not in this manner. After the death of Lord Avestyn, Evynloth had amassed a personal army of those still loyal to him, allowing him to be ready for battle at the drop of a hat.

Below the balcony was Evynloth's private army of Vikings, Dwarves, and a mix of other creatures ready to go to battle in his name. The troops on Lord Evynloth's side contained the most seasoned warriors in the lands and showed no fear for this battle.

After what seemed an age spent staring each other down, Lord Teymark moved his horse forward a few steps, turning to face his small but able army.

"I look out at you all with a sense of pride. We are all here because we want Tera'Loth back the way it was. Many of us here are old enough to remember how things were. Before this debacle, we communicated and embraced diplomacy." Turning toward the castle, Lord Teymark pointed toward Lord Evynloth. "This man and his pathetic army are all that stand in the way of us gaining back what we have lost."

Lord Teymark lowered his helmet and threw down his sword. "Charge." he screamed.

With the lowering of his sword, the onslaught began. Imogen galloped as hard as she could, using a path decided previously. With Matthew by her side, she headed straight for the entrance, flanked by Beelay, Segion, and other soldiers who made a wall of safety for her, allowing her safe passage to the entrance to the castle.

Jumping down from her horse, Imogen looked back to see the utter carnage. Beelay and Segion, who always seemed so reserved, were striking down more men than anyone else. Imogen resisted the urge to watch the battle ensue rather choosing to cast her mind back to the task at hand. With an awkward pat on the back, Matthew left in pursuit of the chest. With a crude map Matthew had drawn for her, she headed for the dungeons to find Richard.

After what seemed like 20,000 steps, she eventually found her way to Richard, who was in his cell, nose deep in a book. It surprised Imogen to see him sitting in relative freedom. The image of this dungeon in her head was obviously inaccurate.

"Richard. I am here to get you out of here."

Richard refused to look up, afraid it was another of Lord Evynloth's tricks to test his resolve.

"Please look at me. You don't know what we are going through right now to get you out of here."

Richard willed himself to look toward Imogen. "I will leave here, child, but it won't be alive."

Imogen looked at Richard in confusion as he said, "We have only a little time before Lord Evynloth fends off enough of them to seek you out, so please listen to me very carefully."

Imogen looked around her for signs of danger as she listened.

"I will give you my blood, but after that, I am leaving this world. I am too powerful to live out my life in peace, Imogen.

You are the last of my line, and I would love to be with you for as long as I can, but there are things about me that would be better if you did not know. I am a liability alive."

Imogen shook her head. Through tears, she argued, "Do you know what we have gone through to get you out of this hole? And all you can do is think selfishly."

Richard shook his head as he walked toward his grand-child. "You are too young to understand why I am making this sacrifice, but I am doing it for you. I would love to be there to see you raise your children and get married, but I can still watch from afar."

Richard extended his hand for Imogen to prick.

Through the tears, she pricked Richard's finger and dropped his blood in the vial.

"There, now you have what you need to make sure Evynloth is unsuccessful in his pursuits."

Imogen closed the vial, placing it gently in her pocket.

"Now do what you need to do to save this world before he finds you."

Imogen, who was now sobbing uncontrollably, shook her head.

Richard blew her a kiss and motioned for the staircase.

At that moment, the pair heard footsteps descending the staircase. Both held their breath, thinking they were out of time.

The shadow on the staircase turned into none other than Segion.

"Oh, I am so glad it's you. I thought we were done for," said Imogen as she leaped on Segion.

"No, child, but you best hurry before we really are done for. You go, and I will stay here with Richard until Afloriana gets here to use some magick on that lock."

Imogen nodded, turning to run up the stairs two steps at a time, leaving Richard and Segion alone. Once Imogen was up the stairs and out of earshot, Richard grabbed Segion's hand through the bars.

"So you told her, then?" said Segion as he looked around the dilapidated cell.

"Yes, I have, and now I need you to do as you promised, and kill me before I do any more harm in this world."

Segion did not bother to argue with Richard about the matter. He had known what needed to happen on this day for a long while now and was prepared to help a friend from being abused by anyone or anything else. Segion did his best to hug Richard through the bars.

"Are you ready, friend?" said Segion as he drew his dagger.

"Yes, please. I am ready. And don't forget to give her all the things I left for her. They will help her understand our past better. I only hope she doesn't make the same mistakes Astrid did."

Segion nodded as he pulled back his dagger. With a hand on Richard's shoulder, Segion stabbed Richard right through his heart.

With the dagger still in Richard, Segion carefully lowered him to the ground. "Goodbye, friend. I hope you will have peace now, and may my ancestors forgive me."

Richard patted Segion's hand, shaking his head as the

light left his eyes. Freeing himself of Richard's hand, Segion ran up the stairs in search of Imogen.

While Richard was taking his last breath below, Matthew arrived in the chamber of his former master. Not to his surprise, Lord Evynloth was waiting for him.

"Ah. My little apprentice has come home. I know what you want, and you are not getting it."

Matthew edged closer to his old master, pulling out his sword, much to the amusement of Lord Evynloth.

"Boy, really? What do you think that will do?" Lord Evynloth said as he attempted to turn the sword to dust.

The sword remained intact.

With a burst of anger, Lord Evynloth lunged toward his old apprentice.

"Very well, if you wish to do this the old-fashioned way, then we shall," he yelled as he charged toward Matthew, only to be stopped dead in his tracks by Afloriana and Drayah, who appeared in front of him. Sensing his anger and the desire to flee, Drayah chanted a spell of binding, but Lord Evynloth dissipated in front of them.

"He was always a coward," Afloriana said. "Oh well, let's get that chest and get you back to my home so you can hold up your end of the bargain."

The entrance to the treasure room was behind a door that was hidden behind a tapestry that hung next to the head of Lord Avestyn's bed. The door opened easily, as Lord Avestyn had never taken many precautions in his own chambers.

As the trio entered the room, they found a treasure trove

of goods that extended beyond their vision. The two lords, with greed, had filled the room floor-to-ceiling with all the stolen treasure they had amassed over the years. In the room's middle sat a cherry-wood chest much like the chest Matthew had left in the attic of Imogen's family's house.

"There is the chest," Matthew said. "Well, we best get this out of here before Lord Evynloth sets his sights back on us."

With that, Afloriana transported her friends and the chest from the castle and on to wait for Imogen in Magicka.

Eventually, Imogen found her way to the room that housed the receptacle that Matthew told them about. They knew it as the Receptus-Chaotica. She approached the receptacle with the vial in her hand. The evil lords used the receptacles to dissolve and destroy anything or anyone with magickal properties. An acquisition of Lord Avestyn's, they used it to get rid of anything that had been a danger to them over the years. In a few moments this would all be over, and Imogen's life—although it would never be normal again—would have peace in it.

But before she could make a move toward the receptacle, Lord Evynloth appeared before her standing guard over the receptacle.

"Stop right there, girl. I won't let you destroy my happiness."

THE DEMISE OF EVYNLOTH ALMACKIA

Imogen and Evynloth stood across from each other. In between them sat the receptacle. Imogen held the vial of blood and Stone water in her hand. Imogen would be damned if Lord Evynloth would get his hands on it, not after everything she and everyone else had experienced to get to this point.

"Imogen, just give me the vial now, and this will all be over. I know you are tired and want to go home to the human realm, where you have peace and safety. You have my word, as your family, I will leave the human realm alone and rule the rest of Tera'Loth as I always wanted."

Imogen spat at Lord Evynloth with all the violence she could muster. "You wanted none of this. It was always Lord Avestyn's plan. I don't think I will ever understand, even in my dying breath, why you let him have this power over you again. He abused you and nearly killed you down in that hole. You could have let him kill you the night that Erika died, but you did not. Why did you go to work for him again?"

In that instant, she saw something in his face. It was pure darkness. The Evynloth she hoped may still be in there was truly gone.

"Don't you see? Now I can take over Tera'Loth by myself and take back the power he stole from me and all the others he locked down in that hole. I decided a long time ago that I wanted more than just Ericka back in my life. I wanted power, as well as revenge for my love."

Evynloth edged toward Imogen as he continued to speak, "He could never figure out why he was getting so weak. He was young by the standards of Tera'Loth. You see, I was already getting my revenge on him with a long and slow poisoning. If Teymark would not have killed him when he did then I would have done it when we opened the gates to lower Necromancium. Lord Teymark aided me in my plans without even realizing it. I wonder how an Elf of his morals would feel about that."

As Evynloth finished his well-rehearsed speech, Beelay and Segion stormed into the room, breaking Imogen's concentration on Lord Evynloth. Turning to see who entered the room, Imogen unwittingly allowed Lord Evynloth to take his chance. In his frailty, he was still able to grab her from behind before the men could make a move.

"*No*," shouted Beelay, lunging forward as Lord Evynloth wrestled the vial from her hand.

Imogen twisted and turned as she fought his grip.

Eventually he got the vial from her without breaking it. Prize in hand, Evynloth cast Imogen to the floor like trash. With the largest grin of victory he could muster, Evynloth edged to the receptacle, his wand raised in Imogen's direction.

On the side of the receptacle sat a lever, which when pulled, shifted the receptacle away from its resting place in the room's center. Lord Evynloth pulled the lever to reveal a deep chasm. It was several meters deep, but one could still make out a circular gate at the bottom. The gate joined together in two pieces. Over the gates, there was a glowing purple barrier. Beneath the gate, dark green figures could be seen, and the sound of banging could be heard any time the figures tried to pass through the gates above them.

"At last, the power and Tera'Loth will be mine." Lord Evynloth laughed as he opened the vial and threw its contents into the chasm.

The room fell into deafening silence as everybody looked toward the gaping hole in the floor. Slowly, a deep rumble was heard from below.

The ground beneath them shook with enormous force. From the chasm, a beam of light shot up through the fortress ceiling. Evynloth screeched. The fortress was collapsing around them, and with it, all the dark magick in Tera'Loth was being sucked down into the chasm that led to Necromancium.

When he looked across the dissipating room at his great-granddaughter, he realized that his chaos was ruined.

"I brought the vial," Imogen said, "but it did not contain

what you hoped for. There is a reason my last name is Welkin. Welcome to the new Tera'Loth. The vial you threw down the hole held the milk of a Stone, but if you were as mighty as you thought you were, then you would have known the Stone was that of a pair, with a sister whose purpose is to suck the dark Magick out of this world and add an extra layer of Stone to the gates of Necromancium. If you were a smart man, you would have sensed I didn't bring the right potion."

"No!," Evynloth screamed, as if the combined agony of his life jumped out to strike him all at once. He tried to lunge for Imogen, but something was holding him back. He screamed as the floor gave way beneath him. and he could do nothing but fall to his death. With no magick at his disposal, he fell, screaming Ericka's name as he disappeared into the chasm below.

Imogen looked on in shock until she was jolted by the sound of Beelay's voice. "Come now, Imogen. We better get out of here before we join him."

With lightning speed, Imogen, Beelay, and Segion fled the fortress as it crumbled around them.

EPILOGUE

Clear of the dangers of Necromancium, Beelay, Segion, and Imogen made their way back to Aflo-riana's home in the capital. They burst through the door to find Matthew in magickal bindings, smoking a pipe and drinking pixie moonshine, his feet propped up on the chest. He was exactly where he said he would be.

"Don't look so shocked. I cannot celebrate without my pipe. Did you think I would not be here?" he remarked with the slightest of grins. Matthew, who was now free of his magickal bindings, approached Segion. "I am afraid that I do have another confession to make," he remarked as he pulled a pouch from his pocket, placing it in Segion's hands with a grin. "We need to hide this or destroy it," said Matthew as the others looked on in shock.

"Is that what I think it is?" said Imogen with eyebrows raised.

"Yes it is, and if we don't hide it then all of this was for nothing."

Segion tucked the pouch into his pocket with a nod. "I will take care of it."

Beelay shook his head before gravitating to the liquor cabinet, pouring a stiff drink, watching on as Imogen approached the chest.

"It seems fitting that they stored it in a chest that looks like the one I began this journey with. Well, there is no time like the present," Imogen said as she choked up a little.

"Can it not wait until morning, child? We have been through hell, and you need to rest. We all do."

With her eyes still fixed on the chest, Imogen shook her head. "No, please, let's do it now."

Segion and Beelay brought the chest out to the carriage before making their way up the Mountains of Memory. Once they reached the top of the mountains, they placed the chest at the edge of the cliffside.

"Well, this seems like as good a place as any to release it all," Matthew said.

Imogen, Beelay, Matthew, and Segion stood before the chest. With their wands outstretched, they spoke the magickal words to break the locking spell.

The locks clicked open, and the lid flew off with great force, allowing all the good magick and spells to spill out onto the winds of Tera'Loth and back to their rightful owners.

As the last specks of magick floated out of Imogen's view, a stillness swept over the land. Turning to descend the mountains, the sky went black. Imogen froze, fearing they failed to rid Tera'Loth of Evynloth. Turning around slowly, her fear became happiness. The sky before her was lit up with the biggest fireworks show to ever grace her eyes. When the last of the fireworks hit the sky, they formed an image of her face and the words, "Thank you," written in all the languages of Tera'Loth.

With dawn returning behind her, Imogen descended the mountains to start her life as a Witch in the new Tera'Loth .

ACKNOWLEDGMENTS

To my publisher, Tony Acree, I will always be grateful to you for taking a chance on me and for helping me realize my dream.

To my editor, Callie Rowland, thank you for your dedication to the craft of writing and your guidance through the editing process.

But most of all, I must acknowledge you, dear reader. Thank you for coming with me on this magical journey to the realm of imagination.

Tara Mier lives in Louisiana with her husband. She graduated in 2009 with a degree in Political Science and International Relations from Victoria University of Wellington. She penned her debut novel "The Quest for Tera'Loth" during the spring and summer of 2016 and has always been known as a storyteller with a passion for reading stories she doesn't guess the plot of within the first five minutes. When she is not drafting stories or thinking up new ideas for stories, she is working her 9-5 as a copyeditor.

www.ingramcontent.com/pod-product-compliance
Lightning Source LLC
Chambersburg PA
CBHW070052030726
47506CB00002B/435